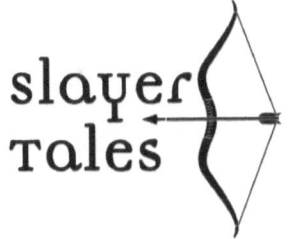

slayer
tales

FORSAKEN BEAUTY

by

USA TODAY BESTSELLING AUTHOR

D.L. SNOW

For my Dad

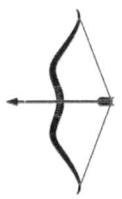

CHAPTER I

Once upon a time there was a poor family: a mother, a father, two daughters and a son, who lived in a small cottage on a plot of land beside the Forest of the Giants. After a year of drought and a meager harvest, the father ventured out on a hunting trip, for his family was going hungry. However, the man never returned...

— FROM THE LEGEND OF THE DRAGON CLAW SCEPTER

Morainia. She'd never been to the place, but it certainly lived up to the legend. Once a rich kingdom, it was now a wasteland of smoking pools of sulfur and crisp blackened hills. There were no trees, no fields, no towns... not even farms to speak of. It was an empty, lonely place. A sad place.

And, oh so many ghosts.

Muriel blotted the moisture pooling at the corners of her eyes. Though she was saddened by what she heard—the moaning spirits of men, women, and children—it was the orange haze blanketing the land, distorting the sun and the sky, that made her eyes water. The smell of brimstone and the acrid taste of the air would remain with her long after their royal procession left.

"Well," said a deep, melodious voice from the mount beside her, "It's not as bad as I remember."

"You've been here before?"

"Almost a year ago."

Muriel cast her gaze from side to side. "And it was worse than this?"

"Yes. For you see, life returns." The man pointed to a pocket of vegetation half-hidden by rubble on the side of the hardened dirt path. Lizard's Tail was growing amid new shoots of Dragon Trees and Snake Grass.

"Oh! Do you think there is more? I should like to pick some for my stores. All of those plants have healing properties, you know."

"I am sure if you were to take but a little, it wouldn't hurt, for I have seen a number of patches of greenery along the roadway."

"Thank you." She met the gaze of the man who rode by her side and quickly looked away. It was folly, spending time in his company. Absolute madness. However, she'd been given no alternative. When one's presence was requested by one's sovereigns, one had little choice but to accept. Muriel had no idea that the man she'd once met in her apothecary shop a month before last summer's solstice, the same man who visited her regularly in her dreams, would be accompanying the royal entourage on this strange expedition.

His name was A'Dale. Allan A'Dale, and he was a man like no other. A man of contradictions, a warrior, a minstrel, a mummer, a soldier. He had hands that wielded deadly weapons, yet he could play and sing with the most adept proficiency. His chin and brow were wide and strong, his lips soft and sensual.

Not that she had any experience with the texture of his lips. Gods above! The mere thought was absurd. As a member of the *sisterhood*, she was chaste and pure. It was the only way to keep her magic potent.

Untainted.

So, she must not spend time thinking about the man.

No matter how soft his lips appeared or how compelling the depths of his eyes.

Though his eyes were so easy to become lost in…

The rich, dark color of his gaze brought to mind a magical drink she'd once tasted, brewed by a holy man who came from far across the Selward Sea. *Cacao*, he'd called it. Sweet and full-bodied and, oh, so delicious. The thick drink stimulated the senses while soothing the soul.

Which was exactly the effect Allan A'Dale had on her.

Muriel shook her head.

No!

The man had *no* effect on her. None whatsoever. What a notion!

"Is something amiss?" the man himself asked in that disarmingly rhythmic baritone of his.

Muriel placed her handkerchief to her nose. "I find the smell rather unbearable." It wasn't a lie. Not exactly. The smell *was* unbearable. However, the smell was not the thing that was amiss.

Before A'Dale had a chance to reply, their attention was seized by the king riding toward them on his great black warhorse, his purple cape flying out behind him, the plumes atop his helmet bobbing with each step. His face appeared carved from granite, stern and implacable.

"Oh dear," Muriel murmured as he stopped by their side.

"A'Dale, a word, if you please."

"Of course, Your Highness." Allan maneuvered his horse closer to Muriel's so that the King could ride beside him along the narrow path. "What is it, Your Majesty? How may I be of service?"

The king removed his helm and rubbed his brow. "How

long have you been captain of the guard, A'Dale?"

"It is going on six months, Your Grace."

"Yes, and…" The king scratched his jaw. "Of course you know my wife. You know the queen."

"A braver woman the continent has *never* seen."

"Aye." The king sighed and turned his head toward the rear of the procession where his wife rode beside the litter carrying the wet nurse and their newborn babe. The fact his face was turned didn't stop Muriel from hearing him mutter, "Nor a woman as headstrong and, on occasion, downright infuriating." The king's words were not meant for anyone else's ears. But of course he didn't know that hearing was one sense that was preternaturally strong in her.

Her *sight*, on the other hand…ah well, that was another matter altogether.

"I am the king. I am to be heeded," he said barely above his breath.

Using her handkerchief, she covered her smile. It wouldn't do for King Cahill to see her finding mirth in his distress. Though the man was good and fair, it was within his power to behead a subject for less than a chuckle at his expense.

Cahill turned to A'Dale. "My wife, that is to say, *the queen*, has many strong opinions."

"Indeed," A'Dale concurred. "One would expect nothing less from the slayer of *Ninn-Arach* - the mother of all dragons."

A'Dale wasn't making mere platitudes. As the only survivor of the dragon hordes of '73 that attacked her homeland of Morainia, Breanna was touted as the best dragon slayer the continent over. She had killed the mythical *Ninn-Arach*, the mother-of-all dragons, and she'd been instrumental in helping Cahill save the kingdom of Lorentia from attack mere months ago. Her skills even rivaled those of Cragmar The Great, whose name was legend.

"Quite right."

The urge to giggle bubbled up inside Muriel as she pretended not to be listening to the conversation between the king and his captain. Though, of course, it was impossible not to.

"Here's the thing," Cahill went on. "When the queen decides a course of action, there is very little that may be done to dissuade her. Her intent in visiting her homeland, while noble, is also perilous and—"

"Your Majesty?" Muriel said, unable to keep out of the conversation any longer. "My apologies for the interruption, but perhaps I may be of service."

"Do not apologize, good woman. In such a case as this, I'm willing to accept help from wherever it may come."

"Might I suggest that *I* speak to the queen? Woman to woman?" Muriel finally allowed her smile to show. "I think perhaps I can persuade her that we have ventured far enough into Morainia for the ceremony to be effective."

Exhaling a heavy sigh of relief, the king said, "Please. I would be forever in your debt."

Muriel turned and weaved her mount toward the rear of the procession. Made up of guards and ladies-in-waiting, wagons and litters, she supposed it was small for a royal procession but by her standards, it was quite the thing. She'd never traveled this far from Lorentia and when she had travelled, it was always by horseback with other members of the *sisterhood*. This excursion was the adventure of a lifetime. However, for a woman who longed for her little shop and apartment off the Highstreet of Lochsend, it was quite enough adventure, to be sure. She was as anxious to turn around as the king was.

She made her way to the queen's side, turned the horse and rode in step with her. The queen was unlike any other, Muriel had no doubt. Wearing clothing better suited to a squire than Her Royal Highness, from a distance her slight frame gave the queen the appearance of a young boy, for she kept her hair in one long plait and it swung against the sword strapped to her back—the very sword that had pierced the eye of the mother of all dragons.

An air of melancholy surrounded the woman. Muriel did not require her *spectaculscope*—an instrument used to see auras surrounding people and objects—to know that the queen's aura was muddy and grey. She supposed the queen was seeing something beside the wasteland Morainia now was, reliving memories of her childhood, of all that she'd lost. She likely saw the kingdom as it once was, teeming with life, rolling green hills and fresh evergreen forests. Lakes and rivers running with clear water. Castle Moray, golden in the distance.

"If I had wed Elwood, perhaps I would be returning now to visit my family, alive and well," the queen spoke in a toneless voice.

She might have thought the queen was speaking only to herself, except that the woman turned to stare at Muriel with empty, grey eyes.

"It is tempting to entertain thoughts of 'what if'. But the exercise is pointless, Your Grace. It only serves to reopen wounds that ought to stay mended."

"Do you feel them?" The queen asked.

"Feel who?"

"The ghosts." Eyes wide, she looked around. "I see them out of the corners of my eyes. Following us."

Muriel could not lie. Not at the best of times and certainly not to the queen. "Yes, Your Highness. I hear whispers of many souls."

"Why don't they leave? Are they trapped?" The queen searched the surroundings as if seeing the souls of her subjects. "Is there something I can do?"

"No. They have chosen to stay."

"Why?"

"I cannot say."

With a gaze as hollow as the landscape, the queen turned forward once more.

"I think we have ventured far enough, my Queen. It's not safe here."

"Not safe?" A snarl forming on her lips. "What do we have to fear here, Good Witch? There is no one here. No one left." She shut her eyes. "Only the spirits of those who died… because of me."

The queen's voice trailed off. She was a proud woman and probably felt tears were a sign of weakness. How Muriel wished she could ease the burden of guilt, but it was impossible.

With a hand to her brow, searching the horizon, Muriel said, "There is one thing to fear, we are too near *her* homeland…" She would not utter the sorceress's name, it was as good as an incantation. "There is no magic protecting these borders, Your Majesty. This land has been claimed by dragons, and even the evil one—whose name I will not speak—can venture here. We must be wary."

The queen laughed. A harsh, bitter sound. "You think I fear *Eleanor*? Queen of the dragons? Bah! She's queen of nothing. There are no dragons left. We killed them all. Remember?" The queen's jaw tightened as she too searched the horizon. "I do not fear her. In fact, I long for a confrontation." The queen withdrew the blade from the baldric strapped to her back. She stood in her stirrups and shouted, "Come, Eleanor. Come if you dare and meet me, woman to…beast."

"Your Highness!" Muriel cried, a feeling of panic rioting in the pit of her stomach. "You mustn't—"

But the queen ignored her. "Eleanor?! Where are you? No more minions to do your bidding? Well, I challenge you to come yourself and face my sword. Once and for all!"

At the sound of the queen's shouts, the procession stopped and waited, as if expecting a reply.

The group was met with nothing but silence.

"You see?" The queen said. "Nothing to—"

A high pitched wail split the calm, the sound plaintive and cross. Turning her horse, the queen moved toward the cry while Muriel scanned the sky with trepidation.

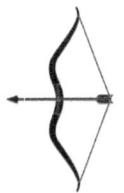

CHAPTER 2

For weeks the family searched for their father for, while he was good and kind, he owed tithes to the landlord and if he did not pay by month's end, the family would lose everything...

— FROM THE LEGEND OF THE DRAGON CLAW SCEPTER

The orange-tinged sky remained devoid of clouds... or anything else, for that matter. Thank the gods. Meanwhile, the queen sidled her horse up to the nurse's litter and pulled back the drapes. "Ah, my daughter. You are awake." After sheathing her sword, she held out her hands. "Give her to me."

The nurse passed the wailing bundle through the drapes of the litter to the queen.

"Hello, Sweetness-of-my-heart," the queen cooed softly to the wee babe with the black curls, just like her father. "I have brought you home for your christening. Is this the place, then love? Have we come far enough?"

Though the babe was only a few months old, Muriel was convinced the child understood what her mother was saying. She stopped crying at the sound of the queen's voice and stared up at her with violet eyes that were knowing and wise. If Muriel wasn't mistaken, they were the eyes of a *true sister*.

King Cahill rode up beside his wife and daughter. "We stop here, then?"

"Yes." She smiled at her husband. "Our daughter has spoken."

She passed the swaddled babe to her husband so that she might dismount and then took the girl back from him, whispering, "How I hate to give you up, even for one second." While she cuddled her tiny bundle, she gave directions to her husband about using some tumbled-down stones for the creation of an altar.

Now that the location was chosen, the king went to work issuing orders that were quickly carried out. Within a short time, a makeshift altar was built and Abbot Dithers donned his ceremonial robes. A regular visitor to the library at Lorent Castle, Muriel was fond of the old abbot and librarian. She'd watched as his eyes had become more and more clouded over the years as he lost the use of his sight. She wondered if she would share the same fate. Though almost completely blind now, the abbot relied on his other senses to great effect and stood beside the altar, holding out his gnarled hands for the babe.

At first Muriel thought the queen would refuse to relinquish her daughter as she clutched the babe to her breast. But the kind old abbot smiled and whispered, "It's all right, my dear. All will be well."

The queen unswaddled her tiny daughter and passed her to the holy man. The babe's arms flailed as he laid her on the altar before beginning a long prayer in Old Lorin, words that few understood anymore.

Being in the practice of intoning prayers and spells in many ancient tongues, Muriel understood the prayer and instinctively translated the words in her mind.

Mother of night and Father of day,
Bringer of rain, wind and sleet,

Giver of light, life and lore,
Creator of the elements,
Keeper of time,
Purveyor of magic and mystery.
I give you this child, born of the stars,
With blood of the ancients and breath of the gods,
Whose fate is but a bud in the springtime of life,
The child's destiny is yet to be foretold...

Once finished, the abbot motioned to Cahill, who withdrew a small flask from his satchel and uncorked it. He took a drink before passing the flask to the queen. She too took a drink and then, holding the flask together, king and queen poured a few drops into their daughter's mouth. He solemnly sang, The Song of Lorent. *All hail the sons of Lorent..., brave and fierce and mighty all. We protect our land, our wealth our people from those who seek to cut us down...*though the word sons was replaced by 'daughters'

Like Cahill, the queen uncorked her own small flask and took a sip. When she passed the flask to her husband, Muriel saw the way his lips twisted in displeasure. She supposed the water from Morainia would be tainted with sulfur. Though it would stink, the properties were not unpalatable and were actually beneficial to the health if taken in small quantities.

The child was in agreement with her father as to the unpleasantness of the drink and the moment she tasted a few drops, she turned her head, scrunched up her tiny face and let out the most spectacular scream.

The queen smiled, as if this was a good sign, and perhaps it was. The people of Morainia had different customs than those of Lorentia, and Muriel, though well versed in spells and potions from other lands, was less familiar with customs.

"Honored Mother, Honored Father. Sisters, cousins, aunts, and uncles. People of Morainia. I return to my homeland with a gift and a promise." The queen spoke loud and clear, as if to an enormous crowd on All Monarch's Day. "The house of Dunvegan tried to destroy us, tried to wipe out *all* of Morainia. They nearly succeeded…"

The child's cries intensified, her little limbs floundering in all directions.

"But they did *not* destroy us. Not all of us. Life returns to this land. I, Breanna of the House Moray, return to my homeland. I present my daughter." She lifted up the child. "She shall be called Hope, for she shall be the future of Morainia. Just as plants return, soon animals and people will follow, and I vow that Hope will one day rule this land. She will sit upon the throne of Morainia as her grandmother did before her, upholding Morainian law in the spirit of all those who came before her. The House of Moray lives on. We could not be destroyed and the kingdom of Morainia shall be reborn. I pledge this with my life."

Cheers broke out from the members of the entourage. The child gave one last cry before hiccupping and looking around at the faces surrounding her. Muriel closed her eyes, listening *not* to the sounds of the living, but rather to the cries of the dead. She could hear the spirits of those Morainians departed, circling them like a spring wind, and she felt the remnants of long lost emotions. Love echoed. Loyalty too. What was the other? Emotions of the dead were more difficult to discern. Things are not the same once a body has crossed over the divide between life and death, but if she wasn't mistaken, the prevailing emotion was…fear.

Someone shouted and a cloud passed overhead.

Was it a cloud, or had the spectres materialized? Muriel squinted at a great black mass that hovered between the earth and sun.

Oh no.

No, it could *not* be!

Why hadn't she sensed it?

How was *it* able to turn up without anyone, her in particular, noticing its approach?

The largest dragon Muriel had ever seen hovered above, impervious to the arrows let fly by the soldiers in their party. The dragon circled lazily in the sky, spouting fire in short, sharp bursts.

Finally, the beast landed and after sucking in an enormous breath, it spewed a fountain of fire and brimstone into the sky so that flaming ash rained down upon the gathering. People ducked beneath cloaks and made panicked attempts to run for cover. But no cover could be found in this barren landscape.

Once the soldiers had stomped out the flames, they circled the group who stood by the altar: Muriel, A'Dale, the old abbot and of course the king and queen. A'Dale had his bow in the ready position and the king stepped in front of his wife and child with sword drawn, protecting his family. The queen had other ideas. Tucking Hope beneath her cloak with one arm, she withdrew her blade from its sheath with her other. How the woman managed to point the blade at the fiery brute without wavering in fear, Muriel had no idea. But then, she was too busy whispering a spell beneath her breath to give the queen's lack of fear much more than passing notice.

Just as Muriel finished one spell and began another, the hideous beast arched its scaly back and convulsed. Its wings spread wide and then transformed into stumpy arms with claws for hands. The reptilian snout contorted as the beast opened and closed its mouth until a head that was not quite human and not quite beast rested on deformed shoulders. The body of the thing remained dragon-like, with tail and legs intact, yet smaller and more agile as it took hopping steps in their direction.

"Am I late?" a garbled voice asked. "I was invited to the christening, was I not? She is my grandchild, after all."

"Eleanor?" The king took a step toward the monster, the tip of his sword pointed at the blood red eyes shining out of the misshapen skull. "Is that you?"

"Oh. Didn't you recognize me, step-son?" The beast looked down at its body. "I suppose my transformation is not perfect, as you can see." The thing made a raspy sigh. "It's those puny people of Dunvegan who have done this to me. The maidens— such nasty little creatures, tasting of dirt—they aren't enough." The fiend spread its stunted arms. "What I need is a *human* maiden. Pure and chaste. It is the only way for me to regain my human form." The creature lifted its nose and sniffed the air. "And I smell more than one in *this* party." The fiend, who had once been Cahill's step-mother, hopped forward, closing the distance between it and the royal family.

"Leave now, or die," Cahill said through gritted teeth.

"Leave? But your wife invited me. Didn't you hear? Why, only a few hours ago she asked me to come. Begged me. And here I am." The twisted lips curled upwards in what could be a snarl or a smile.

A twang, followed by a whistle, alerted Muriel to the arrow A'Dale let loose. But the beast turned its head at the last second so that the projectile bounced harmlessly off her scaly neck. She stooped to pick up the fallen missile and held it up, inspecting it. "You meant to penetrate my eye. You meant to kill me." The thing tsked before snorting fire through its nostrils. The fire was so hot, the arrow turned to ash in the beast's clutches.

"Now, I could kill you all at this very moment." The thing opened its snout and let go a wall of heat and flames so powerful, it knocked the party back. "But where is the fun in that? It'd be all over in one go. Too quick. Too painless. No. You deserve something a little more long-lasting. A little more torturous, I should think."

The thing cocked its head to one side, mockingly. "Ah. The child. I believe I shall take her, thank you very much." It held out its scaly arms as if it actually expected the queen to pass over her baby girl. "Can't have any heirs lying about, now can we?"

Following a nearly imperceptible nod from Cahill, the soldiers attacked, hacking at the beast from all directions. But it wasn't just impenetrable scales that deflected the blades, it was magic. Strong magic.

Black magic.

As if the soldiers were nothing more than annoying gnats, the dragon sorceress batted them away while she moved with her strange hopping gait ever closer to the king and queen.

"Stop or I'll gouge out your eyes," Cahill cried.

"I'd very much like to see you try, my *son*."

Cahill swung with such might that the deflection from the magical shield surrounding his stepmother flung him back twenty feet. With a scream, the queen lunged, but the beast simply grabbed her small sword in its scaly grasp and yanked it from the queen's hand. With its other talon, the creature circled the queen's small neck and picked her up off the ground. A'Dale rushed and swiped at the beast's legs, hoping to find a vulnerable spot, but scales and magic left no part of the thing defenceless.

"No!" the queen gasped, attempting to free herself from Eleanor's clutches with one hand while she held desperately to her daughter with the other.

Through all of the fighting and struggling, Muriel whispered furiously into her cupped hands. She filled the space with the most potent spell she could think of and then opened her hands and blew the incantation, not at the sorceress, but at the baby, screaming in her mother's arms.

With little effort, Eleanor managed to snatch the child from the queen. Once the beast had what it desired, it tossed the queen to the ground at its feet.

"Finally!" it cried. "You shall pay for what you have stolen from me. You shall live with your pain until the day I reclaim the throne."

"No!" Back on his feet, Cahill charged but with a mere flick of its tail, the beast flung the king away once more.

"All hope shall die here today." Eleanor held the screaming infant up to the sky. "I shall finish what my brother Elwood set out to do seven years ago."

"Gods, no," the queen moaned, crawling with arms outstretched, reaching fruitlessly for her baby. "Please!"

"*Please?*" The thing took a hop back. "The slayer of *Ninn-Arach* begs for mercy? How delightful. My heart should break with pity, should it not?" It made a strange sound, smacking its forked tongue against its lips. "The problem is, my dear, I do not have a heart." Eleanor pointed a curled talon at the prostrate queen. "But even so, I shall show mercy. I shall let you live, though I can't take the chance you might try to produce more brats."

A bolt of purple lightning struck the queen, immobilizing her in its dark potency.

"*Quasa indelgasa por finiti.*"

"Oh no!" Muriel cried, momentarily distracted from binding her spell to the child. One of the problems with fighting black magic was that it was nearly impossible to foresee the evil and depravation a purveyor of darkness might conjure. And she had not foreseen *this*. There was nothing Muriel could do to change the terrible spell Eleanor had inflicted upon the queen. But she could save Hope, if given just a little more time to complete the binding.

The creature stood in triumph. "My christening gift, *Queen*

Breanna. I have ensured the House of Moray dies with you, for you shall never conceive a child again, you worthless, dragon-slaying slut!" The beast held the baby's face up to her snout. "Now, observe as *Hope's* life flows from her body to mine."

A collective cry broke from the helpless crowd as the horrid lips of the beast surrounded both mouth and nose of the innocent babe, muffling her wails.

The magic that encircled the beast was so powerful, Muriel could detect a faint humming from its energy as it grew stronger in those last moments before taking Hope's life.

But dark magic, while more powerful than light, always had a flaw. Always.

And the moment the creature tried to draw the innocent soul from the babe into its own soulless body, a white light burst forth, encapsulating the king, queen and child, holding them in a protective bubble while lifting Eleanor up and transforming her back into dragon form.

With one difference. One *significant* difference. Starbursts and lightening flickered around the thing, shrinking it down to the size of a bat.

"What have you done?" the miniature dragon squeaked once the transformation was complete. "Who did this? Where is the witch among you? Where?" The little beast tried to breathe fire, but it was no stronger than a candle flame.

A'Dale, took a swing with his sword, batting the tiny creature high into the sky.

"This isn't over!" a shrill voice cried. "You think you've outsmarted me? You haven't! Your spell was incomplete, you stupid cow. I will return. I will get my revenge!"

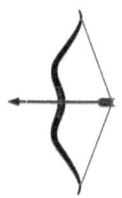

CHAPTER 3

One day, while searching for her father in the forest, the eldest daughter—a child with a sweet and sunny disposition—saw something sparkling high up in the branches of one of the great trees. The girl had a love for all things beautiful and forgot everything in her pursuit to discover what was there. She attempted to climb the tree, but was unable to get her small arms around the trunk. So the next day she returned with her sister and brother, who boosted her to the first branch, enabling her to shimmy the rest of the way up...

— FROM THE LEGEND OF THE DRAGON CLAW SCEPTER

After ordering the rest of the guard to take defensive positions around the royal party, and assuring the few ladies-in-waiting and the nurse that it would be best to stay inside the cover of the litters, A'Dale chased arrow after arrow in pursuit of the tiny retreating dragon. Of course he did not succeed in bringing it down. It didn't matter. It felt good to do something after feeling so helpless during the altercation with the sorceress.

If not for her...for Muriel...

A chill ran up his back while warmth spread inside his chest and belly. She had saved them. Somehow, she had saved them all. Though you wouldn't know it to look at her. She sat on the hardened ground, her head in her hands, weeping. The urge to go to her, to comfort her, was overpowering, but the king and queen were already there at her side, helping her to stand, so he relieved his angst by continuing to fire at the speck in the sky.

"I am so sorry," he heard her say between sobs.

In quick succession, Allan shot off another two arrows until a gnarled hand gently touched his shoulder. "It is no use, my son. Save your arrows for a more substantial target." The abbot squeezed his shoulder and shuffled toward the king and queen.

Giving up his hopeless mission of bringing down the tiny beast, Allan slid his bow over his shoulder and marched up to the group. He dropped to his knee in front of his king. "I have failed in my duty. Do with me what you will."

"Oh, in Cragmar's name, A'Dale, would you stand? There was nothing any of us could have done. Not with swords, anyway, though you tried. Valiantly, I might add. But one can only battle magic *with* magic. Thank the gods for the good witch, who saved us in the end."

"No," the red-haired woman cried. "I have not saved you. I have failed you." She wiped her nose and cheeks on her sleeve before covering her face with her hands.

"Stop!" The queen shoved herself into the center of the small group. "All of you must stop." Her voice cracked with emotion. "The fault lies here." She beat her fist upon her chest, startling the babe held in her other arm. "It was vanity and pride that made me challenge such a powerful sorceress, putting all that I love in jeopardy. Stupidity," she spat. "I am a queen, yet I acted no better than a drunken hooligan spoiling for a fight." With a quivering lip, she took a step toward her husband. "Cahill," she whispered. "Will you ever forgive me?"

The king bowed his head, held out his arms and engulfed his wife and child in his embrace. As the queen adjusted her daughter in her arms, she gasped in surprise. A forelock of Hope's hair that had once been black was now as white as snow. A thorough inspection found that the girl was unscathed. In relief, the king whispered what A'Dale imagined were words of comfort. Whatever was said between the king and queen was inaudible, but perhaps the emotion of the moment played upon the young witch's feminine sensitivity, for she began to cry in earnest while watching the royal family's poignant embrace.

The sound clawed at his heart, much like the acid-covered talons of a dragon, and Allan had to look away. When he turned, he found the old abbot watching him with his milky-eyed gaze. Surely the man was blind, yet he nodded at Allan as if communicating or confirming some hidden message. Probably it was his imagination, for what message could he possibly be trying to convey?

A'Dale's attention did not stray long from the young witch, and when he turned back around, the queen stood in front of her, still clutching her baby.

"Dear, dear woman. Please stop crying. You have single-handedly saved us."

"No. I have let you down."

"Let us down? Don't be ridiculous," the queen said.

"I could have done more. I *should* have known. The spirits were following us, trying to warn us. I felt them but I didn't heed their warning."

"My dear—"

"I didn't finish binding my spell to protect Hope."

"Yet she lives."

"For today.

"What do you mean?"

The witch began to pace, her head down, as if reliving what just happened. "It's a reverse spell, you work backwards through life. I was able to bind a protective shield around her all the way back from death until her coming of age."

"I don't understand."

"From this day until her sixteenth birthday, she is unprotected."

"So finish the spell. Do it now." The queen thrust the baby at the witch.

"I can't. When that…that *thing* tried to steal Hope's soul, she tasted my magic and absorbed the spell. It cannot be repeated nor completed."

The queen pulled Hope against her chest, looking frantically to her husband. "So, we take her back to Lorent Castle and *we* protect her."

The little witch shook her head. "How? Eleanor is a great sorceress. Her magic grows every day. She may not be able to enter Lorentia herself, but she will use any number of evils to try to steal your daughter. Magic, assassins, or more likely, some combination of the two."

A'Dale saw the look of understanding flit between king and queen. The half-woman, half-dragon had tried those very tactics mere months ago, attempting to employ first Zaina, Princess of Fenlock, and then Lord Hood as her assassins. She had very nearly succeeded.

"I can cast protective spells, but I cannot know nor guess the mind of one so bent on evil. I will never be able to foresee the lengths to which she will go to exact her revenge."

The queen licked her lips, considering Muriel's words.

"Today is the perfect example." Muriel fell to her knees in front of the queen. "I failed to anticipate the spell she cast upon you, Your Grace."

With all that had happened, A'Dale had nearly forgotten

the horrible spell that now left the queen barren.

"Can it be reversed?" the queen asked quietly.

"No. It has been bound to you. Until Eleanor dies, a binding spell cannot be broken."

The queen bit her lip as she considered Muriel's words. "I would have given my life for my daughter's. You saved her when I could not. My life, though barren, is a small price to pay for Hope."

The queen spoke bravely, yet A'Dale noticed how her chin quivered when she attempted to smile. "What's done is done." She pressed her lips together. "Now we need to decide how we're going to keep Hope safe."

"We keep our daughter locked away until her sixteenth year," the King said in a stern voice. "We hire a taster for her food, guards posted outside her door, and only those most trusted may enter."

"But, Husband," the queen pleaded, "Our daughter under lock and key? To never see the light of day? To never run in a field or fish in a stream or ride fast through a copse of trees?" She shook her head. "No one should grow up in such a manner. It's brutish."

"Some women find the very activities you described—running, fishing, riding hard—to be brutish. I understand you wish to provide our daughter with a happy childhood, but I would think sacrificing a little freedom for the preservation of her life is worth the cost. Besides, what choice do we have?"

"We must have some choice. We cannot make our daughter captive in her own home!"

A'Dale stepped forward. "Your Grace," he began. "I see flaws with such a plan. Though I do not know magic, I know something about the lengths this wretched beast will go to get what it wants."

"How do you know?" Cahill asked.

"I was once under Eleanor's spell."

"What?" Queen Breanna held her child away from A'Dale and drew her sword. "How do we know you aren't still?"

"He's not." Muriel came forward, a frown marring her lovely features. Even after a bout of tears, she was beautiful. Her eyes only appeared greener, her cheeks flushed and rosy. Her lips? Ah, her lips…so plump and soft.

"I would be able to detect the evil if he were still under the witch's spell."

Perhaps his gaze lingered on her too long, but he could not help himself, and Muriel's eyes widened as she stared, then quickly looked away.

"Explain yourself, man," Cahill ordered.

"It was a potion that was in Hood's—er…Lord Hood, that is to say, King Robyn's—possession when we traveled together. A potion given to the princess, Zaina, by the sorceress herself."

"The love potion?" both the queen and Muriel said in unison.

"Yes. The very one. I did not know what it was, so I put no more than a drop on my finger and touched it to my tongue. That was all it took for me to be under the witch's control. I did her bidding without even knowing I was doing it."

"But the spell did not bind?" The queen asked.

"No," Muriel answered for him, her tone absent, as if deep in thought while speaking. "Potions are not binding."

"What of death potions?" Cahill asked.

"There is no such thing."

"Surely…"

"It's called poison. No spell needed," Muriel finished.

"Ah."

"So how did *you* break the spell?" Cahill asked A'Dale.

"There are two ways to break a love spell," Muriel said, frowning again at A'Dale. "The purveyor of the potion must die."

"And the second?"

"The point is," A'Dale replied quickly before Muriel could answer the king. He'd heard Zaina tell Robyn that proclaiming one's love was the only way to break the spell. Did Muriel suspect that it was *she* who broke the spell for him? That *she* was his one true love and that words he'd whispered inside her shop removed a veil in his mind that he hadn't even realized was there.

It didn't matter. Not right now. Now was the time to concentrate on Hope's safety not on his feelings for the beautiful witch. "It is too easy for the sorceress to infiltrate the castle without ever being there in person," he continued. "Your taster? He could be entranced by the witch to do her bidding, perhaps magically immune to poison. An enchanted bird carrying a poisoned bit of string up to Hope's window. You could be betrayed by the men you entrust to keep her safe—"

"Then it is only us, the queen and I, who see her, who protect her, who taste her food for her."

"Even you are not immune, Your Majesty," A'Dale said quietly. "Who will protect *you* from the witch's clutches? What if she manages to slip a potion into *your* food, one that forces you to raise your hand against your daughter, taking her life yourself? She is not above such a maneuver. In fact, that would be exactly the sort of trick she would play. For pleasure."

"But, surely—"

"It doesn't matter, you see, because she knows where you are and she *will* find a way to get to you and to your daughter. You know her better than I, so you must know that killing Hope will become her obsession."

There was silence among the small group of decision makers until Muriel quietly added, "And we mustn't forget the likelihood that Eleanor will find a human maiden before long.

Once she steals a human soul, she will not be bound by the border of Dunvegan. When that happens…"

Muriel did not finish her sentence. There was no need. A'Dale could see that both the king and queen were imagining the worst of scenarios behind their wide-eyed, empty stares.

"If I might interject," the abbot said in his quavering voice. "I see only one solution to the problem. It is not a perfect remedy and it will be fraught with peril, but I believe it is the only way."

"What? I pray, do not leave us in suspense," the king said, just as his daughter began to cry again.

"The child must be sent away."

"Sent away? Are you mad?" Breanna cried.

"No. I am old, decrepit and blind, but still quite sane, I'm afraid."

"Perhaps the abbot has a point, my love. We could send her to stay with Robyn and Zaina, the king and queen of Fenlock."

The good witch shook her head. "No. It would be the first place Eleanor would look." She took the abbot's hand and squeezed it. If Allan was not mistaken, a secret look passed between the old man and the witch. "Abbot Dithers is correct. Hope must be taken away, but it must be to a place no one knows about." She turned a sad gaze on the queen. "Not even you, My Queen."

The queen hugged her child to her and turned away, as if Muriel were trying to snatch Hope from her arms. "No." She shook her head. "No, there must be another way. There must be."

The good witch closed her eyes and turned her face in the direction of Dunvegan, the birthplace of all dragons and the home of Eleanor and her brother Elwood. In a grave voice, she said, "Even now, Eleanor is spouting magic to reverse the spell. She shall be her proper size in no time. By tomorrow, perhaps, she could return to try to steal Hope again. I may succeed in thwarting her, or I may not. But she will never stop trying, as long as she knows where Hope is."

The queen moaned and fell against her husband. Hope's cries joined in. Allan swore the two voices were joined with the cries of thousands of others. Looking around, he saw glimpses of shadows, strange mists forming and dissipating around the royal family. What manner of place was this? Though the air was hot, a chill ran up the back of his neck.

Cahill held his wife, whispering into her ear words of... what? Solace? Advice? What could the man possibly say to console the queen in such a situation?

A'Dale looked away. The scene was too personal. Too private. He shut his eyes and ground his teeth. The intense feeling of sadness in his gut seemed inappropriate for the Captain of the King's Guard, and he did his best to mask it. When he opened his eyes he found the abbot standing at his side, staring sightlessly at him.

"Your Majesties?" Muriel said in her soft, soothing voice.

The sound clutched at his heart and he pressed a hand against his breast in involuntary response.

"I shall take the babe," the witch said, her voice wavering with emotion. "I shall take her far from here and every day I shall cast a protective spell so that no one may discover us."

"But—" the queen began.

The abbot raised his hand to stop her. "Let her finish, Your Grace."

"I shall raise her as my own. Once she celebrates her sixteenth year, I shall return her to you."

"But you are only one woman—"

"Says the slayer of the mother of all dragons." The red-haired witch glanced at the abbot before continuing. "It is for the best that I take her alone. Eleanor will not expect it. Once she discovers Hope is missing and hidden, she will look for her. She'll assume Hope is being protected by a large party of attendants and guards. She will never believe you'd leave your daughter and heir in the hands of only one."

"Two."

The small group turned to stare at him. A'Dale caught the abbot's smile. "I shall accompany Muriel on this mission, if it pleases Your Majesties."

"But—" This time it was Muriel who spoke up against the idea.

Allan went on before she could finish her objection. "We shall play the part of a family, living a quiet life somewhere in the country far from Lorentia. It would appear more natural, more ordinary than a woman and girl alone."

"Safer too," the abbot added. "A fine idea, young man."

"You would do this, A'Dale?" The king asked.

"Happily, Your Grace."

Muriel shot him a fretful look. "I don't think—"

"Will you teach her how to wield a sword?" the queen asked, interrupting Muriel's objection.

"Of course. She shall learn all manner of weaponry, for I know how important it is to you that she should be strong like her mother."

"Yes." The queen's lip quivered as she cuddled her child. "It is of the utmost importance."

"It is decided, then," the abbot said, placing his hand on the queen's shoulder.

"I should like to discuss this a little more," Muriel said, throwing another pained glance in Allan's direction.

"What is there to discuss?" A'Dale asked, ignoring her look and searching the sky. "You said yourself the sorceress will return soon. The time for discussion must come to a close and we must make haste. We must be away."

"So soon?" Cahill pulled his wife and daughter close.

"I'm afraid so," the abbot said. "Isn't that right, Muriel?"

Muriel squeezed her eyes tight and bit down on her plump lower lip. If not for the fact she was distraught, it would have been a lovely sight. "Yes," she finally managed to say. "I must leave with the child as soon as possible. But the captain's presence is unnecessary. I can take care of Hope myself. I do not need the protection of a…of *this* man."

"Is A'Dale not to be trusted?" the queen asked.

"No." Muriel frowned, speaking as if the words pained her. "He is the most trustworthy of all your guard."

"Then what is the problem?" The king asked.

"Yes," A'Dale said, taking a step toward her. "What is the problem? Why do you refuse my company?"

The witch's eyes went wide and then the strangest thing happened. Although her lips did not move and no sound came from her mouth, as clear as fresh running spring, Allan heard her sweet voice inside his head say, *You know why!*

"I'm afraid I do not understand your objection." He moved to one knee in front of the flustered woman. "But I swear to protect you and the babe until we may return her to her parents. I swear this on my life."

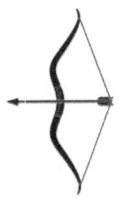

CHAPTER 4

What the child found high up in the tree was a polished crystal, bigger than her hand and shaped like an egg. Forgetting completely about their missing father, the children began the journey home, thrilled to show their mother what they had found. Surely a stone as beautiful as this would pay their rent...

— FROM THE LEGEND OF THE DRAGON CLAW SCEPTER

O h! Of all the forms of punishment, this one was the worst! To be sentenced to spending the next sixteen years with *him*? Alone? Pretending to be husband and wife, raising a child as if she was their own? What had she done to deserve this? Why hadn't she argued more vehemently against the idea and against A'Dale's presence? Why hadn't she insisted?

You know why.

The very words she'd directed into A'Dale's mind repeated in hers. She hadn't objected because there was a part of her—a *dangerous* part—that *wanted* A'Dale to accompany her. Wanted it more than anything...and not solely for his protection.

She wanted it, yet it would be agony. She supposed she deserved such torment for she'd failed the king and queen and, for the next sixteen years, she would pay for her failure.

If only she could hate him. But hate was not an emotion she was capable of conjuring particularly for a man like him.

For three days they had traveled, barely trading more than a few words. After crossing the border from Morainia into Baldane, the small party moved quietly through the woods, staying off the roads and paths, sometimes on the back of the horses and sometimes with only Muriel riding, holding the child, while A'Dale held the reins, leading them through rough terrain. Unlike some men, who found a crying child tiresome, when Hope cried, A'Dale insisted they stop. It was magic that enabled Muriel to feed the babe from her own breast like a wet nurse. Once or twice she caught A'Dale watching, not with the lasciviousness of a lustful male, but with the fondness of a true father.

It was that look that disconcerted her most.

No. Not true. What disconcerted her most was the way he would ask to hold Hope once she'd been fed and how he'd sing lullabies to her in the most beautiful, melancholic voice Muriel had ever heard.

He was doing it now, only this time *she* held the babe in her arms, stroking that stark white lock of hair across her forehead, while he strummed softly on his lute.

"Lullay, lullow, lully lullay,
Baw, baw, me bairne,
I saw a sweet and seemly sight,
A blissful bird,
A blossom bright,
That morning made and mirth among.
A maiden mother meek and mild,
In arms she kept,
A darling child,
That softly slept, while mother sang.

Lullay, lullow, lully lullay.
Baw, baw, my bairne,
Sleep softly now."

Muriel rocked the babe to the sound of his voice and it wasn't until he spoke, asking her a question, that she realized he'd stopped singing.

"Why are you crying?"

"Am I?" She raised a hand to her cheek and found it wet with tears. "Your voice is so…" She kept her gaze on the child, sleeping peacefully in her arms. Thinking better of finishing her sentence, she said, "I can't help but feel Queen Breanna's heartache, even across the distance."

"You mustn't think of her, nor speak her name again," A'Dale chided gently. "The abbot was very clear on that matter. Hope is ours now."

Muriel nodded. "Yes. I know. I am doing my best."

A'Dale set his lute aside and knelt before her. He had a habit of doing that. Was it because he knew it unnerved her so? Taking her free hand in his, he said, "You are doing better than that. It is as if you are her mother by birth. Day by day, I see the love that grows between the two of you."

She snatched her hand away, pretending it was necessary to tuck a loose corner of Hope's swaddling blanket around her wee feet. She wished her reaction would make him walk away, but it had the opposite effect.

Blasted man!

"Why do you rebuke me?"

"You know why."

"No," he said. "I do not."

"You cannot touch me."

"But if we are to be husband and wife, touch is only natural."

"Is it?" she said, her voice sounding unusually sharp to her ears. "I know plenty of husbands and wives who do not touch."

He watched her for a moment before asking, "Do I repulse you so much?"

"You know you do not repulse me." The child hiccuped in her sleep and made a face, as if sensing her discord. "Quite the opposite," she whispered, glancing up beneath her lashes.

A'Dale's grin was sinfully exultant. Muriel sucked in a breath of alarm at the responding sensation swelling in the pit of her belly.

"Then let us make our relationship official. We are charged with living as husband and wife. Let us become such. I know we don't know one another well, but we will, and though our acquaintance is new, I must confess I have loved you since that first day I saw you walking through the rain to your shop. Do you remember? I was with two companions and the princess Zaina. It was *you* who broke the spell of Eleanor's love potion." He took her hand again. "*You* are my one true love."

She did not mean to sigh, but the sound slipped out quite unbidden.

"How I wish I could take my time and woo you properly, but what is the point when the ending must be the same?" He pressed her knuckles to his lips and they were soft. Softer than she'd ever imagined. "Please say you'll be my wife, my *true* wife. In doing so, you'll make me the happiest of men."

His speech, so beautiful, so eloquent, broke her heart anew. Wrenching her hand from his, she thrust the sleeping child into his arms and stood up. "I cannot." She paced one way and then the next. "What you ask is impossible."

With the child secure in his embrace, he stood. "Why?" The word emerged not quite as soft as his earlier speech.

"Because…" She was experiencing difficulty speaking, her words becoming clogged beneath an unexpected sob. "I-I am…a witch."

"I know. And a sweeter witch one could not find."

She shook her head in dismay. Oh, if he only knew the pain of his request! "But…I must remain as I am. I may never marry."

He blinked. "I don't understand."

With hands clenched, Muriel explained, "My magic is only as pure as I am. You see? I must remain chaste. Particularly if I want to remain powerful enough to stop someone like Eleanor."

"You may not love?" he asked, his handsome face showing the first signs of darkness.

"Of course I may *love*."

"Then—" He made a move toward her.

Muriel held up her hands to keep him away. "But I may not *act* upon that love. I may not be married…in the physical sense."

A light of understanding dawned in his rich brown eyes. He took a step back and whispered, "Never?"

"Not while Hope's fate rests in my hands. No."

He blinked and shifted from one foot to the other. "But isn't there some way?"

"No, A'Dale. I'm afraid not. Now do you see why I wished for a different man to accompany me?"

"You knew how I felt?"

"Yes," she said softly. "And my feelings for you are much the same."

"You love me?"

"Yes, or at least, you affect me in a way no other man has. Is it love? Is it lust? I do not know. All I know is I want you, A'Dale, in the way that a wife wants her husband." She did not say, without clothing and in a marriage bed, for that would have been far too forward and dangerous, though it was the truth.

He shut his eyes as a mixture of emotions flitted across his face. "I see." His hands fell to his sides.

Muriel stared at his hands. How strong they were, how sensitive. She recalled how his hands had felt on the few occasions when he *had* touched her. She imagined how they might feel were she to allow him to touch her now. All of her. Caressing her cheek, her neck, her shoulders…her breasts.

If he were to kiss her there, upon her milk-filled breasts, with those lips that were made for kissing, how would that feel? Different from that of the babe, though a suckling child gave a sort of pleasure she'd never expected. But to have A'Dale kiss her there? It would feel so…different.

Mercy.

It took such effort to raise her eyes again. If mere thoughts were so potent, what would it be like to have to live with him? For sixteen years?

There was only one way to manage it. "Please believe me when I tell you that I wish things could be different."

"Do you?"

"Of course."

His smile was sad, but also resigned.

"But it cannot be. Do you understand?"

He nodded once. "I do." His words were uttered so solemnly, it was as if he was making an oath.

She sniffed and nodded. "Good. Now, A'Dale, you must promise me that we will never speak of this again. We will pretend to be husband and wife, but our relationship must be that of brother and sister."

"Brother and sister," he said, nodding slowly. "I understand."

"No touching."

"No touching," he repeated, his hands clenching and unclenching at his sides. "Like brother and sister."

They stood a few feet apart and even though he wasn't

touching her, his aura reached out as if he was. She felt his warmth, his strength, his protection. His love…

Muriel forced herself to back away from the circle of emotions he emitted.

"There is one thing I insist upon…sister."

The word *sister* was said on a sigh, as if it was the source of both pleasure and pain, making it sound anything but familial. "What is it?" she asked breathlessly.

"If I am to be your brother, you must call me Allan."

Eleanor paced the great hall of Dunsmoor Castle where her brother sat at his table, taking part in his favorite pastime. Eating.

"Where, in Cragmar's name, is Fosset?" he bellowed.

Spinning around, Eleanor faced her gluttonous brother. "Do not use that blasphemous name in this house," she huffed.

"Which name? Cragmar or Fosset?" Elwood asked before burping.

"The first of course, you insatiable fool."

"What's wrong with Cragmar?"

"I told you not to say that name!"

"Why?" Elwood pushed an empty platter away and slid another, piled high with pigeon pies, in front of him.

Storming up to the table, Eleanor used her tail to swipe its surface clear of food. The crashing and clanging of toppled platters brought young Fosset and the other footmen running into the room.

"That was uncalled for," Elwood pouted.

Leaning over the table, Eleanor breathed, "Cragmar was a slayer—"

"He wasn't just *any* slayer. He was the *best* dragon slayer to have *ever* lived. Don't forget that, dear sister."

How many times had she cursed the magic that kept her from killing her kin? Too many times to count. If only she had a virgin for each time, she'd be immortal. "I respectfully request that you *not* use that name in this house," Eleanor said through gritted fangs.

"Because *you* are a dragon?"

She'd had it with her brother's insolent mockery. She roared her frustration and when she was done, she spun around, pointing a claw at the nearest man. "You. Come here." Young Fosset was the son of Elwood's former valet, a man who had died by eating a candied apple Eleanor had hoped to use against her brother. Of course it would not have worked. She could not kill her brother, but the simple act of trying had relieved some of her frustration.

The poison had worked splendidly on the elder Fosset, and now his son bowed before her. "Yes, Your Grace?"

"Don't you have a sister?"

"No, Your Grace. I don't. Only brothers."

"And the others? What of their sisters?"

"Barrows has a sister, married and living in Darnell. Clement does as well. But she's also married and living in Darnell. I believe Ernst has one, but—"

"Let me guess, she's *married and living in Darnell*," Eleanor mimicked, her voice rumbling with irritation.

Fosset glanced at Elwood. "That's right."

"Do none of the servants have sisters who are *not* married and *not* living in Darnell?"

Slowly Fosset shook his head. "It is only the Dunvegan servants who have maiden sisters, Your Grace."

"Of course it is. Those disgusting little worms are the only food Elwood will allow me, isn't that right, Fosset?"

"I'm sure I don't know, Your Grace."

As Eleanor sucked in a breath, Fosset glanced fearfully at the king.

"Eleanor, don't you dare scorch my valet simply because you are annoyed with me. Fosset, you'd best be off before you become nothing more than ash upon my flagstones. My sister is in a fiery mood this evening."

Fosset gave one brief nod before hurrying out of the room, leaving the fallen platters behind.

Eleanor chased the fleeing servant with a burst of flame before turning her anger upon her brother again. "You have purposefully removed all human maids from the kingdom, haven't you?"

"You are sounding as paranoid as our sister, Elena. Do you know that?"

"It's not paranoia, it's the truth. You're keeping me in this state on purpose."

Finding a smear of pudding on the table, Elwood ran his pudgy finger through the mess and popped it into his mouth, sucking and slurping with gusto. Once finished, he said, "Of course I keep you in this state. I much prefer your company when you are mostly dragon. If you should ever find a maiden's soul to suck, you know you will leave and who shall I torment then?"

Narrowing her eyes, Eleanor wondered if he really kept her here because he was lonely.

Bah!

A stupid human frailty, loneliness. Something her brother was incapable of. As was she. No, Elwood kept her around for his amusement. That was all.

"Besides," Elwood continued, shifting in his chair and reaching down for a haunch of ham at his feet. "You had your opportunity a fortnight ago to suck a soul and kill the Lorentians and once again you failed."

"I didn't fail. I was thwarted."

"Thwarted. Failed. What's the difference? You had the dragon-slaying bitch at your mercy. Her and her whole party. You should have killed them all and taken the offspring's soul. Easy." He glanced up at Eleanor, then went back to reaching for the ham. "I'm starting to wonder if you don't enjoy being a dragon." He groaned as he stretched toward the floor, his fingers twitching uselessly, inches above the meat. "Seeing as you scared off my servants, would you be so kind as to pick up that haunch for me?"

With a sound of derision, Eleanor stabbed the meat with her talon and flicked it onto the table.

"You see? We make quite a pair." He dusted off the meat and then took an enormous bite. Speaking with his mouth full, he asked, "Why didn't you kill them when you had the chance?"

"Ach! If I had slain the family, all of Lorentia would have raised arms against us. They would have employed their allies in Baldane and Arcana. We would be at war even now. A dangerous scenario when we are out of dragons to protect us."

Elwood wiped his grease smeared lips with his sleeve. "War. Such a messy business." He sighed. "You were right to show restraint. One war is more than enough at the moment."

Eleanor tried, but reptilian eyes were incapable of rolling. Dunvegan had been at war with Darnell for years, though it was mostly for show, orchestrated by Elwood and their sister, Elena, who was the queen of Darnell. Elwood claimed war kept the peasantry occupied.

"Speaking of my depleted dragon stock, what do you plan to do to make amends?"

Eleanor growled. She didn't need her brother to remind her of the fact that she'd exhausted the whole dragon population in an invasion of Lorentia less than a year ago. Now all but a few eggs were gone. "I shall replenish the stock. I told you I would."

"Yes, but you promise a great many things that sadly have never come to fruition." Elwood took another bite of meat. "And now I suppose the Lorents are all safely back in Lorentia? Is that what the scepter revealed?" Her brother grimaced as if the bite of meat in his mouth tasted off. But Eleanor knew he held a special hatred for the queen of Lorentia. He had been betrothed to Breanna of Morainia once upon a time. The chit had snubbed his suit by running away. Though he feigned indifference, Elwood was brutal in his revenge, repaying her insult by destroying the whole kingdom of Morainia. The fact that she'd escaped only intensified his hatred and he would like nothing more than to see her dead…probably after being tortured first.

"Cahill and Breanna have returned safely…"

Elwood grunted at the mention of her name.

"…but the child is not with them."

Elwood raised his piggy eyes. "No?"

Shaking her massive head, Eleanor said, "They have sent her into hiding."

"They have? How interesting."

"Now do you see why I must return to human form? The heir to Morainia lives. She's out there somewhere and there is a spell upon the child, I tasted it when I tried to suck her soul."

"What sort of spell?"

"Reverse protection. Thank the gods it was incomplete."

"You believe the gods played a part in this?"

"Of course. I yet live. Breanna is barren. The child still lives and I have sixteen years to find her."

"To find her? And what shall you do when you find her?"

"This time I will not hesitate in killing her."

Elwood nodded and chewed. His puckered lips slunk across his mottled cheeks in a sneaky smile. "That is something I should like to witness. The problem is, maidens the continent over know of your plight. None are foolish enough to set foot inside our borders."

"What of Niviea? I'm told her sleep-spell is broken. Where is she?"

"No one knows, I'm afraid."

Eleanor leaned closer to her brother. She sniffed. Damn him to the corners of the continent and back…he was telling the truth.

"I need a human soul, Elwood. It's the only way."

He chewed thoughtfully for a moment. "Let me think on it, sister. First replace my dragons and then, perhaps, I shall help you find your virgin."

CHAPTER 5

However, the journey home took longer than it should, for the children fought over who would carry the stone. The eldest said it was hers, for she had been the one to find it and retrieve it...

— FROM THE LEGEND OF THE DRAGON CLAW SCEPTER

Muriel paced while waiting for Allan's return. Which was worse, she could not decide, having him near or having him far away? It seemed the two options were equally difficult to withstand. Today he had gone to trade in the village of Dewsbury, five miles away, and he promised to return before the sun set.

The sky was beginning to turn pink and gold and yet there was still no sign of him. Although they had been given plenty of coins to see them through, Allan had insisted they use their money sparingly. It would look suspicious if a peasant family had more than a copper or two. Once they had decided upon their location and agreed to the tithes—a tenth of all their produce—with the landlord, he had traded one of their horses for a cow, two chickens and a rooster. He'd used some of their smaller coins to purchase supplies, an axe, two shovels, a hoe, some cloth, and cooking supplies.

In the short months since their arrival, Allan had cleared

a patch of land and built a little one room cottage, cozy and warm. She'd started a garden. It would be late, but better than nothing, and she had begun weaving her baskets again in her spare time. But it was lonely. Oh so lonely. Muriel had never lived outside of Lochsend and she hadn't realized how much she depended upon interacting with people until she was removed from them. But Allan had insisted that the less contact they had with others, the better.

How had she ever thought she could do this on her own? It was pride that had made her argue against Allan joining her. Pride and lust. Now, as she waited, startling over ever little sound that came from the forest beyond the clearing, her pride had all but dissipated. Her lust, on the other hand, was as powerful as ever and when she heard the nicker of Allan's horse as he approached, her heart fluttered and her thighs tightened.

Oh gods! When would these unwanted feelings cease?

"Halloo wife!" Allan called, both a greeting and a reassurance. It was Allan's idea that they have a code to greet one another. *Halloo Wife* meant all was well. *I am home, Wife* meant there was something amiss and a stronger protective spell should be cast over the cottage. If Allan should ever ride into the clearing calling, *Wife, where ye be*? She was to take Hope and go down into the hidey hole Allan had built beneath the cottage. That greeting meant danger was imminent.

Muriel greeted Allan with a wave from the doorway, although one hand remained firmly on her stomach in an effort to quell the nervous flutters that began at the mere sight of him. How noble he looked, riding tall, back straight, shoulders wide, like a warrior. His cheeks were ruddy, his thick hair tousled from the wind, his hands strong yet holding the reins with a gentle touch. Seeing him atop a horse was her favorite pose...next to watching him chop wood. If he knew how much time she wasted spying on him as he chopped, he'd be scandalized. But it was impossible to stop, particularly in the heat of summer, his shirt open wide, his sleeves rolled up. Why once, he'd even removed his shirt and she nearly fainted from the vision of his powerful torso, sleek with sweat, as he swung the axe again and again.

Mercy.

Of course another favorite image of him was when he played and sang, his hands moving deftly over the strings of his lute. She loved his hands and marveled at how they could wield a sword with deadly accuracy, yet play a musical instrument or stroke Hope's cheek with the gentlest touch.

An image of Allan holding Hope against his broad chest, his eyes closed, gently swaying while he hummed a lullaby materialized in her mind's eye. Muriel smiled and a peaceful warmth stole across her belly. Yes, seeing Allan with Hope was her favorite thing of all.

"Are you quite well, Wife?" Allan stood not two feet away, a look of concern on his face. "You appear as if you were having a vision?"

A vision? Oh gods. How could she? She'd been standing in the doorway daydreaming about him! She shook her head so hard a few unruly curls popped free of her cap. "I was," she admitted. "But 'tis nothing I can speak of." Muriel could not lie because lies beget lies and would only result in weakening her protective spells. But that didn't mean she had to tell the whole truth either. In this case, the truth wouldn't do either of them any good.

When he went to touch her, in a way that should have been quite natural, she jumped back. His eyes widened the moment he realized what he was about to do.

No touching.

How she wished she could take back the promise she'd made him repeat.

He dropped his arm to his side. "Is it anything of concern?"

"No." Muriel smiled. "Now come in and have your dinner. I'm sure the pottage is stuck to the cauldron by now." Before turning to go inside, she said, "But quietly, for we've already eaten and Hope's asleep."

The mere mention of Hope's name brought a light of joy to Allan's eyes and that light caused a twisting and tugging sensation in the very pit of her abdomen.

Fifteen years, four months, twelve days.

She hadn't meant to keep a tally of the days left until Hope's sixteenth birthday, but she had begun doing it as a reminder of her purpose and now it had become a reflex. Every time she was tempted to give in to the desire she felt for Allan, which was countless times a day, she reminded herself of how much longer she must wait. It helped.

But not by much.

Once they were settled across the small table from one another, Allan with his bowl and bread and she with her small cup of mead, she asked, "How goes the trading?"

"I sold a few baskets for coin." Allan pulled out his purse from the inner pocket of his vest and emptied the contents on the table.

Muriel counted and frowned. "So little?"

"Dewsbury isn't Lochsend, I'm afraid. Prices are always lower for common goods in villages."

"*Common* goods? Is that what you said?" For the first time in their acquaintance, Muriel felt her ire rise against Allan.

Perhaps it was the unusually sharp tone she used that roused Hope. The child made a soft squeak, followed by a thin cry, after which came her usual hearty bawl. Muriel rose to get her but Allan was quicker.

"Let me," he said.

She sat back down, her irritation seeping out of her as she

watched Allan pick up the girl and speak to her.

"Ah, me sweet wee bairn. How's I miss ye, when I's away. Look at ye, rosy and plump, strong and lusty. Just like yer mam."

Was it the way he always spoke to the child in the unfamiliar brogue of his homeland or was it the way he compared the child to her that made all earlier insult dissolve?

"I knows what ye need. A wee suckle." Allan carried the bawling child to the table and Muriel held out her arms to take her, but he didn't hand her over. Instead, he dipped his little finger into his bowl of pottage and then held it gently against Hope's lips. When at first she refused, he sucked the food off his finger himself.

Muriel's pulse quickened at the sight of his sensuous mouth wrapped around his little finger.

Mer-cy.

"Ye donna know what yer missing, me sweets. Yer Mam's the verra best a' cooks, she is. I shuld know, I's been all o'er this great land, I has." He dipped his finger in again and gently touched the soft food to Hope's lips. "The verra best a'cooks. Have a wee taste, me love."

Hope turned her head and kept crying.

"My, me. A stubborn lass, she is." Rather than becoming annoyed, Allan chuckled and dipped again, this time gently inserting his finger into Hope's mouth. "Go on with ye, bite yer ol' da, if ye must."

At first, Hope's cries intensified. But only for a second. Suddenly her tiny body went still. Her eyes opened wide and her little fists stopped waving as she made the sweetest little sucking sounds Muriel had ever heard.

Holding her in one arm, Allan pulled out his stool and sat so that he might feed the child more comfortably.

"How did you know?" Muriel asked.

"Know what?"

"That she was ready for solid food?"

Allan looked up, his eyes shining with love. "Twelve brothers and sisters and I'm the oldest of the lot." He went back to feeding Hope and said, "When they start sleeping light, it means their mother's milk isn't satisfying their wee bellies." He glanced up. "You were cross with me, but a month ago, cross words would never have woken our Hope."

"I'm sorry I was cross."

"I'm sorry I insulted you. Your baskets are anything but common. It's the reason they sold in the first place."

Muriel smiled but something was wrong with her lips. They trembled. She stood and went to stir the fire. Then she went to the door of the cottage and opened it, letting in some cool night air.

"Are you well, my wife?"

"I'm fine," Muriel said, hoping the air would dry the tears on her cheeks. "I just need a bit of air, is all."

Fifteen years, four months, twelve days.

CHAPTER 6

The brother agreed with his elder sister until her back was turned. He tripped her so that when she fell, he was able to steal the stone from her. For the boy had gone hungry too long and was convinced that if he was the one to give his mother the stone, he would be rewarded with an extra ration of porridge...

— FROM THE LEGEND OF THE DRAGON CLAW SCEPTER

W here was she? It was dinner time and she was late. Again. Not wishing to wait and having no desire to eat alone on this day, of all days, Cahill went in search of his wife. It was not a difficult hunt. Though the sun was setting and the spring air still had a bite of frost in it, Breanna was outside in the practice ring, wearing nothing but a tunic and tights, practicing.

Cahill leaned against the weapons shed, and sighed. His wife was beautiful when she practiced, her choreographed moves were completed with grace and fluidity, more like a dancer than a fighter. A deadly dancer. But practicing had become her obsession. Even from the distance he could see how her tunic hung on her slight frame. She lost herself in her never-ending training, often forgetting to eat or outright refusing to eat, even when he sent food down to her.

Pushing himself away from the wall, Cahill approached slowly, as if she were a wild animal that might turn on him if startled.

"Come inside, Breanna. It's dinnertime."

She completed her maneuver before lowering her sword. Turning empty eyes on him, she said, "Don't you know what today is?"

"Of course I know what today is. That's why I'd like to spend it with you."

She ignored him and started another sequence. He'd watched her practice enough times over the years to know this particular sequence involved at least twenty moves, depending on the variations she employed. A haze of red descended upon him, filling his chest, his gut, and his heart, making it difficult to breathe while simultaneously making him feel invincible. He strode up to his wife and grabbed her from behind, covering her wrists where they held the sword and squeezed.

"Let go of me," she gasped.

"Drop this infernal blade and I shall set you free."

She struggled within his arms but did not drop the sword.

"Breanna. Let. Go." He applied more pressure, hoping to force her hands to open. But gods, the woman was strong. She always had been. But now she had a stubborn heart full to the hilt with strained emotions which only added to her strength and resolve.

However, she was not the only one overflowing with repressed pain and Cahill squeezed harder, sure she would drop her sword. He should have known better. His wife—who on good days rarely did as she was bid—was not about to give in to him on a *bad* day. She stomped on his toe, making him momentarily release his grip, giving her just enough time to slip from his grasp.

With a snarl and a look of one possessed by dark magic, she

pointed the tip of her sword at him. "You want me to drop it? You need to best me." Without warning she lunged.

Cahill dodged just in time, yet the sharp tip easily tore the billowing sleeve of his shirt. Looking up in shock, he shouted, "Are you mad?"

Without comment or apology, Breanna strode to the weapons shed and came out moments later holding a sword. She flung it end over end, embedding the blade into the dirt a foot away from Cahill's boot.

"Once you best me, I shall come inside." She moved into her opening stance, feet wide, both hands on the hilt, the sword pointed at Cahill's heart.

"I will not fight you."

"Because you know you shan't win."

"Of course I could best you."

"Really?" His wife smiled, but it was not in kindness or in jest. "Prove it. I dare you."

For a moment, Cahill was taken back in time to the days before he and Breanna were wed. It was here, on this very practice field, that he'd dared her to an archery contest. Oh how different things were then. Although it had been a serious contest, for Breanna in particular, it had also been a game, a courtship game, by two young people destined to be lovers.

But this contest was no game and though they were husband and wife, they had not been lovers in much too long. "I will not fight you, Wife."

She narrowed her eyes at him. "You will, Husband, because I give you no choice. It's up to you whether you face me with a weapon or not." She lunged as if her intent truly was to kill him.

Cahill dove out of the way of her fast-moving sword. Out of instinct, he rolled toward the sword she'd thrown and drew it from the ground. Gaining his footing, he held the blade out in defense. "Breanna, stop."

"No!" She swung her sword in a faux ronde, only to jab instead. This was no play fighting. She was dueling as if she meant it.

Cahill deflected her blows as his wife came at him with one of her most complex sequences, moving in with a half ronde only to step back and swing low, forcing him to jump out of the way before his shins were sliced. Once off-balance, she moved forward again, a left ronde, a right, pushing him back.

She was a worthy opponent at the best of times but now, with the sun well past the horizon and darkness descending, she was deadly and fighting in the dark was pure folly. "We must retire inside," he insisted, circling out of reach of her blade.

"You're afraid of me."

"I'm afraid I'll hurt you."

"Too late for that."

Her words struck deeper than a sword ever could. "Why are you doing this?"

"Because it'll make me feel better." She swung at him.

He easily deflected her offhand attack. "Does this truly ease the pain, Breanna?"

"Yes," she snarled. "Now stop talking and start fighting."

When next she jabbed, he deflected her blade with a long full stroke, forcing her to stumble. She narrowed her gaze and came at him again, growling and swinging. He did not strike but instead deflected with more and more vigor until finally he sent her sword flying.

She cried out and raced after it. Although she was quick, his legs were longer and she was no match for his speed. Cahill tackled her before she could retrieve her fallen sword. He flipped her over and straddled her, holding her arms firmly against the ground. "That's enough!"

She wriggled beneath him, bucking like a wild animal, but

Cahill was determined not to let go. Not this time. "Breanna," he said through gritted teeth, "she is my daughter too."

"Yet you act as if she never was," she cried, writhing and kicking like a fiend. "You never talk about her, you never acknowledge her. You go on as if she'd never been born."

Leaning over so that he was a mere inch from her face, he growled, "It is the only way I can manage her loss. You deal with her absence by practicing swordplay forever and a day. I deal with her absence by never speaking her name because it is too painful." He cocked his head to one side. "Do you truly believe your hurt is deeper than mine? Your method of coping better than mine?

Like that, the fight went out of his wife. She gazed at him with haunted grey eyes.

"Killing me or working yourself to death will not bring her back any sooner."

First her chin began to quiver and then her lower lip. Breanna turned her face away. She hated to show weakness and Cahill could count on one hand the number of times he'd seen her cry. Carefully, he crawled off his wife and then helped her to her feet, pulling her into his arms.

"She's five today," she whispered against his chest.

"I know."

"She's no longer a babe."

"No, she's not."

"She'll have her first wooden sword. Assuming *he* has heeded my wishes."

At least she had enough sense not to use A'Dale's name out loud. As the abbot and witch had warned, a name uttered was as good as an incantation.

"I'm sure he will."

"Do you think they are good to her, the two of them?"

"I'm sure they are. I'm sure they love her."

"Yes." Her chest vibrated unevenly with ragged breaths. "Hope must think *she* is her mother."

"What else would she think? We agreed they could not tell her the truth until she came of age."

Breanna pulled back enough so that she could look up at him. Her forehead creased and her lips pressed together as she tried to maintain control of her features. "She doesn't remember me, Cahill. She doesn't even know my name. She—" Squeezing her eyes shut, Breanna whispered, "Do you know how hard it is? My arms ache with wanting to hold her. In dreams I catch a whiff of her baby scent, sweet and milky, only to waken to a nightmare of emptiness. I want to stay asleep because the waking hours are too painful. I thought I could do it, Cahill, but I can't."

He smoothed a wisp of hair from her face. "You can, my love. You are the strongest woman I've ever met. You can do it."

"In body, maybe. But not in my heart, not where my daughter is concerned."

"You have forgotten the most important thing," he whispered.

"What is that?"

"You do not need to be strong alone."

Her gasping sob broke his heart and before she could turn her face away, he captured her chin and turned her so that he could taste her troubled lips, something he hadn't done in much too long.

At first she shied away, but tonight Cahill wouldn't let her. He deepened the kiss, pouring his suppressed emotions into it, taking her mouth with his, giving comfort but also asking for it in return, plundering her mouth with all the fear, hope, terror and guilt of a man who'd lost his only child and needed his wife now more than ever.

Scooping her up into his arms, he started toward the nearest door to the castle.

"Where are you taking me?"

"Inside."

"I'm not hungry."

"I am." He stopped to kiss her, hoping to show her just how hungry he was.

"Cahill…" She pressed her palms against his chest, as if that could keep him away. "I can't."

"Why not?"

She tilted her head sadly. "There will be no more children no matter how hard we try."

Dropping his forehead to hers, he whispered, "Procreation is not the only reason a husband beds his wife." His exhale was more uneven than he'd intended. "I need you, Breanna. I need you so very much. But more…I need *you* to need *me*."

He didn't kiss her, but only stared into her eyes and waited. She blinked. She licked her lips. Finally, finally she reached around his neck and pulled him close, kissing him like the wondrously sensuous woman he fell in love with.

"I need you too, Cahill. Oh gods, how I need you."

CHAPTER 7

The youngest of the three, picked up a rock and threw it at the head of her fleeing brother. When he fell, she retrieved the stone and hid it in her skirts so it could not be taken away again. When the brother awoke, she pointed at their sister and claimed it was she who had thrown the rock, out of spite...

— FROM THE LEGEND OF THE DRAGON CLAW SCEPTER

The trip up to his bedchamber was made in a sprint. The servants moving through the halls backed out of their way, averting their eyes, perhaps smiling in secret. Bre didn't care. She'd never cared what the servants had thought. She cared even less now. For the first time in five years, all she wanted was her husband and, dragon's breath, the man *could not* move fast enough.

Something had happened out on the practice field. The fierce ache that had gnawed constantly at her innards for the past five years was silenced when her husband kissed her. She'd tried to quell the pain with physical exertion through hours of training, to no avail. The practice only served to dull the ache, but it remained. Always.

"Put me down," she gasped the moment Cahill carried her across the threshold of his bedchamber. She was barely set upon her feet before she tore off her clothes in frenzied anticipation. No, she was wrong. The ache was still there but it was different. New. Or at least, it was a sensation she'd almost forgotten and Bre was overcome with need to slake it…fast.

"Breanna," Cahill whispered, gazing down at her from beneath his dark lashes. For the first time in a long time, she really looked at her husband. His handsome face was still strong and regal, but had hardened and become more angular. Lines creased his brow and the corners of his full mouth. His thick curls were still black but now had streaks of grey running through.

Like Hope.

Bre shut her eyes as an oh-too-familiar pain lanced through her. But a gentle touch beneath her chin and her husband's full, sensual lips tasting hers, teasing hers, beckoning hers to join him, helped to ease the sting.

"Why do you still wear so many clothes?" Bre asked against his lips as she ran her hands up and down his body.

"I was too busy watching you." He kissed her softly once more. "You've lost weight, Bre."

She glanced down at herself. She'd never had a very womanly figure in the first place, and she supposed now, with all the hours of practice, she was even less curvy. But the look in Cahill's eyes told her he didn't mind. His lazy lids and flushed cheeks seemed to indicate he desired her as much as ever. It was a wonder to her how such a man as Cahill desired *her*, even after she'd kept him at arm's length.

She was a fool. Tonight she would make it up to him.

Leaning in to catch his scent, she breathed deeply as she ran her hands up and down his chest. "You highborn men," Bre said with a smile as she deftly undid the tie of his shirt. "Can't even manage to undress yourself."

Cahill smiled, a real smile, and an amazing wave of warmth

washed over her, spurring her on. She lifted the hem of his shirt and he helped her pull it up and over his head.

For a moment she simply stared. Oh, Cahill's chest was the most amazing thing in the world. So broad, so strong. Though she liked to tease, Cahill was not like some of those lazy noblemen who left the defense of their kingdom to others. When Lorentia had been at war, Cahill had led the charge and he still practiced with the guard every day.

Rubbing her cheek against his muscled chest, Bre inhaled deeply before pressing a kiss to his warm flesh.

"Gods, Breanna," he sighed, pulling her close enough so that she could feel his arousal through his breeches.

Ahh. Yes. That.

She trailed kisses down his chest to his abdomen until she kneeled before her husband, working the ties at his waist. Once undone, she loosened the flap and kissed him low on the belly.

"Bre." Cahill threaded his fingers through her hair and held her tight.

With a secret smile, Bre peeled the leather lower, enjoying the sounds of her husband's soft groans.

She carefully extracted him from behind the loosened material and stroked him. Gods above, her husband was a glorious man. How she loved this part of him.

So masculine.

She kissed the tip of him.

So virile.

She opened her mouth and took him inside, running her tongue along the underside of him while she squeezed from below.

So thrilling.

Cahill's grip tightened in her hair. He cursed, using harsh words, his voice ragged and deep.

How could she have forgotten how wonderful it was to take

control of such a powerful man? How could she have denied him this?

Suddenly, she was hauled to her feet. With eyes wild and lips parted, Cahill panted her name. Then he kissed her. If you could call it that. Perhaps crushed her lips in fierce abandon would describe it more aptly. Breanna kissed back with equal eagerness. Needing him, needing her husband. Inside of her. Now.

So when Cahill pushed her to the edge of the royal bed, she gladly fell onto her back, lifting her knees and parting her thighs to show her husband what she wanted.

"Do you know what you do to me?" he asked as he frantically tugged and finally managed to kick off his breeches. "One touch from you and I'm a young stripling again, barely able to contain myself."

"Good. Now come here." Snaking a hand between her legs, Bre gently rubbed her aching flesh. So sensitive. So wet. So ready.

"Let me," Cahill whispered as he kneeled at the edge of the bed, spreading her thighs and taking her fingers away. He lifted her hand to his mouth and sucked each finger, one by one. The pull of his wet mouth drove Bre to distraction. When her husband's lips found her open thigh, kissing first the deep scar that was the result of an entanglement with a dragon that almost killed her, and then kissed higher, she flew to new heights, suddenly reminded of what it was like to sit astride a dragon's neck and ride high into the sky. The thrill. The danger. The fierce speed as it dove, the convulsions racing through the lower part of the belly...

"Oh!"

Nipping at that most sensitive part of her, Cahill held her hips steady so he could lap in between her moistened folds.

"Cahill!"

"Mmm?"

"I need you!"

"Mmm."

"Please."

He kissed her and licked her and nibbled her body until Bre was mad with desire. She'd forgotten how heady it was to have her powerful husband take control of *her*, how very delicious it felt to be at *his* mercy. She bucked and writhed beneath him like she had on the field but this time it was in ecstasy, not anger. She was unable to contain the sensations he drew forth with his lips, tongue and fingertips, having his way with her until her head thrashed incoherently across the pillow.

How long was it before he released her hips? Bre had no idea. It could have been seconds, it could have been minutes, it could have been hours. She lost all sense of time and space until she found her husband lying on top of her, face to face, staring into her eyes.

"I love you, Bre."

"I love you too."

His eyelids fluttered shut and he thrust inside of her, his sure stroke igniting every nerve ending along the way. It was a miracle and for the first time in too long she felt full and complete. How she needed him like this, his large, solid body immobilizing her as he filled her again and again. Why had she denied him? Why had she denied herself? This, *this* was the only thing that eased the pain.

She grasped his powerful shoulders, urging him on, faster, deeper, harder. "More," she begged.

He thrust all the way until he was seated completed inside, his pelvis flush against hers.

Tears leaked out of the corner of her eyes. "Again," she pleaded.

Slowly, Cahill withdrew until just the tip of him remained

inside. The emptiness of his withdrawal made her suck in a breath but then he thrust—all the way—and she expelled her breath in a hearty cry of satisfaction. Pounding her fists against his shoulders, she demanded he do it again. And again.

Her wonderfully fierce husband complied willingly to her demands until she no longer had to ask. Though she did anyway, panting her need like a mantra. *More. Again. More. Again...*

Propping himself up on his hands, Cahill moved with wild abandon, thrusting and cursing, his hair damp across his forehead, his features taut with concentration. How wonderful he was. How handsome and noble.

Bre loved him so much.

She watched as his features contorted, alerting her to his readiness for release.

"Now," she whispered. "Do it now."

Keeping her eyes open took effort, but she needed to see her husband's face and watch his expression as he spilled his seed inside of her. She didn't know why exactly, she just knew she needed it. Still propped on one hand, he grasped her hip with his other and thrust one last time, arching his back and growling at the canopy above. What started as a mere quiver in her belly spread quickly into a massive explosion of heat and fire down her thighs and up her chest so that Bre could no longer keep her eyes open for fear they'd fly right out of her head. Streaks of white and gold popped and flashed behind her closed lids and a strange humming, like a swarm of bees, echoed between her ears.

No matter how hard you try, there will never be another...

Bre's eyes flew open. No. Oh Gods no!

Where is she, Breanna? Do you know? Do you know if she yet lives?

A startled gasp flew out of her mouth before Bre had a

chance to stifle it. She pressed her hands to her ears but it did no good.

You think you've hidden her from me, but I will find her. And, I shall take such pleasure in killing her. There is nothing you can do about it!

"Bre? Bre!"

She writhed and bucked, feeling as if her head was about to explode.

"What is it? Talk to me."

Her husband's face wavered in and out of focus as Bre clawed helplessly at her ears. It wasn't until he shook her that Bre was able to focus on him.

"It's her," she whispered.

"Who?"

"Eleanor."

Cahill swept her snarled hair back from her face. He narrowed his brows in confusion. "Eleanor? Why do you speak *her* name?" He moved closer as if to kiss her but she turned away. "Breanna?"

"I heard her. After we…" Her lips quivered as she tried to form the words but couldn't. "She taunted me." Gritting her teeth, Bre took a deep breath. "She is inside my head." Bre pressed her hands to her temples, squeezing.

Cupping the back of her head, Cahill whispered, "What did she say?"

"I-I thought, I can't…" She shook her head and leaned in against him, shuddering. All the wonderful, glorious feelings of a few moments before had completely vanished. Forgotten. Leaving Bre cold and barren. "I can't do it, Cahill," she whispered against his chest. "She's trying to taint my feelings for you too." She clutched at him.

"Is it working?" he said softly.

Breanna nodded into his shoulder.

"What can I do?"

"You must not ask me to do this again. Not until after Hope returns."

He tried to tilt her chin back up to him, but she wouldn't let him. The witch had not only made her barren and forced Hope from her arms, she had taken the only other source of joy Breanna had. There was only one thing to do.

"Breanna..."

"You should take a lover."

"Don't. Don't say that. Don't do this."

Without looking at him, she got out of bed. She had her shirt on before he had a chance to stop her. But when she went to step into her tights, he got out of bed and held her about the waist. "Breanna, talk to me. Don't shut me out."

Finally, she managed to raise her eyes to his. "I love you, Cahill. Never doubt that. No matter what I say or what I do. You must always remember that I love you."

"Is there nothing I can do?" The desperation on his face only helped to seal her resolve.

"Of course there is. You can continue to hope." Her lips quivered as she said the word, her daughter's name. "And, you must let me do what I need to do."

Cupping her face, he brought her in close again and held her. Bre closed her eyes and held him tight in return. She pressed her cheek against his chest, listening to the thudding of his heart, breathing deeply of his warm, masculine scent. She needed this, needed to remember this. For it would be the last time.

She'd come to a decision. In truth, it had been brewing for many years, but tonight had simply made it more certain. She could no longer stand idly by and wait for her daughter's return. She was done with being at the witch's mercy.

No more. Breanna had to act and that meant she had to

leave her husband and Lorentia behind and find Hope. It was the only way she could keep her sanity.

The only way.

CHAPTER 8

When the children finally arrived back at the cottage, dirty and bleeding, arguing and fighting, their mother asked what had happened. The youngest presented the hidden stone, expecting to be rewarded for what she had done...

— FROM THE LEGEND OF THE DRAGON CLAW SCEPTER

Eleanor waved the dragon claw scepter in a circle, striking the base on the ground. Then, pointing the claw toward the open sky, she shouted, "*Ascendo!*" A host of beasts rose up from the smoking pit of the volcano, flying awkwardly until they jostled into two V-formations.

"*Circuli maioris!*" The beasts flew higher and higher, circling over the heads of the observing party from Dunsmoor Castle. As expected, all heads tilted back, mouths dropping in awe to watch the dragons soar high into the blue, blue sky.

"*Demerguntur!*"

Suddenly, all twenty-two dragons went into a steep dive, plummeting toward the ground at unimaginable speeds. Once Eleanor heard appropriate gasps and screams from those standing on the rim of the volcano, she cried, "*Desinam!*" And swept the scepter in a horizontal motion.

As ordered, the dragons pulled up, hovering a mere body's

length from where the party cowered.

From the massive litter that required ten strapping men to carry it, Elwood clapped as if bored. "Quite a display, sister. You're a natural at commanding dragons." He scratched his head in mock conjecture. "I wonder why that is?"

With another sweep of the scepter, she sent the dragons back to the pit, ignoring her brother's comment. "You asked for your stock to be replenished. I have done so."

"Twenty-two dragons? That is hardly an army."

"There are eighty more and at least fifty eggs ready to hatch." Eleanor used the scepter to point at the smoking bed of the volcano. From where they stood, the dragons could be seen fighting over piles of meat, bursts of flame shooting up from all directions.

"All young and untrained, I'd wager."

"They are in various stages of training," Eleanor replied.

Shifting on his bed of cushions, Elwood held out his hand for the scepter and Eleanor handed it over with reluctance. He pointed at the beasts below. "Some of them are rather puny."

She shrugged. "Apparently puny corpses spawn small dragons. Fear not, for they are as fierce as the rest and perhaps more trainable."

"You're burying the little Dunvegan corpses, are you?"

"I am rebuilding the army as quickly as possible, using whatever means available."

"You sacrificed more than three hundred when you attacked Lorentia. I expect three hundred at least."

Rage boiled in the pit of her hardened belly. "But it's been eight years, Elwood. Eight infernal years and yet…here I am," she indicated her half-human, half-reptilian form with a wave of her talons, "still *mostly* dragon."

"Are you?" Elwood cast a lazy glance her way. "I suppose I'm so used to you this way, I hadn't noticed." He guffawed noisily.

At least when he laughed this time, he didn't spew food out of his mouth and nostrils like he'd done upon her last visit. "So that is why the beasts listen to you so well. You're like a mother to them."

Growling, Eleanor paced to the very edge of the volcano, determined not to give in to her brother's goading. She was running out of time and the dragons weren't breeding as quickly as she'd hoped. She needed a maiden. She needed to transform so that she could search the continent herself because so far nothing she'd done had led to the girl.

After a command from her brother, the litter carrying him moved up beside her and the two men at the front fought for footing along the brittle crust of the lip of the volcano. The man on the left lost his battle as the ground crumbled beneath him. He screamed as he cartwheeled down the steep face, alerting the dragons to his fall. Like a flock of ducks scrambling over a breadcrumb, the dragons half waddled, half-flew to the broken body of the fallen man, tearing him apart in a matter of seconds.

"Now *that* is a sight to whet the appetite." Elwood licked his lips, calling for a basket of food. Fosset hurried forward carrying a large basket and laying out a snack of cold meat and cheese. However, just as Elwood took a bite of a leg of goose, the litter wobbled beneath him. "Hold still!" he cried in displeasure.

Fosset pointed to the empty handle. "You've lost a man, Your Majesty. The weight is…uneven."

"So? Tell these litter bearers they shall become dragon bait if they don't hold me steady!" Elwood's voice boomed, echoing back to them from across the volcano.

From the ranks of soldiers flanking the litter, a man hurried forth, taking the position of the fallen litter bearer.

"You," Elwood said, pointing the goose leg at the soldier.

"What do you think you're doing?"

"I'm holding you steady, Your Grace. I wouldn't want the litter to topple so close to the rim of the volcano."

Elwood chewed on that for a moment. "Hmm. What is your name, soldier?"

"Fosset."

"Fosset?" Elwood glanced at his valet. "Another one?"

"He is my youngest brother, Your Grace."

"Ah, you see, sister?" Elwood turned and pointed the well-chewed leg at her. "That's called loyalty. You likely don't understand the concept because you are too busy plotting revenge, sucking Dunvegan souls and scorching people to ash."

Eleanor didn't bother to comment. It wasn't loyalty that brought the youngest Fosset forth, it was probably the fact that two of his other brothers were litter bearers and he feared for their lives if the litter should falter again. Eleanor only knew this fact because she had made a point of learning all she could about those who served the king in her endless search for an unsullied maiden.

The Fosset family, more than any, disgusted her. She could not abide familial loyalty.

Elwood wiped his greasy fingers on a pillow and picked up the scepter. "So, sister, why did you bring me here today?"

"You know why," she hissed.

"You need a maiden, blah, blah, blah. Well, I need an army of dragons. That was the deal we struck."

"I don't have enough time! It shall take me another eight years to rebuild the stock. I don't *have* another eight years. Once the child turns sixteen, it will be too late." Eleanor swished her tail in annoyance. There was one tidbit she hadn't told Elwood—something she'd seen in the scepter three years ago. Breanna had left Lorentia in search of her daughter and what quickly became apparent was that the dragon-slaying urchin didn't have a clue where her daughter was. However, Eleanor was sure she'd find her, and when she did, she wanted to be close behind. "I promise you, Elwood, I will replace your stock, but first, change me back so I can find the child and kill her."

Elwood tsked. "Unfortunately, you've proven that your promises hold no weight." He sighed with great exaggeration. "I take it you haven't had any luck with the scepter? No hint as to the child's whereabouts?"

"No."

"None of your winged emissaries have located her? Nothing your ravens and bats have picked up in the ether, nothing in the wind?"

"No." Eleanor bared her teeth. "Nothing."

"Yet there is something you're not telling me." He lifted the scepter above his head, peering into the crystal held within the golden claw. "What is it? What are you keeping from me? I must know."

Eleanor growled. Maybe if she told him what she'd seen he'd agree to help. "The bitch is looking for the child too."

"The Morrainian slut?"

"The very one."

"She doesn't know the location of her own daughter?"

"No. That's why I haven't been able to locate her either. But, she's spent the last three years in disguise, searching the continent over."

"And you're *only* telling me now because…?"

"Because I believe she's getting close and I want to be there when she finds her offspring."

Elwood stroked his chin. "This is a pickle, isn't it? My concern is, sister, that the minute you become human, you will leave and I will have no one to tend the dragons. I can't have that. At the same time…" He turned his gaze on Fosset, who seemed to feel his master's stare and visibly shrank in size as he hurried to clean up the basket of half-eaten foodstuffs.

"Perhaps a human emissary is the thing," he said absently.

"Are you suggesting Fosset?"

The valet made a squeak and dropped to his knees beside the litter. "Please, Your Grace, I'm a man servant, not an assassin."

"Fosset is right. It takes too long to train a good valet and the man is just now getting the hang of things. I will not have you rob me of another good man, Eleanor." Rubbing his temples as if this conversation was giving him a headache, Elwood continued, "But the Fosset family have shown loyalty, perhaps that one should do." Elwood used the scepter to point at the youngest Fosset, the soldier who'd taken over the position of litter bearer.

"No!" the elder Fosset cried. "If you must choose someone, choose me, then. Not Duncan, I beg of you!" He supplicated himself by the side of Elwood's litter.

Eleanor bared her teeth in the closest thing she could manage to a smile. You'd think these mortals would learn, but they never did. As far as she was concerned, begging for mercy was as good as begging for death. It was one of the few things she and her brother agreed upon. "Indeed, brother," she said, licking her scaly lips with her forked tongue. "Young Fosset should do rather nicely. Thank you."

What she was doing was wrong. Muriel knew it was. Still, she could not turn away, no matter how hard she tried. She hadn't meant to follow him, she'd been looking for Horny Goat Weed and Shadow Blossoms, both of which bloomed near the stream. It wasn't her fault that Allan was there too.

In the stream.

Bathing.

Naked.

His back was to her—his broad, muscular, *naked* back—and he sat upon a boulder, leaning forward, washing his chest and taking a turn beneath each of his arms. Then he stood.

Mercy! Her throat no longer worked to swallow.

The swoop of his lower back gave rise to the most amazing backside Muriel had ever seen. Not that she'd seen many backsides in her day, but she knew a fine derriere when she saw one. High and taut, she could see the flex of Allan's muscles as he moved through the water, bending to wash his strong legs with a rag.

Don't turn around. Don't turn…

Too late.

Muriel gasped. If not for the sound of the running water, she was sure he would have heard her, in fact, she wondered if he did hear something, for he paused and looked up, searching the forest, listening. But then he went back to washing and Muriel covered her eyes because they refused to shut on their own and what she'd seen was now burned forever onto the insides of her eyelids.

Well, it was as she'd always known, Allan A'Dale was a man. *All* man.

No longer caring how much noise she made, Muriel turned, her basket of freshly picked herbs forgotten, and fled from her hiding spot.

How could she? How could she have been so weak?

It was a short walk back to the cottage, but by the time she returned, Muriel was so out of sorts she could hardly catch her breath. She leaned against the wall of the chicken coop and focused on calming herself. One breath in and one breath out. Slow and easy.

There.

The chickens rustled inside the coop, staying out of the

sun. Bees buzzed nearby searching the garden for blooms and a dragonfly hovered near her as if to stop for a chat. Everything was as it should be, tranquil and peaceful. If she focused, she could still hear the stream, but she mustn't think about the stream, nor the man standing in it.

"Hope?" she called, needing the girl to distract her. "Hope?" Nothing.

The churning in her stomach that had begun the moment she'd spied Allan, turned to dread. Where was Hope?

She ran to the rabbit hutch, but Hope wasn't there.

She wasn't in the garden either.

Picking up her skirts, Muriel hurried up the path to the cottage, calling Hope's name. There was no one there.

Oh gods!

One moment of weakness was all it took. It was as she'd always known it would be. She should not have allowed herself to be distracted. Not for one second. But she had been distracted, so very, very distracted and now Hope was gone.

Gone!

"Mama?"

At the sound of Hope's voice, Muriel looked up from where she'd collapsed on the ground.

"Mama? Are you ill?"

With a hand to her cheek, Muriel stood, forcing a smile. "I'm quite well, my pet. I simply felt a little faint. It must be the heat."

Hope ran forward and put a hand on Muriel's stomach. "Marta says her mother's always fainting when she's got a baby in her belly. Do you think that's what's wrong?" Hope's eyes went wide with delight. "Might you have another baby?"

A fierce jumble of emotions gripped Muriel from the inside, poking and prodding her in all her deepest places. She had to turn away from Hope lest the sensitive girl should see the anguish on her face.

"Mama?"

After two deep breaths Muriel was able to face her again. "I'm fine, pet. But I'm not with child. I'm just overheated."

"Oh." One did not have to see aura's to read the disappointment on Hope's face.

Now that the panic of Hope's absence was beginning to fade, Muriel chided the girl. "Where were you? How many times have I told you not to run off? There are brigands and ne'er do wells all over. Do you know what they'd do if they found a sweet, young child such as yourself?"

With hands on her hips, Hope said, "Mama, I am not a child. I'm nine years old and I know this forest better than any stranger passing through."

"I know you are careful, but there are beings that use magic to hide their presence. Those are the ones that are most dangerous."

"Magic?" Hope lifted her chin. "You always speak of magic. Yet you won't show me what you know." She tilted her head and regarded Muriel with the very same piercing gaze as that of her true mother, the queen of Lorentia.

"I don't know what you're talking about."

"You know magic, yet you won't show your own daughter. Why?"

Blasted inferno! The child was all sweetness one moment and hard as steel the next and the change always threw Muriel off kilter. This was not a conversation Muriel wished to have. It was not a conversation she *could* have.

"Hope. I cannot show you what I do not know." It was not a lie—for Muriel endeavored never to lie—it was a diversion.

Narrowing her eyes, Hope said, "You speak in riddles every time I ask. I *know* you know magic. I've seen you. Why last week I brought home that little lark with the broken wing. Do you remember? The next day, his wing was healed and he flew away."

"It was the poultice. That was all."

The only way to get out of the conversation was to change the subject. In fact, now that Muriel thought on it, Hope had done the very same thing, bringing up magic in order to get out of being chided for wandering off. "You haven't answered my question. Where were you?"

"I'll answer your question when you answer mine."

"Hope! Mind your mam."

The resonant voice of her false husband sent a shiver deep into Muriel's belly. She shut her eyes and took a slow breath.

Don't look at him. Don't look...

Too late. She turned to watch Allan's approach across the yard. His hair was damp and though he was fully dressed, in her mind he was walking straight toward her...still naked.

"Hello wife."

"Husband." Muriel's lips felt stiff as she looked up at him beneath her lashes.

"Hope, apologize to your mam."

Scuffing her slipper against the ground, she whispered, "I'm sorry, Mama."

"Now," Allan continued, his voice deep and firm, "if I hear you speak to your mama in that tone again, I shall have to take a switch to your backside, do you understand?"

Hope dropped her gaze to the ground. "Yes, Da. I'm sorry."

"Go finish your chores. Once you're done, we'll practice archery."

Hope grimaced. "But it's so hot..."

"Hope."

"Yes, Da."

"And no more wandering off, do you hear?"

She nodded once before running off to the rabbit hutch. Together they watched her go. Allan was standing so close,

Muriel could hear the steady thud of his heartbeat and could smell the clean, masculine scent of him.

"She's as headstrong as her mother."

"Yes," Muriel said quietly. Allan was speaking of Breanna, not her. Without knowing why, she placed a hand on her stomach which felt strangely hollow.

She was not prepared for Allan's touch on her elbow and she jumped. He turned her gently toward him and Muriel looked up into his warm brown eyes, questioning, wanting...

"Allan," she whispered.

His nostrils flared as if inhaling his name from her breath. Then he moved his lips, like he was whispering silently to himself. Surely it was an incantation because she was spellbound by the sight. When he took her hand in his, she could scarce breathe and her pulse reverberated between her ears.

"You dropped this."

Muriel looked down to find he'd placed the handle of her basket across her arm.

With a secret smile, he leaned in close. "Were you pleased by what you saw in the stream?"

It took a few moments for her to find her tongue. "Allan..."

He ducked his head so that there was scarcely a breath between them. "Do you think you might return the favor some day?"

"Mercy—"

"I promise, I won't touch. But I should very much like to look. It seems only fair, don't you think?"

The desire to kiss him had never been stronger. The desire to *more* than kiss him—the itch of her fingertips to feel his face, to touch the strong lines of his chest and sweep her hand over the swell of his backside—nearly made her weep. But before she had the chance to do any of those things, things she'd surely both savor and regret, Allan took a step back and then another.

He shut his eyes and a look of pain flashed across his features. "I'm sorry. For a moment, I forgot myself."

Muriel cleared her throat. "As did I." Quickly, she went on. "When I saw you in the stream, I should have turned around and left. I should not have lingered."

"Is it wrong that I'm glad you did linger?"

"Yes, Allan. I'm afraid it is wrong."

"And yet I am not sorry."

She had no reply. Perhaps because there was nothing she could say that would not be a lie for she felt precisely the same way.

"Muriel…"

She turned away, heading back out to the forest to finish her foraging. *Give me strength,* she prayed. *All Sisters both come and gone, I beg of you, give me strength.*

A gentle voice inside her head whispered, *Four years, eight months and three days.*

CHAPTER 9

"Where did you find this?" the mother demanded as she snatched the stone from her child's hand. "It is the most beautiful thing I have ever seen."
When each child cried that they wished to touch the stone once more, the mother held it aloft. "Hands off, for I know what must be done with this..."

— FROM THE LEGEND OF THE DRAGON CLAW SCEPTER

D uncan was close. So close. The moment he'd ridden into Dewsbury, he'd known he was close and the lad at the well had told him the girl lived nearby—by the way he scuffed his boot, bit his lip and shifted his eyes. The coin was merely for confirmation. The problem was, the closer he got to his intended target, the louder the infernal buzzing became between his ears. *She* was there inside his head. That awful *thing* had been his constant companion the entire time he'd been on his quest, her rough hewn voice waking him from sleep, forcing him on from village to village with barely time to eat or rest. It never stopped, except for on rare occasions when he dunked his head under water.

But that could not last, unless he wished for eternal sleep, which, on days like today, seemed like the preferable option, for today it was worse than ever. The buzzing had become so unbearable, Duncan could scarcely see straight. His head swooned as if he'd taken too much drink on an empty stomach.

He passed a tavern and pulled up on the reins. His stomach was empty. Perhaps drink would quell the voice of the queen. He dismounted at the stable and an old stable-hand strolled up to take his horse.

What are you doing? Go get her! Now!

Eleanor. Queen of the dragons.

How Duncan loathed her. Her voice was a lance to a spot right between his eyes, yet he ignored it, finding a modicum of solace in the cool, dim interior of the public house where he immediately ordered a flagon of ale.

"*Never draw attention to yourself,*" his father had repeated more often than he could remember. "*Elwood does not reward bravery. He scorns it.*" It wasn't bravery that had made Duncan do what he'd done when he'd taken his brother's place as litter carrier that day in Dunvegan. It was instinct and Duncan hadn't considered the implications of his actions past that of keeping his family safe, for more of his brothers were litter carriers and in danger of becoming dragon bait.

He guzzled the lukewarm drink, needing relief from his relentless quest, from *her*.

You fool!

He was cursed. His whole family was cursed. The Fossets had been indentured by Duncan's grandfather years ago. Three generations of men from the line of his eldest son—Duncan's father—were to be indentured into servitude in exchange for three parcels of land in Darnell. With his father gone—murdered by the hideous Eleanor, for sport—the second generation of Fosset men had all become servants, all seven of them. He'd seen only thirteen summers when he'd been commanded to join the guard, and at the time, he'd been overjoyed to spend the time practicing for combat with other young men.

Until the day he saw his brother tumble to his death and be torn apart by dragons.

Now a dragon lived in his head.

He finished the ale and ordered another.

You will pay, Fosset. Heed me, you will pay for this.

"She will be there on the morrow," he muttered into his cup before downing the entire thing in three swallows. Was it because he was so close to completing his quest that he willingly angered the queen? Or, was it the knowledge that no matter what he did, whether he heeded the dragon-queen or not, it would do nothing to lift the curse on his family and in all likelihood, they would all die by the sorceress' hand, as his father and brother had before him.

"Halloo?" Allan peered into the darkened smithy. There were no sounds coming from within, no pounding of metal against metal, no hiss of water against hot steel or whooshing of bellows stoking the coals. Strange. Dropping his sack full of baskets, he moved inside, calling out another greeting while keeping his hand firmly gripped on his dagger. A strange shuffling came from behind a door. Pulling the dagger from its sheath, Allan adopted a ready stance as the door creaked open.

Thump, slide, thump, slide...

Allan raised his knife, ready to strike.

"Darwin? Is that you?" A smoke roughened voice called.

"No, t'is another," replied Allan, lowering his blade before the man rounded the door.

"Oh. Hallo," The old smith said when he finally saw A'Dale standing behind the door. "It's you, A'Dale. How ye be this day?"

"Indeed, I am well."

The man searched the smithy. "And no sign of me young apprentice. Gods, but the lad is flighty. A caning is what he needs."

Allan gave his head a shake. What was wrong with him? Why, he knew the old smith wore a peg leg after losing his in a fire years before. But today, for some reason, everything was making him jumpy.

He was being excessively suspicious, that was all. It'd been twelve years, twelve years of living in peace in the heart of Darnell, with no one questioning him or Muriel about Hope's origins, with no hint of evil or the sorceress.

Peace.

No, he did not live in peace. Living with Muriel was torture. Excruciatingly, painful torture. But it was a torture he would not trade.

Going back to retrieve his sack of goods, Allan hoped he gave the impression of one come to do casual business and not that of a man who'd nearly slit the throat of an innocent old blacksmith for no apparent reason.

Now that Allan thought about it, he had seen the young apprentice laughing and roughhousing with some other lads at the town well. They'd all stopped their fighting when he rode past, nudging one another and whispering behind their hands.

He clenched his fist as if he still held the dagger. Blasted paranoia! The lad probably knew where he was headed and was worried A'Dale would rat him out.

"I've got your new scythe and axe. Is it coin or trade?" The smith went to the wall and removed the two implements while A'Dale dumped out the contents of his sack.

"Baskets?" The old man wheezed upon his return. "Bah!"

"Please," A'Dale said. "My wife makes them quicker than

I can sell them." He picked up one particularly fine basket. "Look at the craftsmanship on it. You see? She's worked a whole woodland scene into the weave." Allan punched the inside of the basket, showing its strength. "Beautiful, yet watertight. It's a basket fit for a king."

The old man chuckled, "Do I look like a king? Come, A'Dale. What need have I of something so fine? For my wife? She's been gone nearly a decade already and I've got all the baskets I could want."

Reaching into his vest, A'Dale withdrew his purse. He pulled coins from within and placed them in the smith's open palm. "Here."

The smith tallied the coins then pocketed them. "That should do."

"But you must take at least two baskets as well."

"Why?"

"So I can tell my wife how you raved about them and said you'd never seen their equals. How you insisted upon having them."

"Why would you tell such a tale?"

"To make her happy."

Scratching his thick brow, the old man chuckled. "Ah. So 'tis a love match between you and your woman, is that it?"

"It is." A'Dale smiled and his heart swelled at the thought of Muriel. Though theirs was an *unconsummated* love, it was a love match none-the-less. Next to protecting Hope, Allan's sole purpose in life was to make Muriel happy.

Even if it killed him.

And gods above, it was killing him. You'd think it would have gotten easier after more than a decade. Not so. Muriel was a woman like no other. She was goodness through and through. It was her purity of spirit, kindness and generosity that made him fall even more deeply in love with her day by day.

But just because the love of his life was good and pure, didn't mean his thoughts in regards to her were chaste. Quite the opposite.

Why, he could see her now, the rise and fall of her creamy breasts beneath her dress while she hummed as she brushed Hope's hair. He'd dreamed of those breasts, full and high. He'd imagined how they might feel cupped within his hands. Whenever he had such thoughts, it was as if Muriel could read his mind for her cheeks would blossom with color and her pretty lips would part. The desire to grab her and kiss her so often overwhelmed him. Usually he'd slake his arousal with hard work; cutting wood or hunting or going for a dip in the cool stream nearby.

He could not forget the time he'd caught Muriel spying on him while he bathed and he often found himself envisioning other outcomes to the scenario.

But that was all he had, visions. Fantasies. That and enough wood to last them through at least two winters and enough dried meat for three.

Nights were worse. How many times had he lain awake in bed listening to her soft sighs as she slept, imagining what it would feel like to slide in beside her, to lift her nightdress and fit himself between her thighs? He longed to hear her sigh *his* name with passion and desire, to feel the warmth of her sweet body surrounding him.

With difficulty, Allan forced his attention back to the old man who stooped beside the pile of baskets.

"Very well," the smith sighed. "I'll take these two." He grabbed two baskets and stood. "But I'll most likely turn around and sell them first chance I get."

"As you wish," A'Dale said, stooping to gather the rest. He groaned and shifted where he crouched. As usual, the mere thought of Muriel was enough to fire his loins with painful arousal. Years of unspent arousal. How much longer could he last?

Darwin, the young apprentice, appeared at that moment, a pole across his shoulders and a full bucket on either end.

"Well," the old smith said. "You certainly took your time."

"Sorry, Sir. 'twas busy at the well." He set the buckets down and glanced warily at Allan. "What's 'e still doing 'ere?"

The smith cuffed the boy on the back of the head. "Mind your mouth, boy. Show some respect."

The lad cringed and looked sideways at Allan. "Sorry, Sir. I didn't mean nothin' by it."

"You didn't wish to see me?" Allan asked, hoisting his sack over his shoulder. "Why?"

"Weren't nothing, Sir."

"Darwin," the smith barked. "Mind yourself. Now, take the tools out to the man's horse for him."

There was no mistaking the way the apprentice wouldn't meet Allan's gaze as they made their way to where Allan's horse was tied. It was more than paranoia, he was sure of it. Something *had* happened.

Once he'd secured the bag of baskets to his mount, the boy handed him the scythe and axe and turned to leave. Dropping the tools, Allan grabbed his arm. "Wait." He pulled his purse from his pocket and pulled a coin from it. Holding it up in front of the boy's face, he said, "Why didn't you wish to see me? Tell me the truth now."

With a sullen look, the boy glanced up the lane, then down. "I was afraid t' see you. Afraid t' get into trouble."

"Trouble? Why?"

"Because of what I said."

A'Dale had the urge to shake the boy into being more forthcoming. "What did you say? And to whom did you say it?"

Scuffing his worn boot against the dusty ground, the boy said, "I don't know who it was. They was dressed funny and I couldna tell who they was. But they was asking after you…or your daughter, rather."

"My daughter?"

"Well, they was asking 'bout a girl with a white streak in her hair up in front." The boy patted his forehead. "Just like your girl."

The cold hand of dread gripped Allan's heart and squeezed just as he tightened his hold on the boy's arm. "What did you say?" he asked through gritted teeth.

"Nothing! I didn't say nothing!"

Allan yanked the boy up to within an inch of his face. The lad's eyes shifted. "Liar," Allan hissed. "Tell me what was said. Tell me now!"

Screwing up his lips, the boy said, "Honest, I didn't say nothing…at first. But then, 'e gave me this." The boy struggled in his pocket before pulling out a shiny golden coin.

A gold florin?

There was only one person who'd be so bold as to flash a gold florin around a small village.

Oh gods!

"After me da died, it's been left t' me t' provide for me family," the lad went on, in a plaintive tone.

Allan dropped the boy without thought and jumped astride his horse. The newly crafted farm implements were left forgotten in the dust as he kicked the horse into a gallop, dodging peasants and chickens through the narrow lane of the village.

Why hadn't he listened to his gut? Why hadn't he returned home the moment he saw people watching him strangely? Hadn't Muriel always told him to trust his instincts? That hunches were in truth the stirrings of magical senses in all folk?

Once out on the open road, Allan leaned forward, willing the horse to fly across the miles that separated him from Muriel and Hope. If anything happened to them, if he was too late…

It seemed to take forever before he reached the small fork in the road that led through the forest to his cottage, and before he could even see the smoke from the chimney, he started to shout, "Wife! Where ye be? Come wife? Where ye be now?!"

Fear, like he'd *never* experienced in any battle whether with men or dragons, turned his skin cold and clammy and had his heart beating in time to the horse's galloping gait.

Please, please let her and Hope be safe. Please let them be down in the hidey-hole. Oh gods of old, I beg of you, please!

With dust flying and hooves scrabbling, they rounded the last bend in the path only to pull up to a screeching halt in the little clearing before the cottage. The door to the cottage was left wide open. A tub of wash sat abandoned by the gate, while only two shirts flapped lazily on the line. A hoe sat upright in the garden, as if waiting for its owner to return any moment to finish the job and the door to Hope's rabbit hutch was left open and bunnies were hopping and munching unchecked through the cabbage patch.

There, tied to the hitching post, was a strange black horse, weighed down not only with saddle bags…but with weapons—a sword and an axe among others.

A'Dale slid off his horse and ran as fast as his legs would carry him even though he knew it was no use. He was already too late.

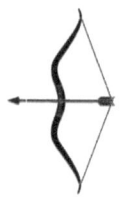

CHAPTER 10

That night, under the light of a full moon, the woman slipped out of the cottage with the crystal concealed in a bag beneath her cloak. Unable to sleep for want of the stone, the children quietly followed their mother down the path that led to the Forest of the Giants.

Deep within the forest was a cave, home of the most powerful magi in the land. Though his location was widely known, few dared to visit for he was ancient, powerful and quick to temper...

— FROM THE LEGEND OF THE DRAGON CLAW SCEPTER

Muriel should have gone to the door to greet him. She'd heard Allan's frantic cries from a long way off, and now his harried footfalls sprinting for the door, fearful and desperate, clearly indicated his trepidation. But she could not leave Hope's side, not while their visitor stood in front of her. Muriel was too busy quietly whispering a protective incantation to move.

Out of the corner of her eye, she saw A'Dale's outline in the doorway. He was such a large man, nearly blocking all the light from outside. She wrenched her gaze away and kept reciting beneath her breath, while his shadow crept inside, a sword in one hand, a dagger in the other. Would his eyes have adjusted to the dim light yet? Would he recognize who it was, looking into Hope's eyes, holding her hands in a death grip?

"Da!" Hope squealed. "Look, we have a visitor!"

"Do we now?" Allan said in a voice she'd never heard before, like the growl of a wolf.

"Yes. Mam says it's her sister, come from afar. I didn't know Mam had a sister. But look, here she is!"

Muriel finished the final phrase of the spell just as Allan realized who their guest was.

"Oh gods!" He fell to his knee in front of the queen.

The queen turned to face him. Although she was slight of frame, her posture and bearing made her appear much taller. "Hello, A'Dale," she said in a low, quavering voice. "It has been too long."

"Your Gr...my lady. I apologize. I didn't recognize you."

"I know, Da. It's because she looks so much like a boy." Hope tilted her head to the side and studied the queen with open curiosity. "Why do you dress like a boy? You'd be much prettier in a dress. I could put something together for you, if you'd like. Da bought some fine linen last month and I've been saving it for something special." She giggled. "If my very own auntie visiting isn't special, I don't know what is!"

"Hope!" Muriel chided. They didn't get many visitors—none, actually—and Hope's naturally inquisitive spirit and talkative nature, while sweet, was not the manner in which to address a royal parent.

"It's all right," the queen said with a soft smile for Hope. "I know I must look strange to you. But I dress this way for a reason. Two, actually."

"Why?" Hope asked wide-eyed.

"First, because it is not safe for a woman to travel alone. This way, I look like a boy so that people leave me be. For the most part."

It was true, the queen looked more like a boy than ever. She'd cut off the long plait of hair down her back and if Muriel wasn't mistaken, she'd lost weight too. Why, unless you knew the truth, you'd miss the very slight hint of a bosom beneath her tunic.

"Second," the queen continued, "dressing this way makes it easier to move when I ride fast. Or, if I have to fight."

"You fight?" Hope whispered. "On purpose?"

"Yes. But only when it's absolutely necessary."

Hope made a face and shivered. "Swordplay is so brutish and unladylike, don't you hate it?"

Oh no! Why did Hope have to express every pert opinion that came into that head of hers? "Hope!" Muriel interjected, "Sometimes our opinions are best left unsaid."

Slanting her head in Muriel's direction, Breanna did not take her loving gaze from the girl. "Don't chide the lass, Muriel. I'd much rather have my...*niece* speak plainly than hear a bunch of simpering platitudes."

Not able to stop herself from wrapping a protective arm around Hope, Muriel murmured, "I couldn't keep her from expressing her opinion if I wanted."

The queen's lips twitched "No. I suppose not." She tilted her head in the other direction to view her daughter from another angle. When she spoke, her voice was soft and ragged. "Tell me child, do you practice swordplay? What of archery?"

"Oh, but I do. Da absolutely insists upon it."

The queen finally managed to tear her gaze away from Hope to nod in A'Dale's direction. "Good. That is as it should be."

Allan returned the nod. Once the queen's attention was back on Hope, he glanced at Muriel and she read unease in his expressive eyes. She understood his concern, for she shared it.

"But mostly I make up my own steps." Hope giggled behind her hand. "It makes Da crazy." She lowered her voice and winked at the queen. "But it makes Mam smile."

"Is that so?" Bre asked. "You create your own moves, do you?"

"Oh yes. I can show you if you like. They're rather pretty."

Oh gods! The queen should not be here. She should not be touching her daughter because the love emitted by Breanna right now was so strong and so palpable, it was nearly impossible to cloak, even with pure magic.

But worse, the very last thing they should be discussing was Hope's combat lessons.

Clearing her throat, Muriel gave Hope a little squeeze of warning—though the child was not likely to heed it, she never did. "I'm sure my sister is famished after traveling such a great distance. Run out to the garden and pull some carrots and turnips. We'll roast that venison your da brought home the other day."

Holding up her hand, Breanna said, "Food can wait. I'm much more interested in watching Hope practice." The queen was grinning now. Exultant. Her eyes shining with love and tenderness. "I should like to see her own moves in particular. Yes, I should like to see that very much."

Everything about Hope was perfect. Dark glossy curls, the white streak giving her an air of maturity and setting off the striking color of her violet eyes. She was a true beauty. Breanna could not have imagined a more perfect child. Sweet, inquisitive, charming, intelligent.

But wait…

What was this?

This was unnatural.

This was an abomination.

Surely the three of them were playing a cruel jape upon her.

So convinced that she was the brunt of some misguided prank, Breanna watch, open-mouthed, occasionally shaking her head and rubbing her eyes, waiting in vain for someone to laugh and explain the truth. For the girl did not brandish a sword nor a bow. Instead, she flaunted a long stick to which was attached an even longer ribbon. That was not the worst of it. She did not employ even the simplest of combat maneuvers.

Oh no. She danced.

Danced!

Twirling and spinning across the grass, flourishing the stick like some mummer at a summer festival, Hope drew designs in the air—curlicues and swirls—the ribbon pirouetted as if enchanted with magic.

Pressing a palm to her forehead to stave off the pounding ache behind her eyes, she turned her attention to A'Dale. She had half a mind to run him through, right here, right now. However, the insolent man did not have the courtesy to *at least* appear chagrined by her obvious anger. His lips were pressed together in a thin line and he held his arms across his chest as if he was not responsible for the disgrace that cavorted before her.

Clenching her right hand in her left, her fingers itching for her sword, Bre said, "In the name of all that is holy, please stop."

But the girl did not stop for she was in her own world, prancing on as if she was the only one there, as if all else had disappeared and she was alone.

Bre blinked.

At the very least, she understood the girl's passion. She recognized the intensity on her daughter's face as she moved across the open grass, humming beneath her breath as she twirled and spun, her skirts flying out around her. How many times had Bre become lost in the movement of the sword she wielded so that hours would pass without her noticing? It was a joy to lose oneself in such a manner, to forget all else—pain, suffering, disappointment—and just be present in the simplicity of movement.

However, the girl's passion for her *dance* did not change the fact that what she was doing was completely and utterly preposterous.

It was after Hope threw the stick, ribbon and all, high into the air, turned a somersault and caught it again, that Bre finally intervened.

"Stop." When Hope still did not stop, she snatched the rod out of her hand. "I said, stop."

"Oh!" The girl's brows drew together in confusion. "Didn't you like it, Auntie?"

"No." Holding the wand in front of Hope's face, Bre snapped it in half and dropped it to the ground.

Hope uttered a startled cry and fell to the ground, picking up the broken pieces of wood. "You broke my wand!"

Hope's crestfallen response only served to anger Breanna more. She turned to the two responsible for this disaster. "I had one request. *One.*" She glanced at the girl on the ground behind her who was sniffling as she tried to fit the broken pieces back together.

Rage boiled in her veins. After all she had suffered, the only thing that had gotten her through was knowing her daughter was being taught how to protect herself. It was not a whim that had made her ask this of A'Dale.

By the gods! It was for Hope's *safety*.

The man's negligence would not go unpunished.

But more important than his punishment was her daughter's training and Breanna meant to rectify the situation.

Immediately.

"A'Dale, two wooden wasters, if you please. I should have

come sooner. It's time Hope was taught properly."

✦ ✦ ✦

"I hate her!"

Muriel slathered Hope's bruised knuckles with a salve, a magical salve, for she had to do everything in her power to keep the girl calm. "Shh, pet. She'll hear you."

"I don't care if she does. She's awful. Make her go away!"

"Hope," Allan chided quietly but firmly. "Mind yourself."

As always, Hope heeded her father, though he could not stop her tears.

No. Muriel reminded herself. *A'Dale is not Hope's father. Cahill is. And, I am not her mother, Breanna is.* How many times today had Muriel repeated those words in her head?

But the queen had been so harsh with Hope, making her practice for hours, striking her knuckles when she missed a shot with her arrows, using the broad side of her sword to strike blows upon Hope's slight frame in order to illustrate the weakness in her swordplay. Tears had run down Muriel's cheeks every time Hope cried out in alarm and injury as if Hope's pain was her own. Yet the practice continued with a ruthlessness Muriel could not bear. She could not watch, but neither could she leave, so she sat by Allan's side, tucking her head between his chin and chest so she wouldn't have to hear Hope's cries of pain. Allan held her close, petting her hair, murmuring soft words of comfort—breaking all her rules—but for once she didn't care.

She's not my daughter. She's not my daughter. The words were a chant echoing between her ears, yet they gave no relief.

"How can she be your sister? She's *nothing* like you," Hope asked through her sobs.

"Shush." Muriel finished wrapping her knuckles in clean

linen and then kissed the top of Hope's head. "Go to bed now. She'll be gone in the morning."

Throwing her arms around Muriel's waist, Hope whispered, "I'm glad *you're* my mother."

Muriel squeezed Hope back even as her heart broke. The voice inside her head whispered, *Oh, pet…I wish that I was, but alas, I am not your mother and I must not forget it.*

After a quiet word with Allan, asking him to remain inside and watch over the child, Muriel went outside to where Breanna sat on a stump, sharpening her sword with a stone.

"I could have you both drawn and quartered for your negligence, you know that don't you?"

"Yes," Muriel replied.

The little queen glanced up, her eyes glassy in the moonlight. "She leaves with me at first light. If you make no fuss, I will pardon you for the wrong you have committed."

"No."

Breanna's hands stopped moving. She sat for a moment, then dropped the stone and stood. Though she was much slighter of stature than Muriel, the fact she had her sword aimed at Muriel's throat made her seem much larger.

"What did you say?"

"I said, 'no'…Your Majesty."

Breanna blinked. She blinked again. By the light of the moon, Muriel saw the tear slide down her cheek, contradicting the queen's grim expression and aggressive stance.

Quietly, Muriel said, "If you take her, *she* will know—the one whose name I shall not utter."

"It is a matter of safety that she learn to protect herself," Bre bit out.

"Yet you come here, putting us all in jeopardy."

The queen's response was a sharp inhalation. In some part of her, she must have known the truth of Muriel's words.

Softening her tone, Muriel said, "Hope may not be the skilled warrior you had hoped for, but it is not for lack of trying. We have tried, by the gods, we have tried. A'Dale has spent countless hours teaching her. He insists upon training every day."

"Then how do you explain her utter hopelessness at it?"

"The girl is as headstrong as her mother and she refuses to engage in the activity. She loathes it." Muriel tilted her head to one side. "Hope couldn't take a life to save her own. It's not in her nature."

The night air amplified the queen's rattling breath.

"You should not have come," Muriel continued quietly. "You know that, don't you? The only thing you've accomplished is to endanger Hope's life." Muriel waited for a response. When none came, she pressed on, her lips quivering as she spoke. "You must leave. Now. For all our sakes." Beneath her breath, Muriel began an incantation, the strongest protective spell she could muster. Even without her spectaculscope, she knew how powerful the queen's aura was at the moment. Love and anger in nearly equal parts was a potent combination, and to anyone with any sort of magical sensibility it would be as visible as a beacon on a mountaintop.

Breanna sniffed. She squeezed her eyes shut and then opened them again. She shook her head as if flies swarmed around her face. The sword shifted in her hands, nicking Muriel's neck.

"I can't," the queen said, her voice raw with emotion.

"Then you shall have to kill me."

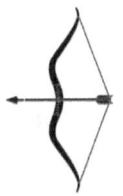

CHAPTER II

From their hiding places, the children observed their mother approach the cave, remove the stone from her bag and quietly enter. Holding hands—friends once more—the children followed their mother into the cave...

— FROM THE LEGEND OF THE DRAGON CLAW SCEPTER

A deep voice came from behind Muriel.
"Over my dead body."
She felt Allan's presence just behind her, the tightly coiled rage and protective instinct was as tangible as the smell of smoke from a signal fire.

"Go back inside," Muriel said. "Stay with Hope."

"Not until she drops her weapon. Not until I know you are safe."

"This is a matter between myself and the quee…and my sister."

But Allan did not go back inside. Of course he didn't. He moved to her side, his sword drawn, pointing it at the queen's chest. They were at an impasse. All on edge, ready to react, no one wishing to back down. Muriel sensed the barely tethered hostility between Allan and the queen and she feared even one small movement could bring on a hailstorm of misguided bloodshed.

So, she did the only thing she could do, she continued to invoke the spell, hoping to dispel the emotional discord that drew in the darkness like a heavy cloud swirling malevolently around them.

"Mama?"

Oh gods, no!

"Mama!" Hope's scampering footsteps brought her into the fray before Muriel or A'Dale could do or say anything to stop her. She positioned herself in front of Muriel, facing Breanna, fitting just beneath the blade of Breanna's sword. "I hate you!" She kicked the queen's shin. "Go away. We don't want you here." She kicked again. "You leave my mother alone!"

Breanna uttered a sound like nothing Muriel had ever heard before. It was the cry of an injured animal, tortured by hellions and the sound not only touched the nerves in her ears but the most profound part of her soul, sending gooseflesh up and down her limbs, rending her heart in two. The queen dropped the sword and fell to her knees in front of her daughter. She held out her hands, pleading wordlessly for Hope to take them, but Hope swatted them away.

"If you ever hurt Mama, I swear to Cragmar the Great that I will tear you apart with my teeth."

Never had Muriel heard Hope speak in such a way. Never had she heard that tone from her daughter. It frightened her.

She's not your daughter. She's Breanna's.

"No," Breanna moaned, her head hanging in misery, her shoulders slumped as if life had fled. Like a kneeling corpse, with no reason to live. No hope.

"Go back inside with your Da, my pet. Your auntie and I quarreled. It happens in families sometimes. It's over now. It's all over."

"I don't want to go back in. Not until she leaves."

Muriel took hold of Hope's shoulders and turned her around, pulling her into her arms. "Do as I say, pet," she whispered.

After hugging Muriel's waist, Hope finally followed Allan back toward the cottage, stopping once to cast a hateful stare over her shoulder. The queen could not have seen the look, for she remained on her knees, head bowed. But the gods bestowed other means of seeing upon mortals and Muriel was certain Bre *felt* the wrath of her daughter even though she may not have *seen* it. For no sooner had Hope looked away, Bre's shoulders began to shake with silent sobs.

Tears pooled in Muriel's eyes in response to the utterly dejected figure of the queen. Settling herself on the ground beside her, Muriel stroked the queen's short hair and hummed a lullaby that Allan used to sing when Hope was a wee babe. After some time, Bre raised her head, wiping tears from her cheeks.

"She hates me."

"She doesn't know you."

Though her expression was blank, tears continued to fall as Bre's stare fixated on the cottage. "Do you know how many times I've dreamed of this day? Of finally seeing her?" She closed her eyes, her face tilted toward the sky. "In my dreams she is the same. She is the infant I gave up and she coos at me in wonder, touching my hair like it's spun gold." Bre reached out at an imaginary strand of hair.

With eyes still closed, she inhaled deeply. "I can smell her, you know. The milky sweetness of her. The scent that is unique to her, to my only child." A breath got caught in Bre's throat. "In my dream, she loves me and I love her and together with her father we live happily ever after."

When she opened her eyes, Muriel caught a glimmer of love shining in her eyes. The light was snuffed out the moment their gazes met.

"Can you even imagine what it's been like? Twelve years has been an eternity." Bre glanced at her hands, her empty hands. "I would have given my life to simply hold her again. To feel the press of her little hand in mine, to hear her say, 'mama.'" The last word hitched on a sob.

"Breanna," Muriel whispered. "When the time is right, Hope will come to love you. She will."

Shaking her head, Bre said, "I've missed everything. Everything. She is practically grown. I see Cahill in her. In her looks and her beauty. There is a glimmer of me too." She inhaled deeply, pressing her lips together. "But she is different than I imagined. I don't know her. I don't know her at all. She is not the child of my dreams. She is someone else and she hates me."

"Dear Queen…"

"But that is not the worst," Bre interrupted. "The worst is that now I don't even have my dream of her loving me to keep me sane. There is nothing left. Nothing."

When Bre's gaze met hers, it was as if the woman was hollow. Muriel saw it as plainly as if she had the gift of sight. Bre believed she had nothing left to live for. The windows to her soul showed only emptiness. Blackness. Loneliness.

Death.

Gods forgive me, Muriel prayed. *For what I am about to do, forgive me.*

Aloud, she said, "Take my hands."

"Why?"

"Because, there is something I can give you. Something to help you through the coming years."

"What is it?"

"I am going to give you the gift of memory." She licked her suddenly dry lips. "My memories."

"You can do that?" Bre whispered.

Muriel nodded and smiled, though the smile ached as it spread across her cheeks. "Yes. By taking my hands, my memories of Hope will become yours." Oh, but there were costs to such a gift. Costs and consequences.

But what choice did she have? She could not send the queen away filled with such sorrow. In such a state, the woman would never make it home, for people who lose purpose attract death like a carcass attracts flies.

Knowing the headstrong queen, she'd ride from here to Dunvegan to challenge the wretched Eleanor, without care that she would surely die. The result of her death under such a powerful sorceress would be the revelation of Hope's whereabouts and that was something Muriel could not allow. Hope may not be her true-born daughter, but she was the daughter of her heart and Muriel would do everything in her power to protect her.

Even from her own mother.

There was only one choice, as far as Muriel could see. She would do this thing, give up part of her soul, transfer her memories of Hope—the very thing she held most dear—if it meant saving the child.

"You must promise me one thing," Muriel said.

"What? Anything. I swear."

"You must never look for us again. You must go home and wait for our return. If you promise me this, I will give you this gift."

"I promise. In the name of all that is holy, I give you my most solemn oath."

"Good." Muriel went to take Breanna's hands, but her own refused to move from where they were pressed against her chest. With a grunt, Muriel forced movement, but her body fought her every inch of the way, knowing what she was about to do was wrong and trying to stop her. It was Breanna who took hold of her fingers with her steely grip, prying her hands from her chest until there was no way Muriel could withdraw.

Closing her eyes, she inhaled deeply and upon the exhalation, chanted softly, *"Memorandi, mia, morei, missa. Missa, morei, mia, memorandi…"*

A light, pure and bright, swirled around Muriel, lifting the edges of her skirt and the tips of her hair. On her next inhalation, the light flowed in through her nostrils and parted lips. On her exhalation, the beam burst forth from her chest, creating a connection between her heart and Breanna's. As the queen breathed, the light made its way up through her chest, exiting through the crown of her head only to be breathed in again by Muriel, creating a perfect circle of perfect light…a sparkling stream by which memories could be transferred and shared.

Never having done this spell before, Muriel was unprepared for how powerless it left her, as all her memories of Hope from the past twelve years—the first days of travel, feeding her, caring for her, nursing her cuts and bruises, cuddling her, scolding her, teaching her, watching her grow into the beautiful girl of today—all of it was transferred to the queen. In return, the queen's memories were transferred to Muriel.

The pain.

The unbearable heartache.

The loneliness.

The utter despair.

When finally the bond was broken, Muriel's grip slipped from the queen's and she collapsed to the ground in the exact place and in the exact position where the queen had lain only moments before.

Never had Muriel known such sorrow. Never had she felt such bone crushing pain. It consumed her until she could scarcely breathe.

"Thank you," the queen whispered, her hand soothing Muriel's brow. "By all the gods of heaven and earth, I thank you."

With every step the horse took, his head pounded like the loudest war drum, reverberating painfully between his ears. It was the drink. He'd had too much. No, not true. He'd had just enough. Wine, ale, mead, Duncan had sampled whatever the Innkeep had in storage and found that after falling heavily into his cups, the voice inside his head became a manageable sort of buzzing instead of the infernal grating commands and insults. The drunken experience was similar to how he'd felt while submerging his head beneath water.

Unfortunately, one could only be drunk or underwater so long before one drowned.

You imbecile!

Holding either side of his head, Duncan moaned. He'd take the pain of a hangover over the sound of her voice any day. The two things together, at the same time, warring inside his skull, was more than he could manage and he slid from his horse, falling to the ground, jarring his shoulder painfully in the process.

Dragon's breath! Get up! Get up! Go get her and bring her to me. She is near. I can feel her. The magic is strong. By the gods, she is near!

Moaning, Duncan rolled on the ground in anguish. Though no longer astride, his head still pounded in time to phantom hoof beats.

Thud-thud. Thud-thud. Thud-thud.

So loud.

Too loud.

As if it truly was a horse.

Cracking one eye open, Duncan looked up.

Ach!

He covered his eyes, for it was too bright. Blindingly bright. Painfully bright.

Hellsfire! He'd never been so hungover.

Slowly, carefully, he opened his eyes again. Two horses looked down upon him. Two horses whinnied at him.

Dragon's breath!

Now he was seeing double. Duncan moaned and curled into a ball on the ground. Rest. He needed rest. She had kept him moving for so long he could not move one more muscle one more mile. If only he could get the voice to be quiet.

"Get up." The voice was louder than ever. It even sounded like it came from outside his head and not from within.

Groaning, Duncan attempted to push himself to his feet. It took three tries.

"What happened here?"

Shaking his head in a sorry attempt to clear his vision as well as the incessant pounding between his ears, Duncan slowly rose to his full height.

"You there. Answer me."

Shading his eyes from the sun, Duncan looked up, expecting to see Eleanor the Dragon Queen standing before him. But, he was either going mad—which was likely—or there was a boy atop a horse, scowling down at him with dagger in hand.

"Who are you?" Duncan asked.

"I ask the questions here. Tell me what happened. Quickly now."

There was something about the boy's voice that was not quite right. It sounded stern and commanding, unsuited to one so young and slight. Duncan moved out of the direct glare of the sun to get a better look at the lad. "Why," Duncan gaped. "You're a girl."

"The matter of my sex is of no consequence." The rider urged the horse closer, blocking out the sunlight, allowing Duncan to see the person clearly. He was right. It was not a boy but a girl. No. A woman. Striking grey eyes pierced him amid a face of slender angles. She appeared in her middle years judging by the lines beside her eyes and mouth and could have been quite pretty if her hair had been longer and her mouth was not set in such a severe line.

"Tell me who attacked you. Where were they headed?"

"I wasn't—"" Duncan did not finish his sentence for a change came over him so suddenly, so completely, his words were ripped from his throat only to be replaced by an unholy, bloodcurdling roar.

It's her!

A cloud of red descended over his vision and a voice that was not his own, howled through his throat, "You!" His body reacted without warning. Leaping with no concern for the dagger in the stranger's hand, it was as if Duncan had suddenly sprouted wings, for he fairly flew at the female, tackling her from her mount and landing solidly on top of her.

She gasped for breath, but he did not allow it. He went immediately for her neck and he squeezed with hands that were not his own, his fingers curling like claws. Through the heavy curtain of crimson, he saw how her eyes bulged with shock and pain.

"You dragon-slaying slut," he snarled in a hoarse, female voice. "How I've longed for this day. How I've dreamed of your death at my hands."

Duncan continued to squeeze despite the fact the woman's face was turning a terrible shade of purple and her eyes glazed and rolled to the back of her skull.

It was awful.

Sickening.

This was not right. He had to stop. He did not kill innocent strangers. He did not harm women. It went against his oath as a warrior and protector. But there was nothing he could do to stop the tightening of his hands around her throat. Nothing.

Eleanor! She is mine! A second voice echoed from the great beyond and as quickly as he'd attacked, Duncan fell back as if someone had pushed him. *She was my betrothed. She is mine to punish.*

Whose voice was that? It was male and slurring. Could it be Elwood? It happened once before that he'd heard the king's voice inside his head. It was the scepter. The one with the dragon claw and crystal. They must both be looking into it, watching Duncan, controlling him together, like he was a wooden puppet on a stick, completely at the whim of their vile manipulations.

Tie her up. Bring her here.

But the child is near. He is my emissary. He will do my bidding.

Of course the child is near, dear sister. He will get her and bring them both back. You see? Then we both shall exact our revenge on the House of Moray. 'Tis only fair.

Once the disembodied squabble was settled, Duncan trussed the unconscious woman as per the bidding of the sinister pair arguing in his head. It was Elwood's promises, both of what Duncan and his family would receive if Duncan succeeded in bringing the woman back alive, and what he would lose if he failed, that hurried Duncan's hand. The woman remained unconscious as he picked her up and lashed her to her saddle. At the very least, he was relieved he had not been compelled to take her life, although he couldn't be sure that hauling the woman back to Dunsmoor Castle was a more merciful fate. Undoubtedly King Elwood had ignoble plans for the woman and she would likely have been better off with a quick, unexpected death.

Duncan shuddered at the thought.

Then, for perhaps the thousandth time, Duncan saw in his mind's eye what would happen if he failed in his mission. It didn't matter how many times he witnessed the horrific scene Eleanor planted in his brain, it was as if it was the first time and Duncan's physical response was immediate. He keeled over as the rush of bread and last night's mead made a reappearance in a puddle at his feet.

Once he'd righted himself and tethered the woman and horse to his mount, Duncan started back along the trail he had set out upon. The directions given by the boys at the well were vague and more than once Duncan took a wrong turn, ending up at a dead end or an abandoned cottage. All the while, he could hear Eleanor muttering in his head to hurry. There was barely concealed glee in her anxious insults but as he walked upon the lonely road, either his pounding headache was beginning to ease, or Eleanor's and Elwood's voices were beginning to fade. Instead of booming between his ears, their voices were more like mosquitoes buzzing within his brain, constant and annoying but no longer incapacitating.

Coming upon a clear-running stream, Duncan stopped and slid from his mount to take a much needed drink. His throat was parched and his tongue swollen from over-imbibing last night. He splashed his face with the cool water and, despite the lingering headache, he felt more like himself than he'd felt in years, as if the waters themselves had magical properties.

The very best of it was that Eleanor's voice was nothing more than a squeaky hinge in the corridor of his mind. There had to be something about this place that blocked her, for it was unlikely she'd be so quiet on her own when he was so close to her intended target.

It was just the reprieve he needed.

However, Duncan was not so daft as to think he could remain here forever. He had an assignment, though a more reprehensible quest one could not find. Regardless of whether he could hear the king and his sister or not, he knew, without a doubt, they would make good on their threats if he did not deliver.

And, the sooner he fulfilled his task, the sooner he would be free forever from the hold of the Dragon Queen. After another quick splash upon his cheeks, Duncan stood and turned, about to remount his horse.

However, that was not to be, for his small captive was no longer trussed but stood before him, a look of grim determination on her delicate features and a sword pointed at his heart.

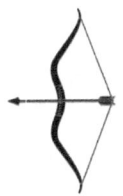

CHAPTER 12

"Who goes there?" A booming voice called out.
"Who dares to disturb me?"
"It is I, oh Powerful One," the mother said, kneeling before
the ancient sorcerer, the stone in her outstretched hands.
"Ah..." From the folds of a cloak, a bony hand with fingernails
like talons, reached for the stone. "A dragon's egg. The most
precious stone in all the land." The sorcerer brought the stone
close to his dark face. The only thing visible from behind the
cowl were his eyes, two glowing orbs shining like small moons
out of the darkness. "You have done well, peasant woman. For
this you shall be rewarded..."

— FROM THE LEGEND OF THE DRAGON CLAW SCEPTER

The young man's eyes grew wide in surprise. Large and brown, they were red-rimmed and bloodshot and he smelled like the filthy rushes swept from the floor of a tavern. How on earth had this man bested her so quickly? It was insupportable. Particularly because she now had a better view of him and Breanna realized he was younger than she'd first thought.

Though large of stature, based on his relatively smooth,

ruddy cheeks and unlined face, he could not be more than a few years over the age of change. He was little more than a youth, maybe only a few years older than her daughter.

Hope.

Ah, sweet, blessed Hope.

She would do anything to protect her, including killing one so young. Slicing through his heart would not be pleasant but she would do it, without question.

Though not without apology.

"I am sorry," she said before lunging and thrusting at the young man's chest.

But for all his size, the boy was swift and he pivoted just in time to deflect her thrust. Still, blood oozed out of a gash in his side, visible through his torn shirt, but Breanna gave it no more than a passing glance before starting in on an offense. However, despite her intentions, her sword wobbled in her hands as if uncertain, giving the lad time to draw his own blade and parry her next blow.

"Who controls you?" Bre asked. She grunted as she swung her sword.

"Do not ask for I shall not tell," the lad replied, easily deflecting her jab.

"The Dragon Bitch speaks through you. I heard her voice. Admit it."

The tall boy continued to easily deflect her onslaught. "And if she does? What's it to you?"

"It is everything to me."

"Good," the soldier said—for he must be proficient in combat to spar with her with such little effort. "You shall have an audience with her when I take you back to Dunsmoor Castle."

Bre laughed. "You shall have to best me and that is highly unlikely." She pivoted, but her movement was slow. Sloppy.

Something was wrong. It was as if she hadn't fought in…years? When was the last time she practiced? Bre couldn't remember.

The sound of clanging metal rang in her ears and Bre panicked because the young man was on the offensive and *she* was on the defensive now. Yet, as hard as she tried, she couldn't remember any of the moves. Her body did not respond intuitively the way it should for one who practices every day.

She did practice every day, didn't she?

She must have. It was something she'd always done. But now…? Now, she couldn't remember. The only memories she had were of living in the cottage in the woods with Hope and A'Dale. Cooking and cleaning. Planting a garden, weaving baskets—of all things—tending rabbits and cuddling her daughter while trying not to think of the man she shared the cottage with.

There were other memories too. The daily chants, humming beneath her breath, speaking words that made no sense to Bre, because they were words she'd never learned.

Why, these were Muriel's memories, not hers! Where were her memories of the last decade? What of the hours she must have spent on the practice field? What of Cahill and Lorentia? There was nothing of her home and husband save that fateful christening day in Morainia and everything that came before. The last twelve years had been wiped from her mind completely.

Now, she had only words and chants to defend herself and what good would that do? The young man had her backed against a tree, her sword arm held firmly in his fist, his blade beneath her chin.

"Let me go," she panted.

"I'm sorry. I can't."

Without knowing why, exactly, she whispered, "*Galdius*

permuto a florem."

The sword she held shivered in her restrained grasp as did the one against her throat. In a burst of sparkling smoke the blade disappeared to be replaced by a bunch of wildflowers.

"What in the name of the blessed ones…?" the lad sputtered, looking at the handful of flowers that he held against her neck. "You're a witch?"

"No… Yes! I am a witch," Bre said. "Now let me go before I turn you into a hog."

"Sorry," the youth replied, tossing the flowers to the ground. "I serve a much more powerful sorceress who will do worse than turn me into a hog if I do not bring you back alive."

Bre may have been out of practice with the sword, but her knee was another story. She brought her knee up, with one swift movement, jarring him brutally between the legs.

"Mother of gods!" the lad cried, releasing her and crouching over his injured groin.

Bre made a spur of the moment decision. Without a weapon there was no way she'd be able to out power the young man. He was too big and strong. Why, even with a weapon…

So she ran. Fleeing from the boy while he was incapacitated was not a savory option—the sort of thing only a coward would do—but after her sorry display at swordsmanship, Breanna had no choice if she wished to save Hope.

Running for her horse, Bre leaped onto its back and kicked the animal into a gallop. She wouldn't head straight for the cottage. No. She'd zigzag her way through the forest, making sure she was not followed before returning to the…

Thunk!

Excruciating pain exploded across the back of her skull, pitching Bre to the side. Blackness peppered with starbursts stole her vision and the last thing Bre remembered was falling into an abyss of icy darkness.

Bre opened her eyes and then wished she hadn't. The bright sun caused an explosion of pain through her head and down her neck. Keeping her eyes shut, she attempted to muddle through the pain in order to assess her situation. By the movement of the animal beneath her, she was obviously atop a horse. A large horse. A strange horse. More disturbing was the fact that she was not alone. Strong arms of a man circled her body, holding her tight so that she could not even move her hand to rub her throbbing head.

There was something familiar about the scenario.

Through the pain, Bre tried to make sense of the jumbled memories spinning around her pounding head. An archery contest, losing her horse to a cheating prince, erotic dreams of the very same prince, sneaking away from Lorent Castle in the dead of night only to be captured the next morning…by the cheating, charming, overly handsome prince.

"Cahill?" She asked, confusion muddying her mind.

"No."

A searing heat sliced directly through the center of her skull. "Hellsbreath!" She cringed in pain. What was going on? "Who are you?" she asked, her voice sounding strange to her ringing ears. "Where are you taking me?"

There was no reply.

Bre tried to turn within the saddle but the man behind her held her too close. She tried to think. No easy feat with memories that seemed nonsensical and random.

Finally the person behind her said, "I am taking you to Dunvegan."

Bre managed to recall that Dunvegan was the neighboring kingdom to her homeland of Morainia and Dunsmoor was the seat of King Elwood. Her betrothed…

Her betrothed?

No. That could not be true. Somehow her brain managed to call up a memory of the neighboring king, sending shivers of revulsion down her spine. She'd never marry Elwood. She'd run away first before having to climb into a marriage bed with such a disgusting, gluttonous oaf.

But wait…

She had run away, hadn't she? Was this man bringing her back in order to force the marriage?

Wasn't she already married? She was sure she'd married a man named Cahill. A prince. A handsome, roguish, cocksure prince with the nicest smile and the most talented hands…

How did that come to pass? How did she come…?

Sudden, horrible images flashed through her throbbing brain: hordes of dragons raining fire down upon her homeland, destroying everything. Her mother and father screaming in pain, her sisters crying. Everyone dying. Everything gone.

Bre gasped, her body going rigid in remembrance.

But the jogged memories continued to unravel. Traveling rough, killing as many dragons as she could. Ending up at Lorent castle, injured and close to death.

Cahill.

Cahill asking her to marry him. The wedding. The wedding night. Newly married bliss. Training some young woman—ah, Princess Zaina of Fenloch—in the art of swordplay. A potion, a skirmish. Another battle.

A baby.

Oh, gods!

Hope.

She opened her eyes and looked about her, ignoring the pain hacking into the back of her head. She recognized this road. She recognized this place. They were on their way to the cottage where she lived with Hope and Allan.

Allan A'Dale.

She sighed.

Allan was her husband and there was no one who was his equal…though they hadn't consummated…

Breanna frowned. Then she shook her head, crying out when pokers lanced the back of her skull.

Dragon's breath! What was going on?

These are my memories. My gift to you.

Oh gods! She had the witch's memories. It was Muriel who lived here with Hope and A'Dale. And now the man who'd captured her was intent on finding her daughter and taking her back to Dunvegan too. There was no uncertainty in Bre's mind about what the Dragon bitch, Eleanor, would do with Hope once they arrived. She'd steal her innocent soul and transform herself back into a human, murdering Hope right in front of Breanna, enjoying every moment of pain she caused.

With desperation, Breanna struggled against the bonds, but the rope and the man who held her was too strong.

He is but a youth, Breanna cried to herself. *Try harder!* But it was no use. She could not free herself. She, the slayer of *Ninn-Arach*, was at the mercy of a mere lad.

"Stop. You must release me," she cried, trying once more to turn toward the boy behind her. "Please. It is of great import that you let me go."

"I'm sorry. I cannot."

The strange thing was, the lad truly sounded sorry, which gave Bre hope. "Don't release me, then. I will go to Dunsmoor Castle with you as your willing captive. But we must turn around and go there directly. Right now."

The lad stopped the horse but his hold did not slacken. "I hope you believe me when I tell you that I wish I could turn around. I wish I could release you as well. But I have no choice."

"What has she promised you?" Bre asked, her voice cracking.

"Land in Darnell and a title for my eldest brother."

"I will do better than that. I am a queen, you see. Of Lorentia. Name your price and it is yours. I will give you whatever you want."

"It is not the reward that motivates me," the boy said quietly. "It is the threat."

"Threat?"

"If I do not return with both you *and* the girl, alive and intact, they will round up my entire family and kill them. To be more specific, they will torture them. Slowly…to death." His body shuddered behind her. "Eleanor uses magic so that I might see. Over and over I have watched my family suffer and die." His hold tightened around her middle. "I'm sure you understand I will do whatever it is I have to do to ensure those horrible visions do not become reality." Even more quietly he repeated, "*Whatever* I have to do."

Tears fell unchecked as Breanna realized the hopelessness of her situation. They rounded the last bend before the clearing in the woods where the little cottage sat and, as a last ditch effort to save her daughter, Bre, shouted, "Husband, where ye be?" It was a warning she and A'Dale had concocted if ever danger should be present. She prayed he and Hope would have enough time to take cover in the little hidey hole beneath the cottage.

No. *She* hadn't come up with that plan. That was one more of Muriel's memories that had superseded hers. In this case, Bre was glad for it and prayed it would work. Her heart pounded fiercely against her breastbone as they made their way down the narrow lane. The young man certainly seemed in no hurry to reach his destination, for which Bre was grateful. Perhaps it would give Hope time to hide.

The moment they came through the trees into the clearing, the young soldier dismounted, dragging her down behind him.

"You're a wily one," he said softly. "I'm not going to leave you alone again."

He pushed her out in front of him and Bre stumbled but his hold on her elbow quickly righted her. "Now," he whispered in her ear. "Tell me where she is."

"I don't know." Perhaps her warning had worked for the garden was empty and the cottage had an abandoned look to it. That was probably their intent, snuffing out the fire so no smoke rose from the chimney. If the guard found the cottage empty, he would likely search the woods, giving them a few moments to escape.

He prodded her toward the cottage and forced her in before him. It took Bre's eyes a moment to adjust and then she gasped. After arguing with Muriel last night, she had slept in the animal shelter so that she might set out at first light. This was the first time she'd been back into the cottage since Muriel had given her the gift of memory. Here in this place, the memories were even stronger. The smells were familiar. The jars on the shelves, the goods in the cupboard, the herbs hanging from the rafters.

Strange. Breanna could have itemized every single thing.

There was Allan's bow hanging on the wall…wait. Where was his bow? Where was his scabbard? Breanna's gaze made a more thorough pass. Other things were missing as well. Tools and implements. Cloaks. Candles.

"They aren't here. Where are they?"

"I don't know," Breanna said but her gaze strayed to the hand woven rug at the foot of the bed.

"What are you looking at?"

"Nothing." She replied too quickly.

Tugging on her bound hands, he pulled her in the direction of the bed. "Perhaps they are here after all."

"No. They are gone."

"If that is so," he said, pushing her to her knees at the foot of the bed, "you won't mind lifting the rug for me."

"Why?"

"I should like to see if there is anything of interest underneath."

"There isn't."

"Show me."

"No." Breanna looked up, defiant. She knew she was giving herself away by being so obstinate but it was her hope that A'Dale would hear and be prepared for their discovery once the hiding place was found.

"I may not be able to kill you," the boy said pointing his sword at her ankles. "But there are tendons that run along the back of your leg. If I were to sever them you would live but you would never run again. It is your choice."

Severed tendons would not do, not when she was going to need to run very soon. Slowly she pulled back the edge of the carpet to reveal what she already knew to lie beneath. The steel ring of a trap door.

"Get up," he said, holding the sword aloft and pulling a length of rope from his belt.

Although tricky to stand with bound wrists, it was even more difficult with the pain inside her head and Breanna, stumbled, off balance and woozy.

"Over here." The youth tugged on her wrists until she stood in the center of the room. He threaded one one end of the rope over the rafter, dropped a loop of it around her neck and then ordered her up onto the stool. Tying off the other end of rope, he said, "I am sorry to have to do this. Truly I am."

More tears coursed down Breanna's cheeks—tears of anger and fear for her daughter—as she stood on the stool completely helpless to do anything, for if she moved even a muscle, the stool would topple and she would end up hanging herself.

With careful steps, the young emissary moved first to the hearth and took the fire iron from the ashes. "Still warm," he muttered before moving back to the trapdoor where he quietly hooked the poker beneath the ring, allowing him to pull up on the door while standing instead of having to crouch.

Breanna couldn't stand idly by. She couldn't. What did she have to lose? "He's coming," she cried. "Take care, A'Dale, he's coming!"

The young man cast an annoyed look at her and dropped the iron in order to draw a dagger from his belt and raise his sword in ready position.

They waited.

Nothing happened.

The boy inched closer, but the black hole in the floor remained silent. After a few moments, the soldier glanced around the cottage as if looking for something of use. "I'm not stupid," he muttered in Bre's general direction. "I'm not going down there only to be ambushed."

"They aren't here, I tell you," Bre said, but was once again ignored.

From her position, all she could do was watch as he yanked a cloth from a hook on the wall and tore it in two. After inspecting the contents of a cupboard, he unwrapped what looked like lard and smeared it on the cloth, then he moved back to the edge of the hole, lit a taper and held it beneath each cloth until they caught fire. He found more cloths to smear with fat and lit those and dropped them in the hole until even Bre could see the light from the fire burning at the base.

"You're going to burn the whole place down," Bre said.

"No." The young man picked up a pail of water that sat beside the hearth, carried it to the lip of the trap door and dumped it. The fire sizzled and popped and then the lad quickly closed the trap door. He looked at Bre. "I'm going to smoke them out."

CHAPTER 13

"I grant you one wish," the sorcerer said.
The woman needed no time to think. "I must pay
tithes to the nobleman on whose land we abide."
"Is that all?" The great magician asked.
"For you may have whatever your heart desires."
The woman's back straightened. "Anything?"
Her small mind filled with possibilities.
"Anything."
"Why then, I wish to be queen, the most feared queen
in all the land..."

— FROM THE LEGEND OF THE DRAGON CLAW SCEPTER

She had an urge to cough but she was much too tired. Bone tired. Like she could sleep for eternity.

Was she dead? It certainly felt like it. For surely someone had sewn her eyes and mouth shut in preparation for the wake. If this was death, then death was a crushing heaviness. Perhaps it was simply the weight of her earthen grave pressing upon her chest. But that would mean she'd been buried alive, which would mean she hadn't died...

Oh gods! Was she alive or dead? She couldn't remember.

"Muriel? Please. Muriel you must wake."

Muriel. Whose name was that? It had a familiarity to it and the voice that had just spoken stirred something deep in the pit of her belly.

She'd have to ask Cahill about the name.

"Mama? Wake up. Please wake up." Her shoulders were shaken and slowly she opened her eyes. A beautiful girl looked down at her, concern evident in the crease of her brow and in her striking violet eyes.

The girl looked up at the man standing above them. "Da! She opened her eyes. She's awake!" Then the girl turned her attention back to her. "Oh, Mama. I was so worried. You were so still and your skin was cool to the touch. I thought...we thought..."

Mama? She blinked, clearing her vision so that she could scrutinize the child more clearly. The girl had Cahill's hair, dark and wavy but for the white streak up front. Her eyes were a mixture of Cahill's blue and her grey. Violet. So lovely. The cut of her jaw was familiar, though more delicate than Cahill's. She knew who this girl was, knew it beyond a doubt. "Say it again," she whispered.

"Say what again?"

"My name."

Casting a confused glance at the man, the girl turned back to her and said slowly, "Mama?"

Tears sprang to her eyes, hot and heavy. They were not tears of sorrow, but of joy. "Oh Hope. It is you." She reached for the girl and pulled her down to where she lay, hugging her fiercely. "Do you know how oft I've dreamed of this day? To hear you say my name?"

At first the girl hugged back and then she squirmed. "Mama, you're squeezing me too tight."

She ignored the child. How could she not squeeze tightly?

She had so many years worth of heartache to make up for.

A set of strong hands tugged on her arms, forcing her to release her daughter. Those same capable hands reached beneath her arms and pulled her upright. "Muriel? What is wrong? What has happened?"

A searing pain lanced the back of her head and she stumbled, completely disorientated by the sensation. Thank the gods, the man—what was his name?—caught her before she fell.

"Tell me what to do, my wife."

Gritting her teeth to wait out the pain, eventually she was able to answer. "Your wife? Are you mad?"

Two gasps, one deep and one soft, echoed between the trees on the lonely road. Her chin was tilted up and she was forced to look at the man who held her much too closely. He was a comely man, to be sure; wide jaw, ruddy cheeks. His brows were drawn together in concern and…confusion?

"You. You are my wife. You are Muriel."

"But I'm the queen. I'm Breanna."

"Da? What is wrong with her? Is she sick?"

"I don't know, my love."

Taking her by the hand, the man led her between two horses and down a game trail to a small pool of water. "Kneel here and look upon your reflection."

She did as he asked, not because he bid it but because looking down was the natural thing to do. What she saw reflected there, was anything but natural. A woman of ample figure, rosy cheeks and curly red locks peered back at her from the water's depths. "No," she whispered. "This cannot be." She touched the reflection with the tip of her finger, erasing the image with the rippling effect of the water and then a shock so great it was as if the earth moved beneath her, pitched her face first into the pool.

Sputtering and splashing, she tried to right herself but the disorientation of her fall mixed with the confusion in her mind made it near impossible. This time, she was thankful for the strong arms of her companion.

A'Dale. Allan A'Dale, a voice whispered in the dark reaches of her mind.

The man—A'Dale—scooped her up and carried her out of the water, lying her carefully back on the ground. He hovered mere inches above her and she couldn't stop herself from reaching for his face. "Allan A'Dale," she whispered.

"Yes," he said, his frown unfurling before her eyes. "And you are Muriel. Hope is our...daughter." He turned and Muriel saw the girl standing behind him.

Muriel frowned. "But she's not our—"

"Shh." He pressed a finger to her lips. "You've been ill. Very ill. You've slept for nearly five days."

"Five days? But...where are we?"

A'Dale looked around as if there was someone lurking behind a tree. "We are traveling. On our way to a new home," he whispered.

"Why?"

"Because it was too dangerous to stay in our cottage."

"Our cottage?" Muriel frowned. She had a vague recollection of coming upon a small plot of land where an even smaller cottage stood—not more than a hut, really—but that was all she could remember.

"Shh," the man intoned.

He had a lovely voice, Muriel noted. Very...melodic.

"Rest," he said. "We have come far enough for today. We'll set out again tomorrow at first light. For now we'll rest."

Yes. Rest. That's all she needed and then she would be as right as rain. Ahh, blessed dreamless sleep. Perhaps that would cure this heaviness in her heart and in her head. Perhaps after a little more rest she'd no longer feel as if she was about to drown in overwhelming sorrow.

"What is wrong with her?" Hope asked as she tucked a cloak around Muriel's shoulders.

"I don't know," A'Dale replied. He let out a pent up breath. "I don't know."

"She thought she was a queen. Someone named Breanna." Hope looked at him with large violet eyes. "Who is Breanna?"

Swallowing, Allan answered, "That is her sister's name."

"Her sister?" Hope wrinkled her nose. "But her sister is not a queen. She is the furthest thing from a queen." Hope giggled at the thought. "Besides, if she was a queen, that would make Mama a princess. And me, as well." Hope twirled on her toe and then bowed. "Princess Hope, at your service."

Allan rubbed his forehead. Now was not the time to discuss the matter of Hope's true parentage. In fact, now was not the time to even mention Breanna's name. With Muriel ill, she was incapable of invoking her protective spells. They were completely vulnerable to the malicious eyes and ears of Dunvegan.

Kneeling in front of Hope, Allan took both her hands in his. "Promise me something."

She nodded in ready agreement.

"Never mention Mam's sister again. Do you understand?"

Hope blinked. Then she wrapped her arms around Allan's neck and gave him a fierce hug. "Gladly," she whispered in his ear.

Later that night, after Hope had fallen asleep, Allan sat up, keeping watch over the small party.

Hope and Muriel. His family.

Except these people, whom he loved with a heart that overflowed, weren't really his family and when Hope came of age and they returned her to her rightful parents, Allan would have no one.

For with Hope gone, there was nothing to keep Muriel by his side.

It was a grim reflection, one he tried to avoid giving occasion to, but in the darkest hours of the night, such ruminations were unavoidable. When Hope's sixteenth birthday came, and he was forced to give her up, what would he do? He ought to provide the king with a dagger so that the man might cut out his heart and throw it on the fire. Surely that would be preferable to going on, broken hearted for the rest of his life.

Giving up Hope was an unspeakable thought. But equally dreadful was the knowledge that in giving up Hope, Allan would also lose Muriel. Though he often entertained the idea that Muriel would consent to become his wife—his true wife, one that shared his heart *and* his bed—once their mission was complete, Allan knew it was all a lie. Muriel was a powerful witch by birth. By marrying him, she would forsake her power and he could not ask her to give up her calling for him. Even if she agreed to it, one day she would come to resent the decision, and that was something Allan could not withstand.

He sighed. For years he had kept the truth at bay by pretending, by not allowing himself to think of the time after Hope came of age. But ever since the queen's visit, the reality of his situation had brought these thoughts to the forefront. How naively and impulsively he had offered his services to the king and queen of Lorentia twelve years ago. If he had known how heartsick the decision would one day make him, would he still have agreed to it?

Yes.

Strange. The voice that whispered inside his head was *her* voice, not his.

Gazing down at the woman who slept a restless, feverish sleep, her cheeks flushed, her lips rosy and parted, Allan experienced an overwhelming degree of tenderness sweep through him. How many times had he thought she was going to die these last five days? Countless times. But she didn't die. She lived, and now, with her head cradled in his lap, Allan chose to ignore the rules between them.

He *had* to touch her. He had to reassure himself that she was alive. That she would not leave him…yet.

He swept damp curls from her brow, his hand straying to her fiery locks. Carefully winding a strand around his finger, he marveling at the silky texture. How good it would feel to bury his hands in her hair, but he stayed the impulse. Instead, he brushed her cheek. So warm, so alive, thank the gods. Though she had a slight fever, the warmth of her skin was a relief to Allan after she'd been unnaturally cold for so many days. He carefully rubbed the crease away from between her brows. Whatever dreams she was having, they were causing her to frown and writhe beneath the cloak that covered her.

Suddenly she gasped and her body went still. Allan's heart ceased beating.

No. Oh gods, no! He would not lose her now.

Leaning close, he turned his cheek, desperate to feel her soft breath upon his face.

Yes. There it was. She was breathing.

With relief, Allan gently lifted Muriel's head from his lap so he could lower himself beside her. Like the last few nights, there would be little sleep for him.

Propped on his elbow, he watched her for a time before

continuing his gentle examination of her features. How angelic she looked when she slept, though she was equally angelic when she was awake. Her skin was soft, softer than her hair even. And her lips. So plump. So sweet. So kissable. One day he should like to test the softness of those lips with his own. Taste them. Surely the inside of her mouth was softer still.

Oh Gods.

He shut his eyes, but the image of Muriel's lips remained upon the inside of his lids.

These thoughts were futile. Frustrating.

He must not torture himself like this.

After a deep inhalation, he opened his eyes again to gaze upon her. Touching her only made him want her more but he could not stop. If Muriel were to never wake up, at least he would have the memory of this to keep him warm on cold nights. With nothing more than the lightest touch, he gently grazed her lips with the pad of his thumb, his fingers delicately caressing the lovely line of her jaw to where her ears peeked out of her hair, the daintiest of seashells in a sea of riotous red waves.

Gods, the woman was beautiful.

Achingly, devastatingly beautiful.

A'Dale was so mesmerized by her features that it took him a moment to realize her eyes were open and she was staring at him. His hand stilled. First shock, then guilt speared him in the gut.

"It's you," she said. Her voice soft, not in surprise, but with some other emotion.

"Shh," he whispered, hoping she was unaware of his hand still at her temple. "Go back to sleep."

She closed her eyes and he went to move his hand but she reached up and stopped him. Holding his hand against her cheek more firmly. "It's been so long," she murmured. "I'm sorry." Her lips quivered and she bit down as if to quell some emotion.

The heat from her cheek and her hand ignited a glowing ember in the pit of his belly, warming him with love and tenderness. He held himself still, reveling in her touch. Considering the meaning behind it. He had seen this before, this sort of reaction in men who'd been unconscious for days after an injury in battle. Often waking up as if they'd been away for years.

Allan exhaled long and slow. Quietly he said, "Do not apologize. I am only glad you are here."

Then Muriel did something he was not prepared for. Her eyes fluttered, she turned her head into his hand and she kissed his palm.

With that one simple action, A'Dale was turned to stone.

Lazily, she looked up at him. "Come. Lie with me."

Hellsfire. Was that desire in her eyes? No. It couldn't be.

"Please."

He had heard her say the word countless times. Never with that tone. Never with that soft hint of longing. Gods above, what was going on?

"I must keep watch," he managed to say.

But the moment she rubbed a feverish cheek against his open palm, A'Dale forgot everything but the woman before him and the years and years of unrequited love. Of unfulfilled need.

"I need you."

I need you. The very words that echoed between his ears. The words he had waited twelve long years for her to say.

"But you said—"

"Never mind what I said." She sighed, but it was the sort of sigh he'd never heard from her before, gentle and gasping. Sensual. "I can't go on without you."

Dragonsbreath!

It had been an eternity that he'd waited for Muriel to say these words. Why was she saying them now? Why here, of all places?

Dammit! A'Dale did not care.

When the woman he'd loved for so many years finally gave her consent, there was only one thing for a man to do.

Make her his.

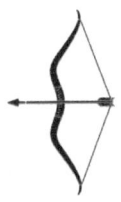

CHAPTER 14

The sorcerer pointed behind the woman. "And the rest of you?
You all had a part in finding the egg. What do you wish for?"
The mother turned, shocked to find
her children had followed her...

— FROM THE LEGEND OF THE DRAGON CLAW SCEPTER

How many times would he have to bear the disappointment? Three soldiers stood at attention in his planning room, none with any tidings of Breanna.

"I am sorry, Your Grace," a veteran soldier named Ansel said with a shake of his head. "I thought I had a lead and followed it to a small village by the name of Dewsbury in Darnell, but the trail ran cold."

Cahill paced. "And you others?"

The other two scouts shook their heads. They'd been gone for a year with no sign of his wife.

"My King," Stutely, the captain of the guard called out as he strode into the room and glanced from man to man. "I came as soon as I could. What news?"

Cahill shook his head, taking a seat behind the wide table that often held maps but now stood as empty as his heart.

"Ah. I see." Turning to the soldiers, Stutely ordered them dismissed by saying, "You may report to the training ring for combat." Once the men were gone, he stood before the table, shaking his head. "Fucking useless pieces of—"

"It's not their fault." Cahill interrupted. "You told me yourself they are your best scouts. I have no doubt Ansel was close, but Breanna will not be found until she is ready to be found." He sighed, glancing at the man across the table from him. Stutely had replaced A'Dale as captain of the guard twelve years ago. A commoner by birth and a mercenary by trade, Stutely was as coarse as they came. As loyal too. He'd been one of Hood's companions, traveling the continent over, as one of the *Merry Men Players*, stealing from corrupt nobility to provide for those less fortunate.

"There is only one thing left for me to do, Stutely." Cahill leaned forward, resting his elbows on the table and his chin on his hands. "I must go after her myself."

"No fucking way."

After knowing him for so long, Stutely's direct manner did not surprise Cahil. "There is no alternative."

"You cannot leave Lorentia. You have no heir, and there is no one to take your place."

"As Captain of the Guard, *you* may take my place. King Stutely. It has a nice ring to it, don't you think?"

With a grim look, Stutely said, "Do not jest, Cahill. You will throw Lorentia into civil war with no heir. Every good thing you've done will be undone. I will not allow it."

"It is not your choice."

"You are not thinking clearly. It's my job to—"

The men were interrupted by a soft knock on the open door. Giselle, one of Breanna's former ladies-in-waiting, stood on the threshold.

"My Lady," Stutely said, bowing deeply.

"Sir Stutely. Your Grace." She curtsied prettily. "May I come in?"

"Yes, come in," Cahill said.

Giselle swept inside the room, glancing coyly at Stutely as she passed. The formidable captain of the guard blushed, something Cahill did not think the man was capable of.

"Your Highness, may I have a word with you…in private?" With a mere tilt of her head, she glanced again at Stutely, whose cheeks flushed an even deeper shade of red.

Cahill suppressed a smile. After so long a time, the wide-eyed young girl who had come to attend his new bride was gone. In her place was a beautiful, self-assured woman who knew her charms and played them like a harp.

"That will be all, Stutely."

"We're not done here."

"I said, that is all."

It was the feminine influence of Giselle that stayed Stutely's tongue. No doubt the man had a mouthful of curse words he wished to throw at him, but he would not do so in front of a lady. Bowing stiffly, he exited the room, leaving Cahill alone with Giselle.

"What may I do for you, My Lady?"

Giselle's smile was pure charm. "I do not come here asking for favors."

"Then why do you come?"

"As a friend." She walked softly around the table until she stood behind him. Before Cahill knew what was happening, her hands were on his shoulders and she kneaded, like his flesh was dough and she was a baker, working out years' worth of tension. "I understand the scouts returned without word of your queen."

How quickly gossip spread and Cahill stiffened as he realized Giselle had heard the disappointing news before he had. "'Tis true."

"I am sorry for this."

He sighed. What difference did it make who heard the news first? It wasn't the first time scouts had returned empty handed, with absolutely nothing to go on. He had almost given up hope. Almost.

"That feels nice," he whispered, appreciating Giselle's feminine touch on his shoulders and neck. Oh how he missed the touch of a woman. Breanna had often done as much, rubbing the base of his skull, down his neck and between his shoulder blades after long hours in the practice field. Giselle didn't have the same strength in her hands, but her touch was welcome just the same and Cahill wondered if she'd had much practice and if so, with whom. Under her adept ministrations, he let his head fall forward, not so much in relaxation but in resignation.

"You know I have taken over much of the queen's duties in her absence," Giselle said quietly.

"Yes," he murmured. He hadn't been aware of her role in handling courtly affairs at first, but in the last few years, the servants and footmen had stopped coming to him with the mundane issues in regards to the running of the kitchen and staff of the castle. When he inquired, his squire had informed him that Giselle had taken it on. "I am forever in your debt."

Trailing her hand down his left shoulder, Giselle came around his side and perched herself on the table in front of him. Taking his hand, she held it in hers, rubbing his knuckles with the same soothing manner. "There is but one duty I have yet to fulfill." Her smile softened when he met her gaze.

"What duty is that?"

She pressed his hand against her heart. "You are a man, Cahill. A man without a wife. A king without an heir." She moved his hand an inch and suddenly he found himself cupping her breast.

He snatched his hand away.

She captured it again and held it to her face. "I am not Breanna. I know you do not feel for me as you felt for her. But feelings are not necessary to sire an heir." She turned her face into his hand and kissed his palm.

Cahill gasped. The sensation was both terribly wrong and...shockingly pleasant. He willed himself to stand. "No."

"You are a king," she said reasonably. "You may do as you wish. I know I do not have the bloodline to become your proper wife, but allow me to be your courtesan, the vessel by which you may father an heir. He will be a bastard, of course, but he will be yours and if anything should happen—"

"Nothing will happen," Cahill said, hands up to block Giselle's persistent approach.

"You are not immortal, Cahill."

"Giselle..."

"How long has it been since you've been with a woman?"

"That is none of your business."

"None of my business? My whole family resides here. What will happen to me, to my sisters, my nieces and nephews, if you die?"

Shaking his head and backing away, Cahill pleaded, "Giselle, I love her, don't you see? Until I know Breanna is dead, I cannot be with another."

"This isn't about love, Cahill." Somehow this tiny woman had managed to back him up against the wall. She placed both hands upon his shirt and looked up at him beseechingly. "This is about your legacy." Her hands made soft circles on his chest. "This is what Breanna would have wanted. You know I speak the truth. You cannot deny it."

Cahill shook his head, unwilling to accept her words even while he heard his wife's voice inside his head whispering, *You should take a lover, Cahill…*

"Even if Breanna were still here…" She sighed with affectation. "The queen is barren. It is your *duty*, as king, to produce an heir."

Dragon's breath! How he wished to continue his denials, but his body warred with him, willing him to take Giselle up on her offer. Right here. Right now. On the map table. Gods above, the woman was temptation incarnate. "Giselle…"

"Yes?"

"Leave."

"Cahill…"

"I am your king. I command you to leave."

She blinked up at him, perhaps sensing how close he was to giving in and wondering if she should push him a little further. But her courtly upbringing got the better of her and she stepped back. Executing a perfect curtsy, she said, "As you wish, my King." Still exhibiting her submissive posture, she looked up at him with a sultry, half-lidded look. "Though… if you should reconsider…" She stood. "You know where my bedchamber is." With a demure smile she turned and walked gracefully to the door.

"Excuse me, Your Holiness," she said to Abbot Dithers who stood outside, leaning heavily upon his young novice, Felix.

Cringing at the unfortunate timing of the abbot's arrival, Cahill took a seat behind the table, exhausted by all that had transpired; the return of the scouts with no news, now this unexpected confrontation with Giselle.

"Is this a bad time?"

"No." Cahill smiled, though the abbot was completely blind and could not see it. "Please have a seat."

The novice helped the abbot into a chair and once the frail old man was settled, Felix quietly left the room to stand outside waiting to be summoned.

"I suppose you have heard the news," Cahill muttered once the door was closed behind the novice.

"Yes. I came as soon as I could. How are you?"

"I am..." Cahill leaned back and closed his eyes. "I am lost, Father. I don't know what to do. I feel as if I am in purgatory where time has no meaning. Life carries on for everyone around me while nothing changes for me." Opening his eyes and leaning across the table toward the old man, Cahill said, "I would welcome any advice you'd wish to give."

"You may not like what I have to say."

"Believe me, Your Holiness, I have not liked what anyone has had to say to me today. Why should you be any different?"

The old abbot chuckled. "Ah. A sense of humor. 'Tis good sign."

Shrugging, Cahill said, "Humor may be all I have left."

After a short silence, the abbot began. "You must act. Doing nothing will be the death of you. As far as I can see, you have two choices."

"What are they? Pray, do not leave me in suspense."

Folding his hands beneath his chin, the abbot said, "Take the young lady up on her offer."

Cahill jumped to his feet. "What? No."

The old man held up a shaking hand to stay Cahill's objections. "She speaks the truth, however much you do not wish to hear it. I have spent my life serving your father and his father before him. You cannot leave the kingdom without an heir, Cahill, it would be disastrous."

"It is impossible."

Tilting his head to one side, the old man said, "The witch did not leave *you* infertile."

"That's not what I'm talking about."

"Then what is it?" The abbot paused with thick grey brows raised. "Ah. Something the matter? Down there?" He pointed a gnarled finger at Cahill's midsection. "There are herbs a man can ingest, if that is your problem."

Cahill cringed, collapsing back into his chair. "That is not the problem I speak of. I am capable—*physically*—of siring an heir." He sighed. "It is my heart that cannot stomach it. Lying with another is a betrayal to Breanna."

"Betrayal? The queen left you. *That* is a betrayal."

Cahill had never heard the abbot speak ill of Breanna before and he could not believe he was doing so now. "Don't you see?" He pounded his fist on the table. "If I give in, if I do this thing, it is as good as giving up. On my wife. On my daughter. Everything." Cahill stood once more and paced, needing to do something to quell the terrible restlessness that was eating him up inside. "I will not give up."

"Ah." The abbot smiled. "There is the conviction of a man fit to be king." He nodded fondly. "Your grandfather would have been proud. Your father, on the other hand…" The abbot made a clicking sound against the few teeth he had left. "He did not have the same mettle as the two of you. He would have bedded Giselle years ago."

Cahill stopped pacing. The holy man had played him. Tested him. Cahill smiled despite himself. "Tell me, what is this other option you speak of?"

"Isn't it obvious?"

"No."

"You must go find her."

"But how? She has eluded my scouts for five years. How am *I* to find her?"

Pressing his weathered hands together as if in prayer, the old man said, "You will find her easily enough. You see, my son, I happen to know where Breanna is and I am sorry to report, she is in grave danger."

✦ ✦ ✦

She'd kept him at arm's length for too long. Why? Why had she denied her feelings? Why had she refused to recognize his? She couldn't remember. Particularly now that he was lying beside her, his masculinity so close, so warm. And his eyes? There was a look of loving tenderness in his gaze that warmed the frigid reaches of her heart.

It must be the firelight that made his blue eyes appear so dark tonight.

She reached for him, twining her hands around his neck and pulling him down to her. She had to kiss him. She missed his kisses.

Oh!

How soft his lips were. How sweet. Was it his lips or hers that were trembling? Perhaps both. Not out of fear or uncertainty, but out of desire. Long suppressed desire.

"You are sweeter than I ever imagined," he whispered against her mouth before deepening the kiss. She gave herself up to that kiss. No longer sweet. It was all consuming. Powerful. He kissed her as he'd never kissed her before. Exploring her lips and mouth like an adventurer, bold yet cautious at the same time.

She could die a happy woman after such a kiss.

Except the rest of her body was not content with mere kisses. In fact, her body felt as if it had lain dormant for too long and was now roaring to life with demands she had long forgotten. "Touch me," she moaned. "I need you to touch me."

He turned away from her lips to groan into her hair. "Are you certain, my love?"

"Yes."

He pressed his head to hers. "It has been so long in coming."

"I know. I'm sorry."

"Don't apologize. It's not your fault."

How good he was. How understanding. Of course it was her fault. She knew it was. But now she would make it up to him.

He nuzzled her neck, which was delightful, but she needed more than nuzzles. Her body ached, throbbed, with both familiar and unfamiliar sensations. So strange. Desire swirled beneath her skin, creating a funnel cloud that would consume her if he did not touch her. It was desire for something she both knew and did not know.

Desperately tugging on the neck of her gown and chemise, she managed to pull the material beneath her breasts so she could guide his head to her bare flesh. "Please."

He groaned and…oh!

Never had she experienced anything so exquisite as the eager suckling of her husband upon her aroused flesh. The sensation stoked a fire low in her belly, something she had forgotten or perhaps had never felt. Yet surely they had done this before. "More," she cried. "I need more."

She guided his hand beneath the cloak to her parted thighs and held him there. He groaned, cupping her through the folds of her gown, yet keeping his hand immobile.

"Please," she begged.

He did not heed her. Something stayed his hand and his labored breathing confirmed a conflict within. "This is not how I foresaw this." His voice was low, guttural.

"I know," she said, taking matters into her own hands and gathering the material of her skirt to pull it up the length of her legs. "But now is not the time for planned seduction. We have our whole lives for that. Now is the time to quench this need between us."

"Oh, my wife," he moaned and swiftly pulled up on her skirts.

Yes, yes she was his wife. And he was her husband. Yet she

had denied him his rights for too long. "You should have taken a lover," she murmured, a tear sliding down her cheek as she wrestled her legs free of her skirts, only now considering how strange it was that she was wearing skirts in the first place.

"How could I when there is only one woman I love?"

She closed her eyes and smiled through her tears. Her smile widened when his finger traced a line up the inside of her bare thigh. She shivered. "I don't deserve you."

"Don't say such things. It is you who is good and pure. It is you who deserves more than me, for I am nothing but a simple man."

And that was what she loved best about her husband. He was king and yet described himself as nothing more than a simple man.

"I love you," she said. "I love you so very much."

"How I've waited to hear you say those words."

"Ah!" She cried out the moment he touched her most sensitive place. How could she have forgotten such a place existed? Such pleasure? It was like nothing she'd experienced before.

She raised her hips to him, pleading for more.

He stroked her flesh, eliciting an unusual dampness that slicked her skin, before pulling away to fumble with the ties on his breeches.

While she waited, she reached down to touch herself, caressing her flesh as he had done, the sensation both familiar and completely new, spreading the strange slickness over herself in preparation for him.

"I have wanted you from the moment we met," he whispered, rolling on top of her. With his knees on the inside of hers, he pressed her open. "I have wanted to make you my wife over and over and over again."

She could feel him at her entrance, heavy and hard, pressing into her, about to penetrate. Oh yes! She wriggled against him, urging him forward, needing him with every fibre of her being because she knew that having her husband inside of her was the only thing that would ease this inexplicable sorrow.

"Darling, I must go slow," he murmured, refusing to press forward as if there was some barrier. "The first time will hurt and I—"

"First time?" She panted. "It has been a long time, I grant you, but we both know this is *not* my first time."

"What?" He pulled away, propping himself above her. There was a look of confusion on his beautiful face.

She groaned. "Oh gods, don't stop now." Digging her nails into him she moaned, "Please, Cahill, I need you inside of me, please."

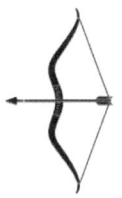

CHAPTER 15

The eldest daughter took a cautious step forward, for she knew beyond a doubt, what she wanted. "I wish to be the most beautiful in all the land..."

— FROM THE LEGEND OF THE DRAGON CLAW SCEPTER

A'Dale had not slept a wink and now breakfast was a quiet, uneasy affair. Even Hope was quiet, perhaps because of the weather. It was a cool, wet morning and they were all cold and tired. Allan was painfully aware of the manner in which Muriel kept her head down, even when he served her bread and sausage. The only time she looked up was when Hope spoke to her. Then a change came over her face. Her smile beamed, her eyes lit up like they reflected a happy, flickering flame.

When she looked at him, that flame went out and a little wrinkle formed between her brows. Then she looked away.

She had called him Cahill.

Hellsfire!

A'Dale stood, needing to move. For each time Cahill's name came unbidden to his mind, his stomach churned, his chest constricted and he had the urge to kill. Preferably the king of Lorentia.

Kicking dirt on the fire, Allan quickly packed up their meagre belongings. They needed to be on the road. They needed to keep moving...

Why had she called him Cahill?

He cinched the saddle too tight and the horse nickered in discomfort.

Had she been dreaming? Had she secretly harbored feelings for the king for these last twelve years? Had Allan been a fool for just as many years, thinking it was him she loved when she never had? Was it the queen's visit that reminded her of the man she truly longed for?

He glanced her way, but she was watching Hope.

"Let's go," he said.

Hope looked at him strangely. He knew his voice was harsh but there was nothing he could say to his daughter to explain.

Not his daughter, Cahill's daughter.

Unconsciously, he reached for his sword and had it halfway drawn when Hope came to put her hand on his arm. She looked up at him with those sensitive, expressive eyes. "Da? What's wrong?"

He shook his head, unable to give voice to his terrible feelings. Releasing his sword, he instead placed his hands on the top of Hope's head and kissed her there, when suddenly he felt Muriel's presence behind him. He turned and, keeping his eyes averted, he asked, "Do you have the energy to walk or do you need to ride?"

"I think I'll walk," she said softly.

He nodded. "And have you...said your daily prayers?" He glanced at Hope and then back at Muriel. Many years ago, Muriel had asked him to promise not to tell Hope about her abilities as a witch which was why he referred to her spells as prayers. He recalled the conversation that had occurred when Hope was no more than a toddling babe.

"I do not invoke spells, Allan, I pray."

"Is that what you call it?"

"It is what we both shall call it. Hope is such a curious child. If she knows I practice magic, she'll want to learn and I'll want to teach her."

"Then teach her."

Muriel shook her head. "Magic leaves a signature in the ether. The last thing we need is a novice invoking spells more powerful than her ability. It would attract unwanted attention. No, the less magic I employ the better."

"Prayers?" Muriel asked. "Is that what I do?"

"Yes." Allan glanced at Hope again. "You pray for protection. Daily."

"Ah," Muriel nodded, though the crease between her brows remained. "Then I shall do so now." She closed her eyes and folded her hands beneath her chin.

Allan could not take his eyes off her. Her pale skin, her rosy cheeks. Her lips moving silently…

Despite the wretched name she'd uttered last night, he still loved her and the urge to pull her into his arms and kiss her—angrily—was so overwhelming, he had to walk away.

"Don't worry, Da. Things will be better once we find a place to live." Hope threaded her arm through his and patted his hand.

He smiled down at her even though he did not believe it. For over a decade he had been living in a sort of fantasy, every day letting himself believe that Hope and Muriel were his family. His true family. The notion had helped him endure the torture of Muriel's presence and his inability to act upon his feelings for her. Now, he could no longer keep up the pretense. Hope was not his daughter and Muriel would never be his wife, for she did not love him. Their new home would not be better, it would be worse. For he had four years left to live with the knowledge that the woman he loved and called 'wife' was in love with another.

It was these thoughts that plagued Allan all morning and into the afternoon, his mind relentlessly replaying the events of last night, over and over again. Each time he heard Cahill's name upon Muriel's lips, his anguish grew.

"Da, you must slow down," Hope called from behind.

He turned. How had he come to be so far ahead? Hope led the horses and Muriel was nowhere to be seen. "Where is your mam?"

Glancing behind her, Hope said, "She is coming but slowly. She is still unwell."

Damnation. He had to get his mind out of this fog. They were in unknown territory and even though Muriel's spells would cloak them from brigands, who knew what supernatural dangers lurked nearby. His job was to protect, regardless of his own emotions.

He waited for Hope to catch up and then untied a bag from the side of one of the horses and pulled out a hunk of cheese wrapped in cloth. "We should eat." He used his dagger to carve off a chunk and handed it to Hope.

"I'm worried about Mam," Hope said before taking a bite. "She's acting strange."

"It is the fever. She will be fine," Allan said with more conviction than he felt.

"Do you think it was a spell that made her so ill?"

Slowly, Allan finished chewing. Then he swallowed. "Spell? What do you mean?"

"Da," Hope said crossing her arms over her thin chest. "I'm not a child and I'm not blind. I know what Mam is. She gathers herbs and practices magic every morning. She is a witch."

Gods! This was not a conversation he knew how to have with Hope. He hated lying to her but he also could not tell her the truth. The only one who would know how to explain things properly was Muriel. He glanced down the path. Where was she?

"Hope, I'm going to look for your mam." He wrapped the cheese and stored it in the food sack. "Stay with the horses. If there is danger, you must scream and you must use this." He handed her his dagger.

Hope's eyes went wide. "Must I?"

"You must, my sweet. Though I doubt it will be necessary."

Allan prayed he spoke the truth. He also prayed Muriel was close, perhaps just around the bend. She was still weak and he should have insisted she rode, but he'd been too angry this morning. He'd let hurt cloud his judgement and now Muriel could be collapsed by the side of the road or worse. He jogged down the path, his pace increasing when he still didn't see her.

A sound in the forest to his left made him stop. Twigs snapped, something moved. Allan turned just as something whistled past his face.

Not two yards away, an arrow quivered where it had sunk into a nearby tree.

The shackles went around her ankles, hands and neck, with a chain connecting all together, forcing Breanna to shuffle slowly into the Great Hall of Dunsmoor Castle, giving her time to observe the stranger sitting on the massive throne, a polished crown upon his thick blond hair, a dragon claw scepter across his lap. Once she reached the edge of the dais, a foot soldier strode forth and swung a club at the back of her legs, forcing her to kneel.

"Breanna, Queen of Lorentia. Heir to Morainia. It is a pleasure to see you again."

Through bared teeth, Breanna said, "We have never met."

The man stood. He was tall and robust with fair skin and piercing blue eyes. He was a man in his prime and might have been attractive if not for the malicious scowl he wore.

He glanced down at himself. "You do not recognize your betrothed?"

"Elwood?" She scoffed. "You are not him."

"Ah, but I am." He stepped down from the dais and came to stand directly in front of her. He used the head of the scepter to lift her chin up. "Why don't you believe me?"

"Because Elwood is—"

"Is what?" He raised the scepter, about to strike if she should answer incorrectly.

She was not scared. He could kill her for all she cared. Hope was safe, that was all that mattered. "Elwood is much older and…ever so much larger."

Throwing his head back, the man laughed. When he regained composure, he said, "Very astute." Yet, his smile was sinister when he continued, "My sister…you remember her, she used to be queen of Lorentia? Now she is mostly dragon. You are acquainted with her, I believe."

"Of course I am."

"Yes, well, she has become quite the sorceress." He spread his arms wide. "We have been experimenting with my *physique*. This one is my favorite. Do you like it?"

"What do you expect me to say?"

"I expect you to tell me how handsome I am." He came closer and snarled, "I expect you to lament the fact you broke our engagement."

Bre snarled in response.

"Ah, but you could have had *this*." He indicated his body with a wave of his hand and then stuck out his lip in an exaggerated pout. "You should not have run from me, little girl. Forcing me to destroy your kingdom. To kill your family." He nodded at the foot soldier standing behind her who yanked on her chains, hauling her to her feet. A malevolent smile spread across his face as he looked down at her. He touched her cheek. "All because of appearances."

Giving her an appraising look, he said, "Personally, I think you would have gotten the better end of the stick. Believe me, my dear, you are no object of feminine beauty."

Lifting her chin in defiance, Bre bit out, "What do you want, Elwood?"

He smiled. "I want you to know I've moved on." He waved his hand dismissively. "I'm letting bygones be bygones."

Bre's body shook with repressed rage and some other emotion that was so deep and dark it could not be named. She knew beyond a doubt that this false Elwood was lying, playing some sinister game for which she was a mere pawn.

"I'm a man of my word, Breanna. Your father and I agreed that our union should bring peace to our lands. It would have. But then you fled and I was forced to keep my promise of war. You see that don't you?"

"War? That was not war. That was an apocalypse." Her lips quivered as she imagined, for the millionth time, her family's death and the complete annihilation of her homeland. "You destroyed everything." If only she had a sword. But then, what would she do with it? Her journey to Dunvegan as Duncan's captive had taught her one thing, she was no longer proficient in battle.

"A consequence of war, I'm afraid." He shrugged as if the loss of her family and kingdom was nothing to be upset about. "In a few months' time, I shall wed a beautiful young princess from across the Selward Sea. An exotic flower, or so I'm told."

"You're disgusting."

"Disgusting?" Putting a hand to his heart, feigning insult,

he said, "Look at me. I'm handsome. Rich. Powerful. I'm a king among kings."

He raised the scepter again, as if to strike, swinging it down but stopping inches before crushing her temple. She did not flinch. Why should she? She welcomed the physical pain. The end to all this. For she knew she would never see Hope again.

Nor A'Dale.

A'Dale?

Breanna blinked. Where had that thought come from?

Cahill. She would never see her husband, Cahill, again.

"Your jealousy shines through, my dear. You can't stand the fact that someone else shall be my wife." He sighed heavily. "Ah, but my once-betrothed, your jealous attempt to wound me is noted and as a show of good faith, I shall invite you to my wedding banquet." He tilted his head to one side in a mocking gesture. "Though a little torture may be in order first."

The doors of the Great Hall burst open and all turned to watch a beast hop through, spurting flames and smoke from its hideous snout.

"Eleanor," Bre growled.

"At least she recognizes one of us, brother," the beast said in a garbled voice. The thing stopped two feet from Bre, its deformed head tilting from one side to the other, taking in Bre's appearance. "I'm in agreement with Elwood. You are not looking well, Breanna. Rather skinny and tough."

The brute stabbed an apple with its talon off a nearby table and forced it into Bre's mouth. Speaking to the king, it said, "Look at her. She will not do for the feast. Not at all."

Elwood came closer, using the scepter to inspect Bre's body, lifting the hem of her tunic to examine her bare belly and protruding ribs. Bre grunted as he walked behind her, dropping the tunic and swinging the scepter against her backside, forcing her to fall painfully once more to her knees on the flagstone.

"You're right," Elwood said. "Nothing but skin and bones. Rather gristly, I fear. I shall have to fatten her up before the feast. I wouldn't want to offend my new bride with such unsavory fare."

Pure, hard hatred coursed through Breanna as she realized Elwood's plan. If it were anyone else, she would suspect it was a cruel jape. But not Elwood. Oh no. The obscene glutton in him would not joke about such a thing. He absolutely intended for her to be present at the feast. Spit and roasted like a pig, served upon a giant platter, forcing his new wife to eat her as a cautionary tale about what would happen if the new bride should ever wrong him, as Breanna had done.

Jerking against her chains, Breanna howled against the apple in her mouth. But there was nothing she could do. Even if she could recall her combat practice, there was nothing in her repertoire that had prepared her for this.

Snatching the scepter from her brother's hands, Eleanor pointed it at Breanna. "Where is she? Tell me and I shall kill you quickly."

Bre shook her head, saliva running down her cheeks from the apple stuck between her teeth.

"You would rather be tortured when it will all end the same? Elwood will marry and with his new wife comes twelve attendants."

The beast dipped its head so close to Breanna's face, the smell of brimstone washed over her, making her eyes water.

"Delicious, unsullied maidens." A forked tongue flicked along the scaly lips of the beast. "I shall suck them dry and return to my human form with twelve lives. You know what that means, do you not?"

Breanna shook her head, not in reply but in desperation.

Eleanor nudged her head with the scepter. "I will find your daughter and I will kill her, sucking her soul so that I shall live thirteen lifetimes. You may as well tell me now and save all of us the time and the torture."

Finally Breanna managed to spit the apple upon the ground. "Go to the seventh level of hell!" she shouted.

A burst of steam streamed from the beast's nostrils. "Torture it is."

CHAPTER 16

After his sister made a wish, the boy approached, a hand to his empty stomach. "I wish to always have more than enough to eat..."

— FROM THE LEGEND OF THE DRAGON CLAW SCEPTER

He withdrew his sword and sprinted back up the path towards Hope. However, when he got there he was too late. A swarthy, one-eyed man with arms the width of tree trunks and a face that resembled a mottled squash had Hope around the waist, his hand covering her mouth.

Hope's eyes were wide with fear, the dagger he'd given her useless on the ground by the horse.

"Let her go," Allan said, approaching cautiously.

The man laughed, a rough, snarly sound. "Nay. The weather's a'changin'. I need me a bed warmer this night."

Cold, hard rage shuddered through Allan. "Let. Her. Go."

The man twisted Hope's hair around his fist and she squealed in pain. "Nay. Drop your sword, and I'll kill ye quick."

Allan did not drop his sword, neither did he halt his approach. There was no way on heaven or earth he would let this man take Hope. "Take the horse. Take what you will. Leave us be."

"I'm no fool." The man twisted harder, forcing Hope onto tippy toes. "This wee chit is the mos' valuable possession ye's got. Now, she be mine."

Noises from all directions surrounded Allan. He stopped his forward advance to take a quick look. Three thugs appeared from behind trees, coming at him from all sides. The men were equally brutish and unkempt in their appearance and Allan gritted his teeth for what was to come. A fleeting thought whistled between his ears like the arrow past his face; if he failed, he would not have to endure another four years of torture before losing the two things he loved most. But, by all that was holy, he vowed he would die saving them.

"There be four of us and but one of ye. Drop your blade."

Allan looked from side to side at the approaching outlaws. "I think not."

The man yanked Hope's head back, revealing her creamy white throat. "You wish to watch her die, do ye?"

Though it went against every single one of his instincts, Allan had no choice but to call the man's bluff. "You said yourself she's the most valuable thing I've got. You won't hurt her."

The man cocked his head to one side and snarled. "Tha's where ye be wrong. I may not kill the lass, no. But hurt her? Aye, hurt her, I will." The man leaned down as if to kiss Hope's cheek and bit her instead.

Allan tasted blood. He *needed* blood.

Pivoting on his toes, he feinted left but lunged right, taking the man on his right by surprise and slashing him across his chest. The thug stumbled backwards, a crimson stain spreading across his filthy tunic, prompting the other two bandits to attack. Between the clanging of metal and the grunts of exertion, Allan could still hear the whimpering cries from Hope.

With renewed ferocity, he parried one blow, ducked from another and swung low, nicking the leg of one man. The man with the chest wound stumbled back into the fray and Allan used his staggering steps against him, forcing him to turn into the path of his companion's heavy blow.

Hope screamed.

What had the brute done? Allan dared not look. To take his eyes off his attackers was pure folly, but his heart screamed with rage and the need to know what the big man was doing to his little girl.

Every suppressed emotion he'd ever felt surged through him, taking over his limbs and his brain, making him a god-like warrior, whirling and thrusting with inhuman speed, incapable of feeling pain. He would kill each of these filthy wasters and then he would kill the beast who held his daughter.

Not your daughter, Cahill's daughter.

Allan's swing faltered, giving one of his attackers time to block his thrust while the other lunged for his chest. He twisted at the last moment but was not fast enough and the tip of the man's sword caught his shoulder, sending a sheet of pain down the left side of his body. He ignored the injury and swung with desperate rage because he knew the effect his blood would have on these men. Blood was a sign of weakness, giving them a taste of victory.

"Skewer 'im, lads. No more messin' about."

With snarls and grunts, the men came at him with more purpose. Allan swung right, then left, then backed away to catch his breath, but his attackers pressed on. His left arm refused to cooperate so he was forced to wield his sword one-handed, blocking blow after blow, the force reverberating through his tiring arm.

"No!"

Was that Hope's voice? Gods! Allan gnashed his teeth

and lunged forward with one last burst of fury. He swung haphazardly, hoping to catch one of the men in a random blow.

Something flashed out of his peripheral vision.

A hallucination from blood loss?

Grunting in pain, Allan deflected a particularly forceful blow and was about to jab when the man to his right made a terrible croaking sound and collapsed, his head hanging at an odd angle, blood gushing from his throat and mouth.

Wiping the sweat and blood out of his eyes with his sleeve. Yes, he was hallucinating, for he hadn't touched the man. Allan blinked. Yet there he lay, his head nearly severed from his body. After shaking his head to clear his spotty vision, Allan noticed his other opponent backing away. He tried to take advantage of the fellow's retreat, but a flash of something red distracted him, making him stumble until he found himself careening off a tree into another, trying desperately to find the balance he no longer seemed to possess.

A high pitched scream, followed by a wet thunk forced him to focus. The third attacker writhed on the ground with a gaping hole in his belly that spewed innards and blood upon the forest floor.

How? How had this happened? He tried to turn, but only tripped on something at his feet. Before him was the body of the largest hood, the man who'd captured Hope. He lay face down in the dirt, the hilt of a dagger protruding from the back of his neck.

Dead.

"Da?"

At the sound of Hope's quivering voice, Allan turned. She was safe. Oh gods, she was safe! He wrapped his good arm around her and together they collapsed against the trunk of a tree. He smoothed her tangled hair away from her face to find her cheeks covered in blood and swollen, but she was alive and that was all that mattered.

"I'm so sorry," he whispered against her matted hair.

"Why?" She pulled back to gaze at him. "You fought so bravely!" Huge tears coursed down her bruised cheeks as she hazarded a wobbly smile. "And Mama…!"

Muriel! Allan looked around, desperate. Where was she? The ambush had required all his attention but now that the ambushers were dead, a certain dread for Muriel stole over him.

"I am here, my daughter."

Allan looked up. Muriel stood before him like some fire goddess, her flaming hair loose and wild, her clothes, face and hands streaked with crimson.

"Are you hurt?" he whispered.

She shook her head and kneeled at his side. "No. But you are." Peeling back his tattered sleeve from his arm, she said, "We must tend your wounds, and quickly. Hope, tear off the bottom of your chemise. I must bind A'Dale's arm." She glanced around. "These four are dead, but there could be more. This is the Thieves Woods and there is likely a whole band of them lurking about. We must make haste."

On the verge of unconsciousness, he watched with detached interest as Muriel calmly and efficiently bound his arm.

"Is this a dream?" he asked, his voice sounding hollow as darkness closed in around him.

"No." She leaned closer, looking into his eyes. When his lids became too heavy to open, she spread them. "You need to stay awake." Then went back to tending his arm, talking to him the whole time. "I am impressed. You fought well against the three, giving me time to circle around Hope so I could take out the leader."

Fighting to maintain consciousness, Allan focused on Muriel. He had never seen her like this, able to wield a weapon with such proficiency. And what was that thing she'd said about the Thieves Woods? How did she know this was the Thieves Woods when he did not? More importantly, how had the brigands found them with her protective spell in place?

Muriel stopped what she was doing to frown at him. "I knew this was the Thieves Woods because I have passed this way before."

Allan blinked. He hadn't spoken out loud, had he?

She went back to tying the binding firmly around his arm and said, "And I know nothing of spells."

"But I saw you this morning."

She shook her head. "You saw me pray, as you told me to."

"Pray? You mean, cast a spell."

"No. I prayed to my ancestors."

"Your ancestors?"

"In Morainia."

"Muriel, what are you talking about?"

"Muriel?" She blinked at him, mouthing her name again as if it was foreign to her. Suddenly her eyes went wide. Her lips parted and she inhaled sharply. She looked wildly around at the inert bodies lying about, soaked in blood. Then her gaze flew to her hands.

Muriel's breath hitched and she wrung and shook her hands as if to wipe off the crimson stains. "What have I done?" she moaned. "Oh *Sisters*, what have I done?"

They sat by the fire, all three of them. Hope's head was in Muriel's lap and Muriel petted her hair absently as the girl slept. Somehow she'd managed a rudimentary healing spell, but she was quite sure there were more powerful ones she could have used. She just couldn't remember them.

It was all so confusing. She stared into the flames feeling… lost. Maybe she could find herself in the flickering light somewhere.

"So you have no memories from the last twelve years?" A'Dale repeated for the third time.

She shook her head, tearing her gaze from the fire to look at the man who sat on the other side of her. She could not decipher the look in his dark eyes. "Not as Muriel, no."

"But from the years before?"

Muriel went back to staring into the fire, trying to recollect that time—her home and shop in Lochsend. It seemed so far away, so distant, almost as if it was a spell she'd read about in a grimoire, the experiences of another, not something she had experienced herself. What felt most real were the queen's memories.

"It is not just memories," Muriel said slowly. "I feel as if I *am* her." She looked at her hands lying gently on Hope's brow. The hands she'd spent hours scouring in the nearby stream. Hands that would never be clean.

For she had fairly butchered those men.

Her hands. *Not* Breanna's, hers.

She shivered.

"Tell me about these memories."

Squeezing her eyes closed, she saw the memories as if they were there on the inside of her lids. Quietly she began to relay them. "I spent…I mean, Breanna spent many years, seven at least, searching the continent for Hope, living a rough, lonely existence." She cringed. As clear as a mountain pond, she could see the endless hours on horseback, through all sorts of weather and terrain. The ramshackle inns and flea-ridden cots. The entanglements with ruffians which, more oft than not, ended in death by her hand. Her fingers twitched in remembrance.

"She was desperate in her single-mindedness." She opened her eyes. "Though the first five years were far worse."

"How so?"

"Traveling across the continent at least gave me—*her*—purpose.

"In the beginning, after losing Hope, her life was without meaning. She had but one pastime. Combat practice." She turned and smiled sadly at A'Dale. "Memories of practice was how I was able to kill those men." She shuddered, remembering clearly hours upon hours, day after day of nothing but swordplay.

"What of Cahill?" A'Dale asked, his melodic voice sounding rough as if he were cross with the king.

Muriel shrugged. "They rarely spoke. I..." The tears that had threatened now broke free. "*She* felt responsible for the loss of Hope. And, she was angry. So angry." Muriel could feel the anger in her bones. She knew it was misguided guilt, for Cahill did not deserve her anger, but it was there.

Suddenly her body gave in to the most intense sorrow she'd ever known and she wept, her shoulders heaving with great, shuddering sobs.

Allan inched closer, but he did not touch her. He did not console her and somehow that made the pain worse.

After a time, once she'd gotten her emotions under control, he asked, "So, the other night, when I...when we...were lying together..." He paused to study her. "You thought you were Breanna and that I was Cahill."

"Yes," she murmured softly.

"You have no recollection of me. Of...us." He gestured to Hope.

Slowly, Muriel shook her head and dropped her gaze. "No." She threaded her fingers through Hope's black hair. So soft. So much like Cahill's. "Every time I look at her, it is like I am seeing her for the first time and my heart feels as if it might burst, yet I am filled with anguish because she is no longer the wee babe I remember." She pressed her lips together. "I have no recollection of her from before I—*the queen*—arrived at the cottage, however many days ago that was."

"How is that possible?"

"It must have been a spell, though I have no memory of how it works. All I remember is kneeling across from one another, holding hands. And then," she paused, rubbing her brow as if that might help the memories return.

It did not.

"Then, waking up, to you looking down at me. Thinking I was *her* and you, my husband."

She glanced at him. The intensity of his gaze took her by surprise. "A'Dale?"

He turned away.

"I am sorry." The words came, yet she did not know what exactly she was sorry for. For some reason she felt she needed to apologize, both on behalf of Breanna and of herself.

After a short silence, the man met her gaze again. His dark eyes shone with strange, unsettled emotions. When he spoke, his voice was deep and resonant, as if his voice were an instrument playing music that spoke to her on some subconscious level.

"Would you like me to tell you about it?"

"About what?"

"About you. Hope." He paused. "Us. Our family."

Squeezing her eyes shut caused the tears clinging to her lashes to tumble down her cheeks. "Yes," Muriel whispered. "Yes, I should like that very much."

Allan proceeded to tell her the tale of the three of them, living simply in a cottage in the woods. He spoke of how she wove with such skill, creating baskets that were works of art.

Of their daughter, who had a gift for befriending woodland creatures in particular, the injured and sickly. He explained how she had kept them safe, weaving spells of protection around their home and cottage. And how they spent their evenings together, telling stories and singing songs to the accompaniment of his lute.

A'Dale was a gifted storyteller and the tales went on for hours as he recounted times of joy and sorrow, funny little occurrences and even the monotonous chores that filled each and every day. She laughed and cried, marveling at the life she'd shared with this man and their adopted daughter.

Yet, at the back of her mind was a seething resentfulness.

She had spent the years in tranquility.

Bliss.

How could she have given up such glorious memories? Why did she trade happiness for this bone-crushing sorrow?

"I must be very inept if my attempt at humor makes you cry," A'Dale said softly.

Shaking her head, Muriel said, "No. You are the very best storyteller I've ever heard. 'Tis the confusion inside of me that makes me weep." She wiped the tears from her cheeks. "And I am tired."

"Of course." The man moved away to make his bed on the other side of the fire.

Why this action caused her pain was a mystery, for she had no memory of this man whom she'd shared a home with. Yet, she missed his closeness and seeing him so far away made her sad nonetheless.

How strange.

She watched him from beneath lowered lashes.

No memory, yet her body reacted to him in ways that were curious. Now that she gave it some thought, she had a memory of A'Dale from Lochsend. He was the handsome Captain of the Guard. She recalled watching for him every morning as he made his rounds, patrolling the town, and feeling a strange thrill in the pit of her belly when he'd stop by her shop to buy baskets.

Her fingers twitched in memory of the act of weaving.

"A'Dale," she whispered, sitting up.

"Yes?" Though quiet, his voice rumbled deep and low, eliciting a familiar achy sensation in the furthest reaches of her belly.

There were so many questions. So many things she'd lost in this horrific exchange. "What is…?" She wanted to ask him about the nature of their relationship but her mouth had gone dry.

He too sat up as he waited for her to finish her question, his gaze never leaving hers, which made the asking impossible.

"There is so much I need to remember." Breaking his gaze, she asked instead, "Would you tell me stories every night? Even if you tell the same ones over and over? Perhaps they will come to feel like they are my own memories, if only I hear them oft enough."

"Of course." He paused and a soft and perhaps sad expression crossed his features. "And do not forget that we have nearly four years left together. That is plenty of time to forge new memories."

Four years? Of course. They must keep Hope hidden until she was sixteen. Then they would return her to the king and queen.

She lay down, hugging Hope close to her, a sense of panic overcoming her.

A'Dale was quiet for a time and she thought he had fallen asleep. But then she heard something, a whisper, an oath? What was it? She'd noticed the same thing earlier. It was as if her hearing was particularly good. In fact, sometimes it was as if she heard things people hadn't even uttered aloud.

This morning she'd heard Cahill's name as if A'Dale was chanting it. Then, this afternoon, clear as anything, she'd heard the thieves hiding in the forest, plotting to ambush them.

Curious.

There it was again. A deep baritone whispering inside her head.

"Did you say something, A'Dale?"

"No." He took a deep breath and exhaled slowly. "'Tis late, Muriel. Go to sleep."

Yes, it was late, yet sleep eluded her, for she'd heard the words Allan had said…the words he'd claimed he hadn't said.

Four years to show you how much I love you. Four years to make you my true wife.

A lonely tear slid down her cheek as she contemplated the sentiments of the man she'd lived with for so many years, a man she barely knew.

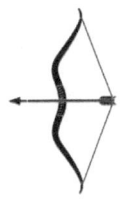

CHAPTER 17

The youngest of the three, who was the most cunning, lingered
behind her siblings, thinking carefully about her wish.
For she wanted each of her family members' wishes for herself.
"You there," the seer called. "What is your wish?"
Moving out from behind her brother, the child said softly,
"I wish to be the most powerful witch who has ever lived..."

— FROM THE LEGEND OF THE DRAGON CLAW SCEPTER

S he was cold.

She did not care.

The split skin on her back burned, the wounds raw and festering.

She barely felt it.

Her stomach was a hollow pit. Bottomless. Empty.

It did not matter, for her heart was much the same.

Death was near and Breanna welcomed it. Prayed for it. For she was sure that death would be like her fevered dreams, perhaps even better, where she would be reunited with her daughter and they would live in a sweet little cottage in the forest, a clear running stream nearby, her daughter dancing in the sunlight, laughing. Later, both of them snuggled together beneath a quilt, listening to A'Dale tell stories and sing in that beautiful and haunting baritone.

Were they dreams or memories? Bre could not tell. The cell had no windows, there was no light. It was impossible to tell day from night, just as it was becoming impossible to remember exactly who she was. For her memories were strange. The ones that were the most recent and the most clear were those that were the most peculiar. Familiar and yet completely unfamiliar.

At times she found herself whispering words, incomprehensible words.

While Breanna recognized her voice, the words were not her own, the language she spoke one she did not know.

You're going crazy.

Death is nigh.

Breanna sighed and leaned against the cold, sweating wall of the cell, allowing the unknown words to slide past her lips. She waited, willing death to claim her.

Then, finally, in the distance she saw a light.

Yes, I have heard tales of this. Death is approaching. Thank the gods!

The light grew closer and closer.

"I am ready," she whispered, aloud or in her head, Breanna could not tell.

Something rattled. There was a screech of metal on metal. The light came closer. So close that Breanna was blinded by it and had to turn away.

Take me across the veil to where my ancestors reside.

"I bring food," a soft voice whispered.

Breanna's stomach rumbled, as if coming awake after a much too long sleep. The scent of onion soup and fresh bread clawed its way through her senses, awakening her hunger, tempting her.

She turned her head toward the light, eyes narrowed. Standing before her was a child. A strange child with eyes that reflected the light like emeralds in a mine. At her feet was a platter upon which sat a steaming bowl of soup and a crusty chunk of bread.

"Who are you?"

"I am a serving girl here in the castle. You must eat."

Breanna let her head fall hard against the stone behind her. This was not death. This was Elwood. Of course he employed children. Of course he wanted her to eat. The man was despicable, but he was also true to his word. He had tortured her and left her on the brink of death, just as he claimed he would.

Now he meant to fatten her up for his wedding banquet.

Let him try. What he had not counted on was her will. She may have lost her ability to fight but she had not lost her steely determination.

"Please eat," the girl repeated.

"Is the food poisoned?" Bre asked.

"No."

"Then take it away."

The girl did not take it away. Torch in hand, she sat down beside the platter and waited.

Bre sighed. "I am not going to eat. You may as well leave now."

The girl shook her head and in the torchlight, it was as if her jeweled eyes cast millions of tiny lights around the dreary cell. That's when Bre noticed the tears.

"Why are you crying?"

"I cannot leave. Not until you've eaten."

"Why?"

"I cannot fail to feed you."

"What will Elwood do?" Bre asked through clenched teeth, marveling that there were further depths to her hatred of the foul king.

An expression of terror marred the girl's features. "It is not him I fear." She leaned closer and whispered, "It is *her*."

"Eleanor?"

The girl nodded quickly, glancing behind her as if suspecting the dragon sorceress might be lurking in the shadows.

"What will she do to you?"

"It is too terrible to say."

"Tell me."

Sniffling, the girl scuttled closer still. "She will suck my soul."

"But you're a child!"

"No. I'm a maid of Dunvegan. My people are small. We are miners, you see."

Breanna had heard stories of the people of Dunvegan. A small, gentle race, used and abused by the conquering king Elwood. She studied the small woman's face in the torchlight. "If she sucks the souls of maids, why is she still a dragon?"

Lips quivering, the girl replied, "We are not quite human. Our souls only slow the progression, they don't stop it."

"Hellspawn."

"That is not the worst of it."

It could get worse? "Tell me," she said, her jaw clenched with pure hatred.

"She will bury my body in the hallowed ground, by the light of a full moon, just as she has done with the others whose souls she has stolen. And then…"

"Go on."

"We will become dragons. Fiends of the sky. Evil, soulless creatures, bent on doing her bidding."

Breanna's eyes flew open. For the first time since waking in the cell, she jerked against her bonds. "No."

"I swear. 'Tis true."

"She is building an army."

"Yes."

"How many?" She turned to the frightened girl. "How many?"

The girl shook her head in fear. "I don't know. Hundreds, maybe? Thousands? I don't know." Her breath hitched before she could continue. "I don't want to find out. Please, Miss. I am so afraid. You must eat. I beg you."

Eleanor and Elwood on their own were malicious and destructive, and together they were a force of diabolical proportions and she had underestimated them.

Again.

She had to do something. She could not die. Not until she bested the siblings, once and for all. The sinister king thought he'd left her with no choice, but the longer he kept her alive, the more time she had to devise a plan to kill him and his sister.

She'd killed Eleanor before, she could do it again. And Elwood would die too, she would make sure of it, for the only thing that mattered was keeping Hope safe and the only way to ensure that was to kill the nefarious pair.

Using her chin to indicate the platter on the ground, Bre said, "Fine. I will eat. But you are going to have to release me."

Wiping tears from her cheeks, the girl smiled and a cold finger of foreboding ran down Bre's spine. It must have been the flicker of the torchlight, for there had been a flash of something familiar in that smile. It was gone now, as the servant peered up at her in weepy gratitude.

"I would surely be put to the lash if I was to unchain you. I hope you understand."

Bre nodded. "Of course." Then she opened her mouth and allowed herself to be fed.

✦ ✦ ✦

The sound of Hope's laughter made Muriel raise her head from her task of weaving wattle. He head was thrown back, her dark hair glistening in the sunlight. She appeared as a mythical creature, not a flesh and blood child. Would she ever get used to the sight of her daughter, half grown? A strange flutter originating in her belly, flew up her chest into her throat.

Hope was helping A'Dale daub the mud across the latest section of wattle she'd completed on the far wall of their new cottage.

New cottage? If only she could remember their *old* cottage. But no matter how hard she tried, she could not. With heavy footsteps, Muriel cut across the clearing and made her way through the trees to the secluded pond. The pond was small but spring fed, so its waters were clear and cool, trickling down the slope at the eastern end in a small stream that would end up in the sea a few miles away.

Muriel knelt beside the pond and looked down. She sighed and touched the water as if ripples could change what she saw. Though her reflection said one thing, Muriel's memories told her something quite different. Yet when she stared at herself, old memories came to life. They were memories of a different time and place. She remembered owning an apothecary shop and selling baskets. She remembered her cozy apartment above the shop and being quite content, collecting herbs and magical ingredients, practicing spells while administering remedies from her shop, hung with baskets of all shapes and sizes. The baskets had been her one vanity, the prettiest, most durable baskets in Lochsend.

Muriel looked around. It was late summer and the perfect time to harvest for weaving. There were all kinds of grasses here that would be useful. She began collecting, finding the activity soothing when very little else was.

"Mama?"

She caught her breath.

Oh, that word, that name! She gazed lovingly at her daughter and a long forgotten memory resurfaced as if it had just happened. It was a recollection from that fateful journey to Morainia for Hope's christening. Hope had started to cry and when Breanna had held her, the wee child had gazed at Muriel. Why, she'd been hardly old enough to focus, yet Muriel had seen something in her gaze. A *knowingness*.

She saw the same thing now.

"What are you doing?" Hope asked, startling Muriel out of her memory.

"Why, I..." She glanced around. What was she doing? She had lost track, for it was all Muriel could do to sift between her own memories and those of the queen's.

Grass.

Wattle.

Weaving.

"Why, I was going to pick some grass for baskets." She smiled. "Once the walls are complete."

Hope's beaming smile touched a spot deep in Muriel's chest. "Da says there's only the thatch left and we shall finish that tomorrow."

"Then I had best pick my materials before it gets dark."

Hope took her hand. "May I come? There is something I wish to speak with you about."

"Of course."

They entered the clearing, hand in hand, and A'Dale stood, shirtless and covered in mud. Her abdomen contracted at the sight.

Was it the fact that he was half-clothed and appeared so... manly that resulted in this strange fluttering throb?

Or, was it the way he watched her, his dark eyes full of an emotion that looked suspiciously like love...and something else?

Hope released her hand and scampered off to follow a butterfly. Muriel smiled after her, wondering at how she could be one moment so care-free and child-like and the other so knowing and wise beyond her years.

Pressing a hand to her belly, Muriel turned back to Allan. "You need to bathe, A'Dale. You are a sight."

Looking down at himself, he grinned and his expression was mischievous as he stalked toward her. He didn't stop until he was standing directly in front of her, forcing her to look up, the heat from his bare skin intermixing with hers. "Perhaps tonight I shall tell you the story about how you used to spy on me when I bathed." He winked. "Scandalous. But true."

He turned and strode toward the pond, whistling and leaving Muriel to watch him go, her mouth hanging open while something continued to gnaw on the tender flesh in the deepest recesses of her belly.

CHAPTER 18

The magi's strange eyes changed from white to red.
"Come closer, all of you."
The mother and children kneeled before him,
trembling from the power emanating from the ancient one.
"What you are about to receive is a reward, indeed. But it is also
a curse...do you still wish to receive these gifts?"
Without hesitation, the children and mother nodded their assent.
"Very well." The sorcerer removed his cowl revealing a skeletal
face with glowing eyes. He reached for the woman and wrapped
his bony fingers around her neck and squeezed...

— FROM THE LEGEND OF THE DRAGON CLAW SCEPTER

Eleanor sat upon the throne, peering into the crystal held in the scepter's claws when the doors to the Throne Room opened. A local girl entered, small and child-like, though there was something about the look of displeasure on her face that was incongruent with her small stature.

"Get down," she cried, pointing at Eleanor. Her voice sounded like the mewl of a kitten and Eleanor's instinct was to singe the girl with a burst of flame. Except that this was no ordinary local, it was her brother, and no matter how much she wished for her brother's death, she was not able to kill him. It was part of the covenant her family had struck in order to obtain their power.

"Off my throne and spell me out of this insidious body."

Eleanor hopped down from the golden seat, making a screeching, cackling sound of laughter. "Change you back? But I like you like this." She came closer. "So small. So innocent." She smacked her scaly lips. "So tasty."

"Change. Me. Now." Her brother glanced down at his tiny female form. Then looked up. Oh how she enjoyed the fact that she positively towered over him.

Of course she did not heed him. She was enjoying this far too much.

"You were marvelous by the way. I watched the entire performance in the scepter. Compelling. If not a king, you could have become a famous mummer, traveling the land, entertaining the nobles. So moving. So convincing." Smoke poured from her nostrils, curling through the air in playful, wispy shapes.

"*Please, Miss. I'm so afraid. You must eat. I beg you,*" Eleanor mocked, her garbled voice pitched high in her attempt to sound like a miner maiden. "The tears, brother. How on earth did you conjure such a thing as tears?"

His hands clenched, likely with the desire to wrap around her scaly neck. But they were much too small.

"I merely thought of you, your stinking snout too close to my face," he said in the high girlish voice of his enchanted physique. "It is amazing how easily I can drum up the horrid stench of you."

His insult only resulted in more laughter. "How easily you tricked the grimy slut. It's a wonder Breanna ever had the brains to escape you before."

"May I remind you, sister-mine, that Breanna bested you. Killed you, in fact. In your own palace, I might add."

Waving the scepter in a wide arc, Eleanor muttered, "Bah. Lorentia made me lazy. The truth is, I should thank the bitch. It is because she killed me that I have become stronger and more powerful than ever."

She waddled toward Elwood, holding the family scepter aloft. "Now all I require is the reassurance that you will donate the twelve ladies-in-waiting who attend your bride. The dragon army is complete. All I need is to regain human form in order to leave Dunvegan. To exert my power outside the borders."

"I have already told you, you may have them."

"And your bride?"

"I haven't decided. I must meet her first. Perhaps I shall find some use for her. I should like to make her fall in love with me before handing her over to you."

Eleanor blew a joyful column of flames at the already blackened beams of the ceiling. "You have no idea how amusing you sound, saying such ridiculous things in your current form."

"Oh, I know precisely the degree of ridiculousness." Her brother indicated her dragon form with a wave of her tiny hands. "Now, I command you to change me. Else I may reverse my decision about relinquishing my betrothed's attendants to your nasty care."

"You wouldn't."

"I would."

Growling, she weaved her massive head one way and then the other. "Oh, very well," she conceded, waving the scepter in a figure eight while intoning, "*Reformabita primogenitalis.*" A yellow light flew from the scepter's head, swirling around Elwood in a vortex of shimmering light. His tiny body arched, and then…exploded.

"What have you done?!"

Each finger, each toe, blew up like a cured goat's bladder filled with mead. His tongue grew next, too big for his mouth, lolling fat and useless against his chin until that too grew so large he gargled nonsensically. His stomach stretched so fast and so large, his skin was in danger of bursting open—ah what a sight that would be!

Finally, finally, the light receded and Elwood was left, lying face up on the flagstones, staring at the charred beams above. His over-sized head too heavy to lift, his arms too weak to push himself upright.

She had returned him to his rightful form and it seemed, by the sputtering, angry noises he made, that he was displeased with this outcome.

"Change me back," he managed to mumble.

Her thin, lizard lips curled back in a hideous smile. "Too long you have been pretending to be someone else, brother. I shall change you into whichever form you wish, before your bridal party arrives." She hunkered down even closer, breathing brimstone breath directly into his face. "But for now I think it best that you remember who you *truly* are."

He tried to turn his head but his neck was so thick it would not move.

"Do not forget that I have the power to reveal your true self at any time. Those maidens are mine. Do not threaten me again."

With that Eleanor stalked toward the exit, her claws making clicking sounds along the stone. "Fosset," she called once she reached the door. "The king requires some attention. I suspect he's hungry as well. Prepare his favorite foods. Oh, and locate his bucket. He's in a foul mood."

✦ ✦ ✦

"Again!" Muriel demanded. Her voice carrying across the open space of the meadow. "Get up so we can practice again."

Anger gnawed on the back of Allan's throat as he strode around the cottage to find Hope sitting on the ground, her head to her knees, her wooden practice sword forgotten. Weeping.

Muriel nudged her with the tip of her sword. "Get up. You must practice until you get it right."

"Enough!" A'Dale shouted before crouching beside Hope and whispering in her ear, "It's okay, me bairn. Your mam's not herself."

With a sob, Hope threw her arms around A'Dale's neck and allowed him to pull her to her feet. With tears streaming down her cheeks, she glared at Muriel. "Why are you acting like *her*?"

Quietly, Allan added, "Muriel, this has got to stop."

With the utterance of her name, it was as if the part of her that was truly Muriel sat up and finally listened. She blinked and then covered her mouth in horror. Drawing Hope into the circle of her arms, she whispered, "I'm so sorry, my pet. I am only harsh because…I never want to see you hurt. Ever."

Hope's expression faltered. She sniffed. "It's okay, Mama. I understand."

The love for his daughter surged through Alan, taking him by surprise, stinging the backs of his eyes. Or, perhaps it was only the northern wind. Glancing around at the fallen leaves and the naked trees, Alan said, "Winter is coming. We have many preparations to make for the change in season." He put a hand on Hope's shoulder. "Your rabbits must be tended before supper."

Hope met his gaze and nodded. But, instead of turning

away, she tilted her head to one side and gazed directly into his eyes. For a moment it was as if he stared into the eyes of Hope's true mother, Breanna. The difference being that Hope's gaze was softer. Soft, yet firm. How was that for a contradiction?

Just when he was about to ask her what she meant by her probing gaze, she grinned, flicked her gaze in Muriel's direction and then winked, before scampering off to tend the rabbits.

A'Dale watched her go, puzzled, before turning his attention to Muriel. "We agreed years ago that Hope did not have the nature for sparring."

With trembling lips, Muriel said, "Four more years, A'Dale. We cannot be complacent in her safety. If the girl cannot defend herself, what good is she?"

"Do you hear yourself? Gods, woman. How can you say that?" He turned as if to stride away, but then, thinking better of it, spun back around, his anger no longer concealed. "What good is she?" he shouted. "Why, she is our daughter. She is as good and pure as ever there was. Too sweet-tempered to wield a weapon." He took a step toward her, lowering his voice. "You once knew that and understood it because she was so much like you."

Muriel's lids fluttered in confusion.

With a sigh, Allan continued. "We once agreed I'd continue to teach her, because it was a promise we'd made, but that you'd keep her safe."

"I'm sorry," Muriel said, pressing her hands against the side of her head, her face an expression of pain. "It is as if there are two people living inside my skull. Two minds in opposition." She sighed. "Br—" she stopped before she said the Queen's name. "*Her* will is so very—"

"Stubborn?"

A small smile touched her lips. "I was going to say strong."

There. There it was. A glimpse of the woman he loved.

Softening his voice, he said, "Hope is not made for combat. It is a losing prospect, trying to teach her." The urge to take her hand was strong, but Allan overcame it by stooping to retrieve the fallen practice sword. "You always said it was unnecessary and that you could protect her in other ways."

"How? How am I to protect her?"

"Why, magic. Of course."

Muriel shook her head sadly and walked in the direction of the cottage.

A'Dale strode to catch up. "What is it? Have you forgotten so much?"

She stopped, her gazed fixed upon her open hands.

"Muriel?"

She was silent so long, he wondered if she'd heard him. But finally, in a sorrowful voice, she whispered, "The little I recall is no longer potent enough to protect her."

"Perhaps it will come back. If you keep practicing, that is."

"No." She opened and closed her hands as if seeing something there in her empty palms. Finally her glassy gaze met his. It was filled with sorrow and...shame? "I am no longer pure."

Taking her hands, A'Dale said, "Not pure? But Wife, we have never...that is to say, we have not consummated anything. Our relationship is platonic." Surely impure thoughts did not count.

Tugging her hands from his, Muriel smiled sadly. "I do not refer to chastity."

"But, you once told me—"

"I have taken life, A'Dale." She wiped her palms down the front of her apron. "Not once, but..." She showed him her hands. "The blood of *three* men stain my hands."

"Three men who would have killed you and Hope." He reached for her again, but she kept her distance.

With eyes large and bright, she beseeched him. "Magic cares not for right or wrong. In its eyes, I have sent souls to the afterlife, and whether the act was noble or not, I am tainted. The only course I have now to best a sorceress as strong as the one we hide from, is to practice the same sort of magic that she does." She blinked and a lonely tear fell from her lashes to the bloom of her cheek. In a much lower voice she said, "Is that what you are asking me to do?"

Bowing his head, A'Dale said, "Of course not."

"Then we have no choice."

"Yes we do," a sweet voice rose from behind them.

Both Allan and Muriel turned. They had been so caught up in their conversation they had not heard Hope's quiet approach. How much of their conversation had she overheard?

"Mama, *I* am pure. I have not killed anyone." She wrinkled her nose. "I *hate* swordplay."

Muriel sighed. "Yes, I am well aware."

"I am also chaste…I think." She glanced up at A'Dale, "What does chaste mean, Da?"

Clearing his throat, A'Dale replied, "That is a discussion for you and your mother."

Innocent, inquisitive eyes turned to Muriel.

"Of course you are chaste, my sweet. For the word refers to the joining of a man and a woman." She touched Hope's hair. "And you are but a girl."

"I am nearly a woman, Mama."

"You will become a woman when your moontime is upon you. Not before."

Hope's sweet features crinkled in thought. Suddenly a light came into her eyes. "Oh. Now I understand. You speak of joining of men and women to make babies, like my rabbits do."

"Yes, my love."

A'Dale choked. Irrational rage blindsided him at the thought of his daughter with some lust-crazed male. His grip tightened on his sword while Muriel seemed completely oblivious to his distress.

"Now run along and fetch a bucket of water for supper."

Hope's expression changed again. Her soft lips hardened. Her violet eyes narrowed and her delicate hands fisted on her hips. "No. I hardly think it fair that you should discuss me without me present. Don't you think I should have a say in my own protection?"

"Of course, darling. But this is a matter that is…" Muriel looked to him for the right words, but A'Dale was still overcome by the notion of Hope's virginity being compromised by an undeserving brute. Therefore his reply was little more than an angry grunt.

"It is because you speak of magic. You think I don't know, but I do." Hope gazed at Muriel with guileless violet eyes. "You're a witch."

There was panic upon Muriel's features when she glanced at him.

Before either could protest, Hope continued, "I'm your daughter. It's time you teach me what you know."

"You may be my daughter, but that does not mean you are suited to practicing magic."

"Oh, but I am." Hope gently took the wooden waster from his hands, a resolute expression hardening her delicate features. "Uitta permutto en finis." She waved the sword in a figure eight and a sparkle of light transformed the wooden sword to a stick with a ribbon fluttering from the end.

Allan exchanged a bewildered glance with Muriel.

Hope handed the baton to Muriel and then stood before the two of them, her small fists propped upon her hips. "How do you think Da recovered so quickly from his wounds after the ambush in the Thieves Forest? *You* certainly didn't do that."

"That wasn't you?" Allan asked, quietly.

Slowly Muriel shook her head.

"See?" Hope said with stubborn pride.

"But…that is a complicated spell. How—" Muriel's fine brows drew together.

"Oh, Mama. I've watched you every day for almost thirteen years. The plants you pick, the words you whisper when you think no one is listening. Why, sometimes you even whisper them in your sleep. They're so pretty, like little poems. I've been reciting them for as long as I can remember."

"No!" Muriel dropped to her knees in front of Hope. "You mustn't. It's dangerous to do such a thing when you don't know the meaning or the intent."

"Then teach me." Hope looked down at her like the true princess she was; wise beyond her years with a resolve as fierce and stubborn as her royal parents.

Swallowing hard, Allan said, "I agree with our daughter." For some reason the word *daughter* got caught up in his throat. "But I know not the ways of magic. You must make this decision yourself, Muriel. I will help in any way I can."

Rubbing her temples, Muriel shut her eyes and took a deep breath. She began to whisper and while most of the words sounded foreign to Allan, he caught the word, sister, repeated again and again. Suddenly, Muriel's body convulsed and Allan was sure she was about to collapse, so he sprang to her side to steady her.

Her eyes popped open.

A strange voice spoke through her. "*Come closer, child. Take my hands.*"

What was this? What had Muriel done? Icy fingers slid along his spine as he observed a complete transformation in the woman he loved.

CHAPTER 19

*The children were too stunned to move. It was not until their
mother lay dead on the floor of the cave, her body limp,
her eyes rolled back, that they cried out in alarm.
"You killed her!" The oldest of the three sobbed.
"This is not reward, this is treachery..."*

— FROM THE LEGEND OF THE DRAGON CLAW SCEPTER

H ope approached Muriel without fear.

"*Yes. We recognized you from the first, we did.*"

Cocking her head to one side, Hope whispered,
"Are you the one who speaks to me sometimes inside my head?"

A soft look came into Muriel's eyes. "*So, you have heard.*"
Muriel's lips quivered into a smile. "*It was me, though I am not
the only one.*"

Hope's eyes shone with enthusiasm.

"*Do you understand what it means to be initiated into the
sisterhood?*"

Hope's head went to bob up and down but she stopped
herself, changing her mind at the last moment. Her expression
fell. "No," she said. "Not really."

"*It is a calling. For life.*"

Hope smiled. "And that is what I want. What I have always

wanted."

"Do not agree too quickly. Like all things, there is a balance that is required. You will receive great gifts, but in return you must be willing to make great sacrifices. Your body is very young to understand, but your soul has lived many lifetimes. It is your soul that I address."

Hope glanced his way. Confusion, excitement and fear were at war upon her bonny features. Allan drew himself to his full height. "It is your choice, my sweet girl." But how the choice terrified him. She was too young to make such a monumental decision. To never know love? To never be a mother and hold a wee bairn in her arms? 'Twas a sacrifice indeed.

"Close your eyes, child. Listen to the voice inside of you, for this is your soul and she has lived a hundred lives. She will never lead you astray."

Hope's lashes fluttered closed and her lips parted as she mumbled beneath her breath. Her eyes moved erratically behind her lids as if she was asleep and dreaming. Suddenly she cried out and yanked her hands from Muriel's grasp in order to cover her mouth.

"Ah. You have caught a glimpse of your future."

Hope made a sound that had Allan at her side, wrapping her small body in his embrace. "What happened? What did you see?" he asked, shaken.

Hope's slight form trembled within his arms as he stroked her hair and hummed a soothing tune like she was the babe of yesteryear.

"I'm going to die, Da," Hope said.

Holding her tighter, Allan cooed, "No, my sweet. I promise I will protect you."

The soul inside of Muriel tsked. *"Do not make promises you are likely to break. We are all fated to die. You cannot make the girl immortal, A'Dale."* Muriel's unfocused gaze settled on Hope.

"The vision I saw," Hope started softly. "Is that what will happen if I choose the sisterhood?"

"*No one knows, child. Not even those of us on this side of the veil can predict the future for certain.*" Muriel's head lolled back as she gazed up at the sky. "*Millions of souls making seemingly insignificant choices every day constantly alter the path of the universe.*

"*What you saw was one possible outcome for your future. A warning. Nothing more. The tapestry of your life is not complete. The pattern may be changed. Every choice you make alters the weave.*" She paused. "*The choice you are faced with now is the most significant of this lifetime. So choose carefully, child.*"

If there was ever a decision that Allan wished he could make for Hope, this was it and his hand moved instinctively toward his belt to where his dagger was buckled.

Finally Muriel's gaze found his and for the first time, Allan noticed that her green eyes were completely black. "*…there are some events that are destined to occur no matter what choices are made to avoid them.*" She turned as if seeing the world in ways that his eyes could not see. "*Unfortunately, we never know which is which.*"

"Stop speaking in riddles." Allan held Hope tight. "She's only a child. She can't make this decision." It took effort to control his breath. "Please. Tell us what to do. I beg of you."

In direct contrast to his frustration, Muriel's face was the essence of peace. "*It is not my decision to make. Neither is it yours, A'Dale. Nor is it Muriel's.*"

Hope struggled within his arms, shrugging his hands from around her. She turned to the sister speaking through Muriel. "Then I know what I must do."

"*Are you certain?*"

"Yes. It is what I was born to do. I wish to be initiated."

"*You are a true sister. You will make a most powerful witch.*

But before initiation you will be a novice."

Hope smiled, and a beam of sunshine squeezed through the clouds to fall upon her head. "When shall we start?"

For the fifth night in a row, Muriel awoke from restless sleep. Her knees pressed together in friction, rubbing away the unsettled feelings that seem to make a home in her belly. Though she suspected the dreams were caused by the uncertainty she felt over Hope's training, there was another restlessness that was unnamed. Her dreams were like the spells she'd forgotten, memories she'd given away. She could sense them but could not access them.

Rolling over, she could make out the shape of A'Dale sleeping on his mat upon the floor, lit by the glowing coals inside the hearth.

A strange throbbing sensation between her thighs had her sucking in a sudden breath. It was not the first time it had happened. She slid a hand down to the juncture of her thighs, wishing to quell the strange sensation, yet that only made it more intense.

"I have kept myself from Cahill too long," Muriel muttered. The words had no sooner left her mouth than she covered it, realizing that she had spoken as if she was the queen.

Oh, when would it end? When would she be herself again?

Though she had spoken quietly, it was as if the words were the crow of the cock and A'Dale sat up.

"Muriel?" There was something about the way he said her name, softly, like a lover, that elicited an unusual tightening in the back of her throat.

"I did not mean to wake you. Go back to sleep." She rolled over, hugging Hope to her chest, all the while strange images of a man—sometimes Cahill, sometimes Allan, sometimes a bizarre mixture of the two—invaded her thoughts: talking softly to her, touching her, kissing her passionately on the lips.

After two more nights—a full week—of restless, unsettled, sleep, Muriel was at her wit's end. Winter was on their doorstep and the nights grew colder and darker. That meant that more time was spent in the lonely cottage, just the three of them, by the hearth. On this night, A'Dale brought out his lute and succumbed to Hope's pleading that he sing her favorite, *An Ode to Little John.*

T'was a wee lad, only ten hands tall,
So slight, so fair, but loved by all.
His courage, 'twas said, was bettered by none,
And that is where our story's begun...

When A'Dale came to the chorus, Hope joined in.

"Tell me his name," Allan sang.

"'Twas Little John," Hope cried.

"A dragon he tamed."

"'Twas Little John."

"The soldiers he shamed?"

"'Twas Little John."

"Of immortal fame?"

"'Twas Little John!"

Muriel watched and listened, amazed anew at how Hope could be so serious when they practiced spells by day, but how young and innocent she appeared now as she sang and clapped along with her father.

The image of the two of them brought a tide of warmth that infused her flesh like the mixing of two simple compounds that mingled together in a potion, creating something quite new.

After the song ended, Allan sang an epic ballad about the Slayer of *Ninn-Arach* and Hope's eyes fluttered closed even before the song ended. Allan carried Hope to bed and tucked her beneath the bedclothes, a sweet and loving act.

"Why are you crying?" he asked when he returned to sit with her in front of the hearth.

"Do not fear. They are happy tears."

A'Dale ladled some mulled wine into a cup and handed it to her. "I am glad," he said. "I should very much like to see you happy again all the time, as you once were."

She sipped the spiced drink, gazing into the firelight, trying to remember what it was like to feel happy most of the time. The task proved impossible, for there was an underlying sense of doom that pervaded her entire spirit.

"She was so unhappy," Muriel murmured.

"Ah." A'Dale drew his chair closer to hers. "You have taken on a great burden, my wife. Know that you do not need to bear it alone." In an action that was both natural and unusual, A'Dale took her hand, rubbing the backs of her knuckles with the gentlest of touches.

Her gaze lingered on the way their hands appeared together in her lap: his large, strong hand holding her much smaller one. The sight was…comforting, The sensation of his touch, on the other hand, was something more than comforting. Something that provoked the restless yearning inside of her.

Without considering her actions, Muriel reached tentatively for Allan's face; her finger tracing the ridge of his brow, down his cheek, marveling at the rough texture where whiskers began.

"Muriel?"

Her fingers hovered just over his lips. How warm his breath was. How much she longed to feel his soft breath against her mouth and even other parts of her body.

What a strange notion.

A'Dale's nostrils flared as he drew in a sharp breath before taking hold of her questing fingers and drawing them away from his face.

"You mustn't," he said as he laid her hand upon her lap. "I am not made of steel."

She frowned. What did that mean?

Before she had a chance to ask, A'Dale rose and began to bank the fire for the night. "'Tis late, Wife. You best get to bed while the cottage is still warm."

Snow blew outside and A'Dale was thankful for the warm cottage, a smokehouse full of provisions and a belly full of stew. Yet, this night, like so many before it, would inevitably feel like the seventh level of hell, for Muriel's restless dreams had awoken him again. She made soft, moaning sounds, not like she was in pain, but rather as if she was experiencing extreme pleasure. The soft sighs would have fired his loins if not for the fact that he knew it was not him who figured in her dreams, but Cahill.

How often had she uttered his name in sleep? Too many times to count. So many times that Allan had fashioned a new target for archery practice in the shape of a man...wearing a crown. While piercing the dummy in the head and the heart gave him some relief by day, it did nothing to help him during the night.

This night, a cold, damp wind whistled between the chinking and Allan rose to add wood to the fire. With the increased light, he could make out Muriel's shape beneath the bed clothes, shivering.

Taking one of his own blankets from the floor, he gently laid it over Muriel and Hope before returning to hunker down in front of the fire.

"A'Dale?"

Allan turned. "Yes?"

"Thank you for the blanket, but you will surely freeze without it."

"I will be warm enough."

Silence. And then, "There is another solution to staying warm."

"Is there?"

"Why, of course." She sat up, inching closer to Hope. "There is room in the bed for all three."

"Muriel…"

"There is no need for anyone to be cold tonight."

Ah. To share a bed with his family. It was the very thing he'd always longed for and yet would present a whole new form of torture.

"Please, A'Dale."

"I'll come keep ye warm if you promise me one thing." At least he would be warm in his own personal hell.

"What's that?"

"You must call me Allan."

Her silence lasted only a moment. "Come…Allan. Keep me warm."

He removed his boots first before sliding beneath the blankets. The bed, while plenty large for Muriel and Hope, was a tight squeeze for him, with barely room to lie on his side. He snugged himself up to Muriel's back, wrapping his arms around her waist and held her tight.

It was heaven and hell all at once.

"Allan," Muriel whispered after a few moments.

"Yes?"

The silence dragged on before she continued, "What is the nature of our relationship?"

Of all the times to ask, why did she have to pose this question now? Did she sense his dilemma? Could she feel the hint of arousal through all her skirts?

"Allan?"

Her use of his name was like an incantation, binding him to her. "We are husband and wife."

"That is not what I ask."

"Are you asking me if I love you?"

She shifted within his arms. "Yes."

He gently nestled his face into the crook of her neck and shoulder. "With all my heart," he whispered.

She was holding her breath, for her chest stilled and no air escaped her. Had he shocked her? Should he have lied?

No. It was time she knew the truth.

Even with all the changes in her these last two seasons, he still loved her and always would. There would never be another woman for him, whether they ever consummated their relationship physically or not.

Finally she released her breath and drew another into the deepest part of her chest. "Allan?" His name was whispered so softly, at first he was uncertain as to whether it was his imagination until she repeated it.

"Yes?"

She took a deep, quivering breath. "And…do I…?"

This time his answer came much more quickly. "You have never said it, but I believe you love me too." He closed his eyes, breathing in the scent of her skin. "Or at least, you did, once upon a time."

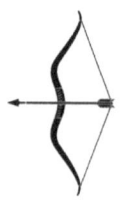

CHAPTER 20

"You children do not understand the ways of magic." The sorcerer stood and nudged the body of the woman. "For the universe demands balance, a trade-off of one thing for another." He made for the door of the cave, calling over his shoulder. "Bring your mother's body, we must act quickly if you are to receive your reward..."

— FROM THE LEGEND OF THE DRAGON CLAW SCEPTER

He had known this day would come and had dreaded it for months. What would his punishment be for failing, for even though he had delivered the queen of Lorentia into Elwood's clutches, he had failed on the other count, of finding the heir, and he had always known he would pay for his failure.

Now here he was, shackled and being led into the Throne Room of Dunsmoor Castle, the dragon queen in attendance and the handsome king upon the throne.

"Ah, the youngest Fosset," the fake Elwood said when Duncan knelt before him. "I believe you have grown since last we met."

How to answer? "Your mercy while keeping me alive in the dungeon—"

"Enough. No more sniveling. I abhor it."

Duncan clamped his jaw shut and kept his head bowed, awaiting something, but he did not know what. Would his death come swiftly? Doubtful. Torture was more likely. Perhaps the sorceress would turn him into a hog or worse.

"Bring in the others," the king commanded.

Duncan dared not look, though he clearly heard the double doors open and the shuffling gait of more than one prisoner, followed by the firm step of the guards.

"Duncan?"

Upon hearing his name, Duncan hazarded a glance up to find all five of his remaining brothers advancing, legs in shackles, hands cuffed and chained together by collars around their necks. He jumped to his feet but was struck down by the nearest soldier, a hard blow between his shoulder blades that knocked the air out of his lungs.

"A family reunion. How delightful," the king said as he reached for a pie from the table beside the throne and took a large bite. "Might I just say how disappointed I was in your father for up and dying before fulfilling his duty to me?" He munched thoughtfully on the food before continuing with a full mouth. "Though he did manage to sire the lot of you, however much you've continued to disappoint."

"Kill them all," the beastly queen said. "Better yet, allow me to perform the service."

"No!" Duncan crawled forward on his knees, his body tense in expectation of the blow that would surely knock him low once more. "I beg of you. Take my life but spare my brothers. It is I who failed, not them. I take full responsibility."

"There are few things that disgust me more than familial loyalty," Elwood said. "Wouldn't you agree, sister?"

"I loathe it." She held out her taloned hand for the scepter. "Though martyrdom is equally unpalatable."

"How shall we break them of it?"

Once Elwood had passed the dragon-claw scepter to his sister, the queen's serpent-like tongue flicked out between her scaly lips. "I know just the way. Give the boy a dagger."

The shackles were released from his wrists and he was dragged to his feet. The man nearest him, a captain who had trained him in combat, removed a dagger from his belt and passed it to him. He kept his gaze distant, as if he didn't recognize Duncan.

"Now," Eleanor said, hopping forward and raising the scepter in an arc. "It is only fair that a life be traded for the life you neglected to give me." She pointed at the line of men, Duncan's brothers, who ranged in age between one year older than him and twelve. They regarded him with resigned terror.

Waving the scepter in front of Duncan's face, she intoned a spell in her hideously harsh voice. Immediately, Duncan felt his hand tremble where he held the dagger. A force he could not name drew him forward, as if the dagger were a powerful sentient being and Duncan was at its mercy.

"You will kill one of your brothers. Choose which one or I shall choose for you."

"No!" The more Duncan tried to open his grasp in order to drop the dagger, the firmer his hold on it became. When he realized how futile it was, he covered his right hand with his left, attempting to turn the tip of the blade towards himself.

The beast hissed her displeasure. "You will not take your own life, you sniveling piece of meat." She waved the scepter once more and the blade jolted in his grasp, forcing him to lurch toward his brother, Dawson, who was closest to him in age. Dawson's eyes grew wide with fear, his mouth fell opened to speak or cry out but the blade slashed without warning, opening his gullet from ear to ear.

His brother's eyes rolled back before his body crumpled to

the flagstones.

"No!" Duncan jerked back, the possessed blade, bathed in blood, slipping from his hand and spinning across the floor to land at the feet of the guardsman, who picked it up, wiped the blood on his stockings and sheathed it once more.

Rage rushed through him and Duncan lunged for the dragon queen, only to be cast away by a sweep of the scepter.

"Go find the child," she hissed. "For every year you do not return without that little bitch, another of your brothers shall die."

Cahill sat in the corner of the public house, drinking a cup of mead and using a crust of bread to sop up the remnants of his stew. The room was full tonight; a party of travelers had arrived, he'd seen them outside earlier, and a more colorful, interesting caravan he'd *never* seen, even in Lochsend. It was a large group of at least a dozen women and perhaps twice as many men of all shapes and sizes and nationalities. The women were painted, it was the only way to describe them, their faces artful canvases that caught more than one side-long glance. While their bodies were completely covered in flowing robes, he could not tell if the rest of their physiques were painted as well.

However, no sooner had they arrived than the women were corralled up to their rooms by dark skinned men with shaved heads save for a square of hair at the crown that was kept long and tied with a cord. The men also wore robes and carried curved swords holstered at their hips. Cahill noted the protest from the ladies upon arrival and even though he could tell they were angry, the language they spoke was lyrical in its intonation and he recognized it as Semetian.

Semetia was a long way across the Selward Sea. What were they doing in Baldane?

The leader of the party was a tall, well-built man, dressed like a wealthy merchant, with fair hair and prominent scars upon his cheeks. He had the look of a scoundrel but in a way that he'd wager women found appealing.

Cahill leaned back into the shadows where he sat, thinking about the merchant. He had seen his face before, in fact, he knew the man. His name was Arthur Bland and he had traveled together with Lord Hood, now the King of Fenloch, as one of his companions. Bland had also helped to save Lorentia from a dragon horde attack over a decade ago. Before Hope.

Despite Bland's help, Cahill trusted him the least of all Hood's men and had not decided whether to make himself known to him or not.

"All virgins, that's what the innkeep said," a squat, furry man said to his companion when he returned to his seat at the bench nearest to Cahill's.

"Virgins?" The man's companion sneered. "I should like t' balls a painted virgin, I would."

"Not likely. They're under heavy guard. On their way to Dunvegan, or so the innkeep was told." "Dunvegan? Whyever would they want t' go there?"

"The king hisself ordered twelve virgins from across the Selward sea. I suppose if you was the richest man on th' continent, you'da spent the coin in your coffers just the same."

"Gah," the man guffawed. "If half the tales of the King of Dunvegan be true, the painted lasses would be better off with the likes of us."

The two men laughed and went back to their meals and drinks, making up stories about ways to sneak upstairs and corrupt one or more of the foreign ladies.

The news had Cahill watching the door and when Arthur

Bland appeared, settling in at a bench on the other side of the smoky room, he knew what he had to do. The question was, how to make contact?

It was when the innkeep's son appeared to collect the empty bowls, that Cahill made his move. "Do you see that gentleman over there in the corner? The one with scars upon his cheeks?"

"Aye, sir. I do."

Cahill passed him some coins and said, "Let him know that an old friend wishes to speak to him. I shall wait for him by the stables."

The lad frowned, surely thinking that Cahill wished to caused trouble. Though Bland was well dressed, he had the appearance of one who drew trouble wherever he went—whether of his own making or not.

Undoubtedly, Bland would be leery of the message himself and Cahill had to be careful. He pulled his cloak around his shoulders and with a stoop to his shoulders, as if he was much older than his age, he made his way to the door and outside.

Evening had fallen and a cold northern wind whipped around his feet causing the heavy cloak flap against his legs. The ground was frozen and ice cracked beneath his boots as he made his way around a small courtyard, keeping to the shadows, not wishing to be seen until he knew it was safe.

After waiting by the stable for some time, a tall man appeared silhouetted at the door of the inn.

Interesting. Bland was so sure of himself that he would meet a stranger alone?

No.

Two more men followed, swords drawn, moving briskly across the courtyard.

Stepping out from the shadows, Cahill called, "Arthur Bland, I bring greetings from the Lorentian Court."

"If you are a citizen of Lorentia, you are far from home,

friend." Arthur held his sword at the ready as he cautiously approached.

"That I am, good sir. As are you." Cahill flipped his cloak over a shoulder, revealing his sword. "I wish to speak in private." Then he showed him his empty hands. "I give you my word, I mean you no harm."

"The oath of a stranger is one I rarely honor."

Moving carefully into the glow of the lantern light, Cahill hoped his identity would be revealed. "I assure you, I am honorable. And, we are not strangers."

"Your Maj—?" Bland began.

With a sharp shake of his head, Cahill cut the man off before he could complete the word, *majesty*. "A word, sir."

"Of course." Bland turned to his men, instructing them to return to the inn. Once they were out of earshot, he said, "What are you doing here? Where are your men?"

"I am alone."

"Are you mad?" Arthur glanced around, as if expecting soldiers to materialize out of the wind. "I had heard you were unwell, but this is insanity."

"My ill health is a rumor, started by my own men. I travel alone so that I might cross borders unnoticed."

"For what purpose?"

Cahill drew Bland toward a woodshed at the back of the stables. Though there was no one around and the wind was too loud for voices to carry, he could not take any chances of being overheard. Once he was certain of their privacy, he said, "I am on a quest to save my wife."

"Where is she?"

"Held in the dungeon of Dunsmoor castle."

"How long has she been there?"

"Too long."

"Are you sure she's still—"

"Yes," Cahill interrupted, not wishing to hear Arthur articulate his worst fear. "She is alive. I have no doubt."

It was obvious that Arthur was not so certain, but then, Arthur didn't know Breanna like Cahill did.

"You have heard that I make for Dunvegan, I suppose," Bland said.

"I had heard, yes."

"And, you wish to join my party?"

"Quite right."

Arthur rubbed a scarred cheek. "I am sorry. I should like to help help, but…"

"I will pay for your assistance, of that you can be sure. You have only to name your price."

Head down, Bland paced, contemplating the offer. After a few passes, he stopped. "I do not doubt your ability to pay. I doubt your ability to save the queen and my ability to escape unscathed. There is more at stake here than you know." Arthur glanced back at the inn.

"You speak of your cargo."

"Not cargo. I lead a royal entourage. The Semetian Princess Solaya will wed Elwood to open trade routes between the continents. If I deliver the princess and her attendants unsullied, I am guaranteed enough wealth to buy a fleet of ships and to monopolize the transport of trade between the kingdoms across the sea."

There it was. Arthur's motivation was greed, pure and simple. At the very least, the man was honest about it.

"The loss of such a thing is a great risk, even to aid an old friend," Arthur added.

"So, your answer is no?" Cahill tasted bitterness on his tongue.

Expelling a deep breath, Arthur said, "When faced with an obstacle, there is always a way around. Always. Come to my room later tonight. I believe together we might find a solution."

In a burst of sparkles, a stick spun in the air, rising higher and higher until it sprouted wings and flew off, a pretty red cardinal. How was it possible that Hope knew so much magic and had been practicing it unbeknownst to her for so long? Muriel had spent the last few weeks testing Hope and her knowledge and had been surprised—and shocked—at every turn.

Was I secretly teaching her? she wondered. It was completely possible as Muriel had no memories left to inform her of the truth.

"You didn't teach me," Hope said quietly as she dusted the snow off a stump and sat down.

"How did you know what I was—"

"I can hear you." Hope tapped the side of her head. "In here. Not all the time, only sometimes." Her smile was sweetly innocent. It was the smile she had perfected in order to get her father to give her whatever she asked for. Against A'Dale, it worked every time.

Allan.

It was Muriel's turn to smile secretively for even the unspoken sound of his name created pleasant little shivery sensations inside her belly. The image of his large, warm body fitted so wonderfully behind her, his arms wrapped around her, infused her with warmth. Why, she hoped the season never changed and it stayed cold forever, for she did not want him to return to the floor.

"Mama?" Hope placed her hand on Muriel's arm and gazed up with her striking violet eyes. "Are you unwell?"

"I am well, my pet." She pressed a hand to her tummy and

sighed. "What has become apparent is that there is little, if anything, for me to teach you."

Hope frowned. "That can't be. There must be so much more to learn. I'm only a novice."

"And I am sorely out of practice." She rolled a stump close and sat across from her daughter, taking her hands in her grasp. How delicate they were. And warm.

It is magic that keeps the body warm, the blood flowing, the heart full.

Startled, Muriel looked around for the source of the voice.

Ah, sister. You have given away so much of yourself.

"Yes." Muriel whispered. "I fear it was a grave mistake."

Do not regret the decision to trade memories with the queen, for it was done out of love and there is nothing more pure than a sacrifice made in the name of love.

Was it the warmth from Hope's hands that heated her own? Or was it her own abilities that flushed her with pleasant warmth?

"Will you help me?" Muriel asked aloud. "Will you help me remember?"

"Remember what, Mama?" Hope squeezed her fingers. The girl had spoken the truth about not hearing everything, for she obviously could not hear the conversation going on in Muriel's mind.

What has been given away cannot be restored. The outcome of your decision has brought much hardship, but will bring blessings as well, as is the natural order of things.

"Balance," Muriel murmured.

Yes.

"Mama?"

Hope's voice was nothing more than a distant echo.

"But how am I to teach Hope if I do not remember?" Muriel asked.

You won't teach Hope.

"But...?"

We will teach her. Through you.

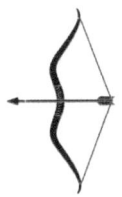

CHAPTER 21

Dragging the body of their mother between them, the three children followed the ancient one along a path to the farthest edge of the forest where the landscape changed from lush and green to barren and stony.
"What is this place?" the boy asked.
"This is the birthplace of all dragons," came the reply...

— FROM THE LEGEND OF THE DRAGON CLAW SCEPTER

B re whispered the strange words that she'd uttered every day for the last six months in the language she knew but didn't understand. The words were a spell, more remnants of Muriel's memories, and welcome memories at that, for once complete, the shackles around her wrists and ankles opened. She carefully removed them and then finding the sharp stone hidden in the cracks of the floor, she made a mark upon the wall, a tally that helped her to keep track of time. Once done, she. tiptoeing to the back of the cell. The young girl who brought her food every day wouldn't be there for several hours and Breanna used the solitary time to exercise and practice her combat maneuvers, for she had learned her lesson when faced with the young soldier in the woods. She vowed she would not be bested by a mere lad again.

The movement accomplished another task; it kept her body fit which in turn helped her retain her sanity—a part of her she would surely have lost by now if she had been chained to a wall day in and day out. It was what Elwood and Eleanor wanted, for her to slip slowly into madness while they fattened her up for the wedding feast.

Bre closed her eyes and imagined herself back at the practice field of Lorent Castle. Within moments, a change came over her, and she could feel the grass beneath her feet, the sun upon her face and the wind in her hair. She moved with soft steps, barely making a sound as she completely her maneuvers with imaginary sword in hand. She was so taken with her practice that it took her a few seconds to register the clanging of metal and the sound of footsteps coming from down the corridor.

Her eyes sprang open.

Not enough time!

Leaping back to her position by the wall, she had only enough time to refasten the wrist shackles while her anklets lay open by her legs. She let her head fall against her chest and closed her eyes, feigning sleep.

The cell door screeched open and Bre heard the soft step of the Dunvegan maid as she approached with her tray. It was only when the crockery clattered as the tray was set down beside her, that Bre pretended to wake.

"Where am I?"

"The dungeon," the maiden said in her soft voice.

"Who are you?"

"I am but a serving girl, come to bring you food." There was resignation in the girl's voice, as Bre asked the same questions of the maid every day.

Bre rolled her head along the stones behind her, as if it took great effort to move her head. "Who am I?"

"You are a prisoner."

"Ah."

"And I bring you good news."

"Am I to die today?"

"No. You are to be given *two* meals a day. The king is merciful indeed."

"Merciful indeed."

"He says you must get nice and plump."

"Plump," Bre repeated absently. "Nice and plump like a roasted rump," she said in a sing-song voice. "Nice and plump like a camel's hump." She giggled—a sound she had not made since childhood—though this laugh bordered on lunacy.

"Just so," the girl said, moving closer to inspect the flesh on Bre's arms. "Not fat enough yet." She brought a spoonful of fatty broth toward Breanna's mouth but before Bre could open, the girl dropped the spoon and gasped. "What is this?" She took hold of the unclasped anklets.

"What is this?" Bre repeated, letting her head loll forward.

"Your anklets are open."

Peeping through half-closed eyes, Bre asked, "My anklets? What are they for?"

"To keep you here."

"If I am not here, where am I?" she questioned. "Is this a dream? Have I crossed the veil?"

"I am certain they were secured after I left," the girl muttered. "Who has been to see you?"

"I dream of dragons sometimes. Ugly, filthy things."

"Eleanor," the girl hissed before securing the anklets around Bre's legs once more and Bre allowed her to do it while remaining perfectly still. Once done, the maiden scuttled up to Bre and bent down to whisper into her ear. "You musn't tell a soul I know. Do you understand?"

"I musn't tell, I musn't tell." She swung her head back and forth as she muttered the phrase over and over again.

She could feel the girl's gem-stone gaze flickering upon her. Bre continued to chant. "Musn't tell. Musn't tell."

"Quiet now. You must eat."

"Must eat. Must eat." Like a newborn chick awaiting its mother, she opened her mouth and closed her eyes while making a humming sound at the back of her throat.

"You are completely mad, aren't you?" The girl sighed. "Such a pity. I should have preferred for you to know what's going to happen to you."

The quickest route to Dunvegan was to cross through the kingdom of Morainia. The last time Cahill had visited that barren land was for Hope's christening. He had no desire to revisit it ever again except that by doing so he would shorten his journey by days, perhaps even a week, and he didn't need Arthur Bland's doubts to remind him that every day his wife spent in the dungeon was a day she came closer to death.

Despite Bland's initial response to Cahill's request, after meeting with the merchant up in his rooms at the inn, the men had devised a plan. While Cahill would not travel with the party, he would pretend to be a member of the entourage. A messenger sent ahead to notify the king of their pending arrival. Bland had proven himself to be a master of disguises, fashioning clothes for him that resembled those of the foreign guards and providing a paint that would color his skin many shades darker so that he would appear Semetian. His long hair was shorn, save for a square at the crown and it was styled in the mode of the Semetian's guards. The transformation was remarkable and even Cahill did not recognize his own reflection in a looking glass provided by one of the Semetian ladies.

After a week of travel, Cahill approached the border of Baldane and Morainia and though he was in a hurry to cross into his wife's kingdom, he slowed his mount to a walk as the road, that would once have been well-traveled, became scarcely more than an overgrown path which brought him through the Forest of Giants to the border. What he found at the edge of the forest came as a shock. The landscape, while lonely and desolate, was covered in green despite the season.

What magic was at play here?

He rode carefully down the stony path into the valley ahead and once on flat ground, Cahill dismounted. Crouching low, he touched the shoots that covered the ground. Thin strands of twining grass, green as a summer lime, covered blackened soil. Snake grass. Though it was winter, the ground emitted heat as if warmed from below. Steam rose in the distance and as Cahill approached, he saw a pool of steaming water, surrounded by low bushes.

"Not bushes," he said aloud as he grew near. "Dragon trees." Kneeling beside the pool, he cautiously touched the water and found that it was not boiling but merely warm, like bath water. Cupping a handful, he brought the water to face and tasted it. Though still sulfurous, the water was palatable.

It was a sign. If Breanna's homeland could come back to life, she must still live.

And Hope, his daughter and heir to this land, must also live.

With renewed energy, Cahill mounted his horse and kicked the animal into a run. He could feel Breanna here, her ancestors, her people. He was meant to come this way, to witness the rebirth of this land. One day soon this place would be habitable again. But first he had to find his wife and free her.

"Gods of this place," he called, urging his horse into a

gallop. "Direct my path and give me strength so I might save your queen."

As Muriel prepared the morning fare, she tried but could not dismiss the sensations from her unsettled dreams. It was impossible when the subject of her dream sat at the table watching her.

Allan.

His name was a word she had whispered in her dream, the syllables sighed with pleasure, as if she had truly experienced his kisses and lovemaking and not just dreamed about it.

It was torture. Beautiful, wonderful torture.

When the three of them sat around the little table, breaking their fast, she could scarcely raise her eyes to meet his. Though it was a chilly morning, her cheeks were warm from the perpetual blush staining her cheeks.

"You look well this morning, Mama," Hope said with a sweet smile. "Don't you think Mam looks exceptionally well today, Da?"

"She does indeed," Allan said, mussing the hair at the the top of Hope's head. "Though I ne'er find fault with your mam's appearance. Not today nor any other day of the year."

"What foolishness," Muriel protested, though she could not help her smile. "Finish your porridge so we might begin our lessons."

"What will you do today, Father?"

"There is much to do: the roof is in need of repair where it leaked last night. There is always wood to chop, water to haul..." He cast a sidelong gaze at her.

Muriel looked away. Did Alan suspect her of spying? It was hardly lady-like, but after he'd confided to her that she'd done it in the past, she'd been curious as to why she'd do such a thing.

So, she'd followed him one day.

And the next.

Even in winter, the man removed his shirt and washed himself. Such a private act, something she should not watch. However, regardless of propriety, she was compelled to return day after day.

Why did the sight of his bare chest thrill her?

Why was it that when she attended to her own ritual of washing, using heated water from the kettle, that she imagined Allan in the shadows of the cottage, spying on her? Such a strange thing to wish for, but she did it nevertheless, and the sensation of the warm water on her skin was made more exhilarating by the thought.

The sound of Hope's stool scraping against the floor as she stood brought Muriel's thoughts back to the present.

"Eager to begin, my pet?" Muriel asked, rising to put away her own empty bowl.

Hope nodded with enthusiasm and the two of them donned cloaks in order to begin their daily lessons in the out-of-doors. Muriel loved this time with Hope. It was as she'd always wished, to one day be able to instruct a novice in the art of magic. There was only one thing she wished for more. She wished that she was able to remember the daily lessons.

However, the benefit to her was that with each day that passed, Breanna's memories became more distant as well.

Once the two of them were seated in their positions inside the fairy circle behind the cottage, Muriel began the chant that would call forth the sisters from the other side of the veil. Like every other day, a warm glow began in the pit of her stomach and spread like the most soothing spiced wine through her veins. She tilted her head to the gray winter sky and closed her eyes, opening herself so that she might become the instrument for the spirits of the sisters she called forth.

She never remembered the exact moment of the transformation, she only ever recalled coming back into herself, always noticing how the sun had somehow magically crossed the sky in what felt like mere seconds. This time when she opened her eyes, Hope sat at her feet, holding her hands, a look of extreme pleasure on her features.

"Oh Mam! That was the best lesson yet!"

Muriel squeezed Hope's hands. "What did you learn?" Strange how her throat always felt dry as if she had spent the entire day chanting without stop.

"I learned about the magical properties of love."

"Magic performed out of love is the most powerful magic there is," she said, beaming at Hope.

"Those are the exact words that *Sister Wilda* used. Do you remember?"

"I'm afraid not," Muriel replied. "It is merely the instruction of my superior from my days as a novice that I recall. That is all."

Eyes glistening with excitement, Hope rose and spun around inside the small circle of stones that had been erected for the purpose of their lessons. Hope had told her that the two of them had built the fairy ring together, but of course Muriel had no recollection of it.

While her lack of memory saddened her sometimes, the joy that blossomed in Hope as she learned the art of the mystics more than made up for it.

She learns quickly.

Ah, 'twas sister Wilda.

If she continues along this path, she shall be the most powerful witch the continent has ever seen.

The prophecy should have given Muriel comfort, but for some reason, a chill ran down her spine as if someone had dropped a handful of snow down the neck of her cloak.

Hope ceased her dance and threw her arms above her head, reciting a spell that was unfamiliar to Muriel. The air within the circle glistened and sparkled like diamond dust dancing in the ether. A gust of wind came up and swirled the sparkles in all directions and instantly Muriel's sense of foreboding was replaced with one of love and contentment.

She stood. "It's time to begin preparation for the midday meal. If there is still light, we shall continue later."

Hope clapped her hands, her violet eyes sparkling. "I shall join you shortly." She scampered off in the direction of the privy and Muriel watched her, marveling at how blessed she was to have Hope in her life.

Allan too.

On her way back to the cottage, she stopped to listen for sounds of A'Dale in the smokehouse or at the chopping block. There was nothing save a warm sensation that heated her through at the thought of the man.

Ahh.

She was blessed, indeed.

Contentment vanished when a northern wind whipped up around her, licking her legs like an icy tongue, bringing upon it the sound of Hope's desperate cry.

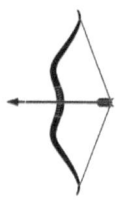

CHAPTER 22

The sorcerer commanded the children to dig a grave for their mother. And so, using hands and rocks, the children did as the sorcerer bid. When the grave was large enough for their mother's corpse, the children stopped, exhausted and filled with grief. "Why did you stop?" The ancient one asked. "Keep digging until I say it is enough..."

— FROM THE LEGEND OF THE DRAGON CLAW SCEPTER

"You are not dying, my pet," Muriel said as she stroked Hope's back. "It is your moontime."

"My moontime?" Hope repeated slowly, eyes wide. She blinked. Then, a slow, delighted smile blossomed across her cheeks. "This is what moontime means?"

"Yes."

"So, I am a woman?"

"Well…yes, but…"

"I am a woman!" Hope danced and skipped across the snow-covered ground, her skirts spinning out around her. She twirled once more before clapping her hands and tilting her chin to the sky. "Oh, *Sisters*. Thank you!"

Muriel wiped a tear from her cheek. Only yesterday a babe, and now…a woman.

Too soon!

From some deep recess in her soul, the voice of the queen cried out in grief.

The lessons had made it easier for Muriel to push Breanna's memories aside so that they did not overshadow her own. Today, however, Breanna's memories mirrored Muriel's own sentiments.

Despite the moisture pooling at the corners of her eyes, she reached for Hope and grasped her hands. "My sweet. It is a day to celebrate, indeed. I shall prepare a special meal. Whatever you like."

Hope's cheeks were flushed and her eyes alight. "But I must go through the Rite of Womanhood and Initiation."

Muriel paused. She shook her head. "I am afraid it is too dangerous to allow."

Hope narrowed her gaze. "Don't all witches go through it?"

"No. Not all—"

"The powerful ones do. You went through it, did you not?"

"Of course, but—"

"Why should I be any different?"

"Because you are special."

"You are biased, mother. I am no more special than any other."

A more erroneous statement could not be made. "There are reasons that I cannot explain. You must trust me, daughter. You cannot complete the ritual."

"But the *Sisters* wish it. I didn't understand what they meant before, but now I do." Hope's grip tightened and Muriel felt the strength borne of magic that coursed through the girl. "It is destined, Mama."

Thank the gods A'Dale chose that time to emerge from the forest, a brace of ptarmigan over his shoulder. "Are you well?" he asked Muriel, no doubt seeing the tears upon her cheeks.

Before Muriel had a chance to reply, Hope sprang into Allan's path.

"Da! I am a woman!"

Allan frowned as he met Muriel's gaze. Then his eyes widened in understanding and what followed was a dark, protective scowl.

Hope, for all her perceptiveness, gave her father's mixed reaction no mind as she prattled on excitedly, "I shall go through the Rite of Womanhood and Initiation, something the most powerful witches must do. It is the most sacred time in a woman's life and I shall return a true witch." She spread her arms with joy. "Oh, I am so very blessed!"

Allan took hold of Muriel's arm and turned her roughly toward him. Rarely had she witnessed such hostility on his features. "What ritual does she speak of?"

"It is the Rite of Womanhood, where a witch makes her pledge to the sisterhood."

"What is involved in this rite?"

"A witch takes only the clothes on her back and spends her entire first moon in nature. There she is provided for and learns her purpose and her path."

"Alone?"

"Aye."

"I forbid it."

Muriel nodded. "I am of the same mindset. It is an important and sacred rite but—"

"Important?" Hope stepped between the two of them, her chin held high. "It is the *only* way for me to access the strongest, purest magic. You know this better than anyone, Mama."

"It doesn't matter," Allan said, taking hold of Hope's shoulders and turning her toward him. "It is my sworn duty to protect you. I cannot let you go. I am sorry."

Squaring her shoulders, Hope confronted her father. "I am

the one who is sorry, for you do not have a choice in this, Papa." She turned to include Muriel in the discussion. "This is my path. The decision is mine." Gone was the dancing child and in her place stood the promise of the woman Hope would become. Strong-willed. Certain. Immovable.

Powerful.

Hope closed her eyes and whispered an incantation, one that Muriel was familiar with as she had used it often in Lochsend, many years ago. The spell stripped fear from the hearts of men, thus it was often used before battles. How clever of Hope to use it on her father, for it was fear that ruled Allan at the moment.

His body jerked, his chest drew up and out as if pulled by an invisible cord. Once released, he blinked before smiling and drawing Hope close against his broad chest. "Ah, me wee bairn," he whispered in the heavy accent of his homeland. "I's'll never be prepared t' let ye grow old. To me you's'll always be the babe I sang t' e'er night."

"I know, Da. I know."

Hope lifted her face from her father's chest and beckoned Muriel close and for the first time in thirteen years, the three of them wrapped their arms around one another and held each other tight. A true family.

"You can sing to me now if you like," Hope said, nestling her cheek against Allan's chest.

Allan's deep voice cracked as he began the old lullaby that was her favorite.

"I saw a sweet and seemly sight,
A blissful bird,
A blossom bright,
Lullay, lullow, lully lullay,
Baw, baw, me bairne."

✦ ✦ ✦

The kingdom of Dunvegan appeared even more desolate than Morainia, but appearances could be deceiving, for Dunvegan mines produced precious stones which Elwood controlled. The riches were so great that Elwood was considered to be the wealthiest man on the continent. The people of Dunvegan clearly did not share in his wealth. Their strange towns, hewn out of soft stone formations, were forlorn little villages. Only the colorful doors that marked the mounds as homes gave any gaiety to the place. It was outside of one such village that Cahill stopped to reapply the stain that darkened his skin. He sat upon a stone as he completed his task, marveling that he had managed to travel this far.

Dunvegan, purported to be the birthplace of all dragons, was a dangerous place. Cahill knew more than most the truth of the legend, for his step-mother was from this land and had not only called upon dragons to raid Lorentia, she had become a dragon herself. It was she that Cahill had to avoid, for surely the dragon queen would see through his disguise and if she knew who he was, not only would he face certain death, but so would Breanna and every subject in his kingdom.

He would not allow it to happen.

He mounted and rode up a meandering path. After cresting what he thought was a hill, Cahill found himself on the lip of a low volcano. His horse whinnied and made snorting sounds as it shied away. Within the depths of the volcano came rumblings and rustlings as if the volcano was about to erupt. His mount turned and hurried down the opposite side of the volcano along a well traveled path, clearly eager to get as far away as quickly as possible. Just as the ground leveled out, something overhead blocked the sun and Cahill raised a hand to his brow to see what it was.

A large dragon circled above.

Hellsfire!

Though there was no way his horse could have seen the thing, it was as if the animal could sense the beast's presence. His mount reared, nearly throwing Cahill, before galloping blindly ahead. It wasn't until the path took a southern turn that Cahill managed to slow his steed into a trot. He turned in his saddle in order to make sure they were not being followed by the beast. What he saw behind him stole his breath and stilled his heart.

Where before there had been only one, the sky was now black with dragons. They traveled in V-formation each consisting of seven beasts and Cahill counted at least fifteen such formations.

An army of dragons.

There was only one reason to build such an army. Elwood and Eleanor planned on war. But with whom?

He need not ask.

Never had his mission been more dire. He had to find Breanna and return to Lorentia for he was not fool enough to think that Eleanor had forgotten the kingdom she once ruled.

Though the road to Dunvegan had been long, his horse seemed as keen as he to arrive and as Dunsmoor Castle appeared on the horizon, the animal galloped straight for the walls.

Leaning over his neck, Cahill whispered, "You may be even less safe inside those walls, my friend. In the event things go awry, I thank you now for your faithful service."

The path upon which he rode joined with a roadway and Cahill caught up to a merchant's caravan. He skirted around the slow moving wagons and soon after came to a halt at the castle's bridge where he was greeted by armed guards.

"Who goes there?" A big brute of a soldier asked.

"I come in peace. I am an emissary from Semetia, with news of King Elwood's betrothed."

The soldier ordered him to dismount and roughly divested him of his sword and dagger before shackles were clamped around his wrists.

"Take the messenger to the Great Hall," the guard commanded. "The captain will know what to do with him."

Three men came forward and directed him inside the castle walls at sword point.

"Is this how you greet a friend?" Cahill complained as the eager soldiers drew blood through his thin Semetian garments.

"Assassins come in all forms," was the man's reply. "On with you."

He did not need to be commanded, as Cahill was more than willing to move inside the castle walls. Now that he was here, he could *feel* Breanna was close and even though logic told him she must be holed away in the dungeon, he could not help himself from searching every figure and face for something familiar.

What he saw inside the walls was in stark contrast to the dreary landscape: gardens and greenery, fruit trees and animals of all shapes and sizes. As for people, apart from the soldiers, of which there were many, most inside the walls were the child-like folk, native to this land. Their colorful eyes sparkled out of solemn faces like gemstones in the rock and Cahill felt an empathy for their cruel existence. He vowed to himself that once his family was safe, he would return and liberate this land and these people from the tyrant Elwood.

The castle itself was opulent, with floors of marble and tapestries of the finest silks hanging from the walls. Cahill was led toward two massive wooden doors, carved with a scene of dragons raining fire on a village.

"Halt." Just outside these doors that surely led to the Great

Room, a soldier with plumes upon his helm that marked him as captain of the guard stepped forward. "Who is this?"

"He claims to be an emissary from Semetia."

The captain approached, sword drawn. Pointing the tip at Cahill's chest. "Explain your presence."

In the soft language of the Semetians, Cahill uttered the formal greeting with a tilt of his head, as was the Semetian way. Then, in an accent he'd practiced, he said, "I come bearing news and wish to speak to the king."

"The king is indisposed."

"I shall wait."

"You will relay the message to me."

Cahill drew a breath as he considered his options. Perhaps it was best if he did not come face to face with the king. In that way, he did not risk coming face to face with Eleanor as well. "The Semetian entourage passes from Baldane, through Darnell, and shall arrive within the next fortnight."

"Is that all?"

"Only that the Princess Solaya is eager to arrive and wed the king."

"And her attendants? She travels with twelve virgins?"

Nodding, Cahill said, "Everything is as promised."

"The king shall be pleased." Sheathing his sword, the captain motioned to the three behind. "Take him to the dungeon."

"The dungeon?" Cahill protested.

Removing a club from his belt, the captain strode forward.

"I am a goodwill ambassador, I—"

The captain raised the club and before Cahill could finish, he swung.

Pain exploded inside his head before everything went black.

✦ ✦ ✦

This time when the maid approached down the corridor, Breanna was not taken unaware. It had been a fortnight since her meals had doubled and she vowed not to make the same mistake again, so she half-lay, half-sat in her position against the wall, all shackles in place, when the cell door screeched open.

"Where am I?" Bre whispered her usual greeting

"The dungeon," the maiden replied, as always.

"Ah yes. I am to wed the king."

"Indeed, you shall attend the feast." The girl kneeled beside her and Bre opened her mouth to accept the food. However, before the bowl of broth was gone, the sound of clattering footsteps could be heard coming their way.

Setting the food aside, the maid got up and went to the door. Through half-opened lids, Bre observed as a group of soldiers dragged a prisoner along the corridor.

"Who is this?" the girl asked as the men approached the cell.

"A Semetian messenger bearing news of the princess's arrival."

"Hmm." The girl moved along the bars to get a closer look at the captive. "He appears large for Semetian."

"And heavy," the soldier added.

"What news did he give?"

"The party shall arrive within a fortnight."

"Indeed? How fortuitous. Put him in the cell at the end of the corridor."

"As you wish."

How strange that a simple serving maid should have sway over the king's men. But more shocking than the young woman's authority was the fact that Breanna had so little time to enact her plan for escape. She had no doubt the wedding and feast would take place as soon as the party arrived. She could be dead in days.

The girl returned and finished feeding Bre, though her attention to the task was sloppy and distracted.

"I must bring mutton next time. Perhaps a pie." She poked Bre's stomach. "Still too skinny."

"Too skinny…" Bre muttered and then pretended to faint.

The girl slapped her across the cheek to rouse her before taking hold of her chin and tilting her face up.

Cowering in an attempt to hide her anger, Bre whimpered.

"You will die. You understand that, don't you?" The maid's normally soft voice sounded unusually harsh. What was she trying to do? Warn her?

Bre blinked and met the girl's jeweled gaze. "I welcome death."

A small smile touched the maid's lips. "Then you shall get your wish."

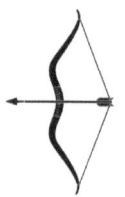

CHAPTER 23

*Full of fear, the children dug until
the pit was large enough to hold them all.
"That will do," the sorcerer said. He kicked the body of their
mother into the pit with them and then, holding the beautiful
stone aloft, intoned a powerful spell which caused the earth to
shake and the sides of the pit to cave in upon the family, burying
the dead mother and her children, alive...*

— FROM THE LEGEND OF THE DRAGON CLAW SCEPTER

Pulling his cloak around his shoulders, Duncan let the horse walk down the lonely road. Night fell early at this time of year and he should find a village inn to take shelter; not so much for himself but for the animal. In his attempt to find the girl as quickly as possible, it had been three days since he'd last stopped and allowed the horse a rest. But, despite his sense of urgency, pushing the animal past its limits would only add more time to his quest and less time to save his brothers.

This time when he left Dunvegan, he had struck out in a new direction, a road that took him toward the sea and like last time, the queen's voice was constantly in his head, reminding him of his family's fate should he fail. His days were haunted by the look on Dawson's face when he slit his throat. Horror. Disbelief. Betrayal. He barely slept because nightmares plagued him, dreams where he not only took Dawson's life but that of each of his other brothers as well.

So he rode on, determined. This time, he would not fail.

A cold north wind whistled through the trees, swirling a skiff of snow from the road around the legs of his horse. With head down, the animal stopped walking, refusing to go any farther. Duncan slid from the saddle and dropped the reins over his head to pull.

"I promise we'll stop at the next habitation."

Whinnying in response, the horse tried to tug away but Duncan held firm until the animal gave in and followed him. The going was slow and he had no idea how far they walked, time had lost all meaning. The full moon had lit their way until clouds gathered, covering the moon, making the road even darker and more difficult.

And dangerous.

"Death would be a relief," he muttered to himself.

I will not allow your death. The garbled voice of the dragon-queen rang between his ears. *Not even by your own hand.*

It was true. He had tried to take his life, more than once. Each time he had been thwarted by the queen who somehow controlled him, even from a distance. It was the family scepter. Legend had it that three hundred years ago, Elwood's family had made a pact with a disciple of black magic. They were promised power and riches, all made possible through the Dragon Claw Scepter.

What had they bargained in return?

No one knew. For it seemed as if they had everything. Wealth, power, and the loyalty of dragons to do their bidding.

"There." Duncan stopped. "What is that?"

Firelight flickered through the trees and Duncan led the

horse from the roadway toward the light. He tied the animal to a tree before creeping along quietly to investigate the source of the light before making himself known. A group of hooded men sat around a fire. The fact that they wore identical hooded cloaks and were chanting, or humming—the sound was a low buzz like that from a hive—told him they were from an order of some kind, though whether friend or foe, he could not be certain.

Staying hidden in the trees, Duncan waited until the chanting stopped, which coincided with the moment that a cloud covered the moon. Sword drawn, he stepped quietly from out behind a tree and approached the circle of men.

"Who dares to bring a weapon into the sacred circle?" A man from the opposite side of the fire stood, removing his hood. His eyes glowed as if two tiny moons were embedded in his sockets.

"I am Fosset and hail from Dunvegan."

"What brings you to these parts, so far from that place?"

"I am on a quest for the King."

"This is the one?"

"Yes."

"He seeks the girl."

Voices rose around the circle, though with heads bowed and hoods in place, Duncan could not tell from which seated figures the voices came.

"How did you know?" Duncan asked the men in general.

"Leave your weapons over there," the standing sage said, pointing to the shadow of trees. "Then we shall tell all."

"Who are you?"

"We are The Seers and we have seen you, Duncan Fosset of Dunvegan. We know whom you seek and we know where you may find her."

The cottage was quiet. Too quiet. And Muriel could not sit still after seeing Hope off with nothing more than a cloak to keep her warm. For the fifth time in the last hour, she went to the door and stood in the opening, letting the cold winter wind steal her breath away in puffs of icy fog.

"Come inside, Muriel."

"How can you remain so calm?" She shut the door and leaned against it, observing Allan sitting by the fire and whittling a figurine.

"I am as worried as you. But we must have faith."

Returning to the fire, Muriel set her sewing basket on her lap. "She cast a spell on you, do you know that? It was before she left, a spell to remove fear."

Allan frowned and put a hand to his heart as if there was something missing and he had only now realized it. "She is powerful for one so young."

"She may become the most powerful witch ever," Muriel spoke softly, gazing into the firelight. She closed her eyes and bowed her head as tears welled up.

A'Dale came to kneel at her feet. He took her hands in his and rubbed the backs of her knuckles. "Why does her power upset you so? It is a blessing, for she may defeat the sorceress all on her own."

Muriel's breathing hitched, making speaking difficult. "Magic is not like swordplay, A'Dale, where the more you practice the more powerful you become. It is about balance." She squeezed Allan's fingers. "The more power you have, the more you must forsake. The universe demands it."

"Balance?"

"In order for Hope to become powerful, she must undergo the very worst of trials." She shook her head as tears streamed down. "The sort of things she must endure far surpass what I can imagine."

"But Hope is good and pure. You have always said purity is essential for magic. Surely her trials cannot be so very bad."

"Oh, Allan. The tests will be terrible. It is only if she remains benevolent that her power will grow, yet the tests will be designed for her to question that benevolence."

"Is there nothing we can do?"

"There is only one thing we can do for her. And it is the key to defeating all evil."

Allan lifted his hand slowly and wiped a tear with the pad of his thumb. "Tell me, Muriel. What is this one thing?"

Covering Allan's hand where it lay upon on her cheek, she whispered, "Love. We must show her love. No matter what."

"Yes." He gazed deeply into her eyes. "Love is powerful indeed." He smoothed a stray lock of hair off her forehead. "You and Hope have taught me this."

"Allan…"

"I have loved you for so many years." His hand slid around behind her head and he drew her forward.

She touched his face—only the second time she had done so—and let her fingertips explore the contours of his cheek and jaw. "I suspect it has been the same for me."

"Woman," Allan said raggedly. "I have waited for you." He took hold of her questing fingers and squeezed. "I beg of you, tell me how much longer I must wait."

Muriel cupped his jaw with her free hand and said, "There is no longer a reason to wait any more."

Allan's eyes grew wide and then narrowed in sadness. "Because you protected us."

She smiled. "My chastity is secondary to something as potent as taking a life."

His gaze heated her cheeks, the warmth spreading down

her neck, across her chest and pooling low in her belly. A strange pulsing sensation throbbed between her thighs and she squeezed her legs together beneath her skirts.

Releasing her hand, Allan brushed her cheek with his knuckles. "Please do not sacrifice yourself in any way to be with me. If there is even a crumb of a chance that you could regain your power—"

"Allan, giving you my virginity is not a sacrifice. Quite the opposite. I'm beginning to think it is as important as all the other needs of the body. Eating. Breathing..."

A dark look came into his eyes. "And your memories? Do you still harbor memories—even if they do not belong to you—for the king?"

"Cahill?"

"Yes."

Was that the reason he had kept his distance this past season during their nights staying warm together? Because of what happened that one night on the road? Muriel moved her head from side to side. "All thoughts of the king have been banished, and practicing magic has helped to create a barrier." Tentatively, she touched his lips, whispering, "It is you and you alone that occupies my thoughts."

"Gods." Taking hold of her face, he pulled her to him and kissed her on the mouth. His lips were soft and sweet to start, but then began moving more aggressively over hers. What kind of kiss was this? So wet? So all-encompassing. His tongue swept over her mouth—a strange thing, indeed—resulting in her wishing to do the same to him. When she opened her mouth to try, his daring tongue pushed past her lips and entered.

She drew back. "Oh!"

"Do you not like that?" Allan's brows drew together.

Muriel touched her lips, considering. "No. I—I think I

liked it very much."

He groaned, an odd sound, like he was in pain. "Would you like to try?" he whispered against her lips.

"Yes please. Very much."

He kissed her softly and Muriel parted her lips in order to use her tongue, first to graze Allan's top lip and then the bottom. She was beginning to understand that the sounds he was making—that seemed as if he were in discomfort—were actually sounds of enjoyment. How strange. Did she make the same sorts of sounds?

She tried it again, only this time venturing further into his mouth. How warm and soft was the inside of his lips and then…

His tongue touched hers and…what a marvel! Delicious shivers coursed through her, lighting her up as if she was practicing magic.

Yes. The feeling was comparable to how one felt when conducting a spell!

"Muriel…"

She loved the sound of her name, particularly the way Allan said it. Soft but with an undertone of need.

"Are you absolutely certain?"

"Yes."

He stood and drew her to her feet, not to lead her to the bed, but so that he might pick her up and carry her there. Though it was only a few feet away, she wrapped her arms around his neck and gazed up into his face. Such a good face. Strong, sensitive, masculine.

He set her down on the bed and then removed his boots before crawling up beside her. "So oft have I contemplated this moment. I thought I might go mad with want."

Had it been the same for her? Had she lived in close quarters with this man for years wanting him as he wanted her? Given how strongly she felt now, she had no doubt that she had harbored the same desires—a physical craving for him—for perhaps as long as he had.

"And now that the time is here, I want to savor it." He loosened the tie at the top of her shirt and slid the material down her shoulder. "To touch you..." His calloused fingertips were exquisite against her virgin skin and without really understanding why, she arched her back toward him. Yearning for his touch.

Or his mouth...

For he kissed her shoulder and rubbed his face against her, breathing in her scent and Muriel responded wholeheartedly. She grappled blindly with the buttons on his vest and the ties on his shirt, aching, hungering for him.

"My love." He moved to the side in order to tear off his vest and pull his shirt over his head.

There. Oh yes. There he was.

His chest was so broad and so muscled. She ran her hands along his shoulders and down the front of him. So warm and soft, yet hard too. How would it feel to have him lie atop her, skin to skin? To feel the weight of him? She needed to know and was desperate to experience it. Loosening the ties of her overdress, she pulled the two sides apart, leaving only the thin material of her chemise between them.

Allan groaned before cupping her breast, his large hand squeezing her flesh as he used his thumb to tease her nipple through the material of her thin shirt. When he leaned down and placed his mouth over the hardened tip, a jolting shock tore through her chest and she clutched at him, digging her fingernails into his broad shoulders.

"Allan!"

Yanking on the damp linen, he exposed her for the first time and gazed down at her as if she was a sacred relic that invoked awe and supplication.

"So beautiful." He touched her again, tracing around the dark nipple, down her rounded flesh and beneath. "So very beautiful." When this time he drew her nipple into his mouth, she cried out. Oh the pleasure!

The last time she had *lain* with Allan, it was as if she was someone else—trapped in a dream that faded as soon as she woke.

Dreams and memories that belonged to someone else did not compare. This? This was so much more.

Why, it was more than magic!

She writhed in ecstasy beneath him, finding the gentle suction divine yet unsettling because her body yearned for more. Something else entirely. Parting her legs, she drew her knees up on either side of Allan so that she could press her very core up against him. Frustration struck as there was far too much fabric separating them, so she reached between in an attempt to rectify the situation.

With a groan, Allan rolled away, pushing himself to his feet.

"What are you doing? Where are you going?"

"Nowhere, my love. I simply need to disrobe."

"Ah."

"And then, I shall disrobe you."

"Oh."

"Do you find the notion shocking?"

Pushing herself into a sitting position, Muriel said, "Not in the least." She shrugged out of her overdress and tossed it to the floor.

He captured her hands. "It is not a race."

"Yet my breath comes fast as if I am in the midst of one."

With a groaning sort of chuckle, Allan raised her hands to kiss them. "It is the thrill of what we are about to do. But believe me when I tell you that the longer we draw it out, the more pleasure there will be."

"Have we not drawn it out long enough?"

How she loved Allan's eyes and the way they smiled when he did. Or was that love shining from the dark depths?

"There are many different ways that I've imagined this would go, but the one constant is that I remove your garments, piece by piece, as if uncovering a treasure. Please do not rob me of this pleasure."

He untied his leggings and pushed them down his powerful thighs. It was the first glimpse Muriel had ever had of his entire body. Or at least, the only one she could remember, for it was possible she had seen him thusly during her supposed spying sessions.

His backside was well rounded, his legs defined by muscle and sprinkled with hair, but it was his manhood that was most startling. That part of him stood out from a base of dark curls, thick and proud. He stroked his own length as he gazed down at her lying on the bed, and the sight sent a thrill of desire down her throat, all the way to that tender bit between her thighs.

Reaching out a hand, she asked, "May I?"

He came closer, placing one knee on the bed. "If it pleases you."

She tentatively touched the skin that covered him. So soft. Yet beneath the softness was a solid mass of muscle, a delightful contradiction. She raised her gaze to gauge his reaction.

Hi lips were twisted and his eyes squeezed closed.

"Am I hurting you?"

"Oh no." He guided her hand to wrap around his girth and, with his hand over hers, squeezed. Hard.

His member twitched inside her closed fist. "Surely this is too much," she gasped.

"It is not nearly enough." He removed her hand and crawled

up beside her on the bed.

"Why do you look as though you are in pain?" She rubbed the crease between his brows.

"It takes a great deal of concentration to hold myself back from what I wish to do."

"What is it you wish to do?" she asked as she ran her fingers down his cheek and along his jaw.

"Make you mine."

She paused in her exploration of his face. Meeting his gaze, she whispered, "That is what I wish for too. Please do not hold back."

He made a growling sound at the back of his throat. "You do not know what you speak of. The things I want…I fear I may hurt you."

Pushing herself closer, she placed her lips against his. "You will not hurt me, for I am yours and you may do with me as you wish."

CHAPTER 24

What happened in that ghastly grave? No one knows. But when the light of dawn touched the disturbed soil, the family emerged... changed. None more so than the mother...

— FROM THE LEGEND OF THE DRAGON CLAW SCEPTER

Braced above her, Allan gazed down with dark-eyed tenderness. "I wonder if you have any idea…"

"Shh." She pressed a finger to his lips. "Make me your wife."

His lids fluttered closed as a soft moan slipped past his lips. "How I adore you." He leaned over and kissed her, a combination of the soft, warm kiss that she loved and the demanding one which she absolutely longed for. Shifting his weight, he twined a leg over hers and held onto her face in order to kiss her more thoroughly.

Sighing into his open mouth, Muriel wriggled beneath him and the hand that cupped her jaw slid down her throat to the loose neck of her shirt and beneath. How could that part of her be so incredibly sensitive? Why should her nipple covet the roughness of his thumb? What prodded her hips to rise up and off the mattress as if seeking something?

"Mmm. My love…" Allan drew away. "Lie still for me."

Muriel obeyed, as if an animal caught by a predator, hoping its stillness would provide camouflage from the carnivore's attack. Unlike the prey, however, she longed for Allan to attack. Longed for his mouth, his teeth; she even longed for him to bite her.

He moved so that he was propped by her side and pushed her long chemise slowly up her legs and thighs, revealing her skin inch by inch. He caressed each newly exposed part of her: propping up her leg to caress the backside of her knee, the inside of her thigh, higher and higher until the soft shirt was bunched at her midsection, revealing the very juncture of her legs.

"Allan..." she whispered, feeling overexposed and reeling from it.

"So beautiful." He gently opened her legs and moved between, petting her mound and down. "You are so warm here."

"Oh..."

"Wet too."

He did something then. He touched a part of her that she hardly knew existed. Except of late because it was the source of a strange throbbing sensation that often took her unaware at moments when she thought of him.

She cried out as her hips flew off the mattress.

He held her down and did it again, a little swirl with his thumb right on that part of her.

"Allan! What is that?" She gasped, clutching at the bedclothes beneath her.

"Your pleasure."

He did it again and she moaned, reaching for him. Needing more.

His curious fingers probed lower and deeper until suddenly Muriel felt a single digit slide deliciously inside of her cunny and she screamed with pleasure.

"Gods," he murmured, sliding out and back in.

"Allan! Oh, please, Allan!" Where had this desperation come from? Why did she feel as if Allan was a conjurer, casting a spell on her body that would cause her to burst into flames if he did not keep doing what he was doing? Or, better, doing something else, like lie atop of her and enter her with something other than fingers.

With both hands at her hips, he pushed her chemise up further, helping her half-sit so that he might pull it over her head, leaving her completely bare.

"Wife," he whispered in awe. "Oh my beautiful wife." He leaned over her, kissing her softly before gently pushing her onto her back and moving over her, kissing her lips, her jaw and throat. He moved lower still, tasting the indent at the base of her neck and then moved to her breasts.

So divine.

She threaded her fingers through his hair and held him there, reveling in the sensations that radiated across her torso and down. But she could not keep him in place for long. He moved lower, kissing the underside of each breast and then her tummy and hips.

"Allan?"

"Shh."

He nibbled the skin on her hips and caressed the sensitive skin at the crease where thighs met pelvis. Her body convulsed and then he did the most shocking thing. With palms on the inside of her thighs, he opened her wide and gazed upon her most private parts.

"What are you doing?" She pushed herself onto her elbows.

"Looking at you."

"Why?" Muriel tried to squeeze her legs together, for she felt more than exposed, she felt the heat of wanton sexuality overcome her and she didn't know what to do about it.

Allan held her legs wide and met her gaze with a hazy, lusty look in his eyes that told her he liked what he was doing, liked what he saw.

"Watch me," he whispered.

She could scarcely do anything but, for it was so compelling, watching him stroke her mound, swirling his fingers around and around and the sight added to her shameless desire.

"Oh!"

Allan grazed her pleasure again and Muriel collapsed onto her back so that she might lift her hips toward him, pulsing up and down, an instinctual motion as his fingers tickled and teased her womanly flesh.

"Stop playing with me, Allan."

"Don't you like it?"

"I do, but—"

He slid a finger inside and she wailed both in satisfaction and in frustration. "That. I need more of that!"

"Oh wife." He crawled on top of her, settling his weight on her for the first time. Brushing hair from her eyes, he whispered, "It will hurt. I am sorry for this." With one hand between them, he guided his manhood to her opening and thrust.

A sharp, stinging sensation, followed by the most delicious pressure ignited her womb and Muriel gasped.

Allan stilled. "I am sorry."

"Do not apologize." She smiled up at him as she realized that his body was joined fully and deeply with hers. What a wondrous thing! Oh, to never have experienced this? Was any amount of magic worth the price of relinquishing something so marvelous as this?

Slowly, slowly, Allan withdrew and Muriel immediately felt the loss. "What are you doing?"

"Only this," he groaned as he withdrew all except his tip.

Then he thrust again and Muriel screamed.

"I have hurt you." There was remorse in his voice.

"No." Muriel clutched at his buttocks, holding him close. "Not at all."

He gazed into her eyes as he repeated the process, the slow withdrawal, the sudden thrust.

"Yes."

Again he did it, and then again, and Muriel suddenly understood the look on Allan's face before, for there was pain, but it was tempered with so much pleasure. How strange. How wonderful. And when Allan increased the tempo, Muriel was thankful because her body craved whatever he was doing. The friction created by his most intimate parts, finding a home inside of her again and again and again.

"Muriel," Allan said, as if pleading for something. "Gods, Muriel."

"Yes, Allan. Yes." For she would give the man anything he asked for. Whatever it was, the answer was yes.

He pressed down on her shoulders, holding her captive beneath him as his hips moved faster and faster, his body meeting hers with more and more fervor until a tingling, throbbing something-or-other broke inside of Muriel's womb, sending flashes of magical impulses out in all directions, making her moan and writhe in the most intense and delicious bliss she could imagine.

"What...?" She gasped, not able to finish her sentence because the rippling pleasure stole the air from her lungs.

With a grunt, Allan leaned forward and thrust two more times until he was embedded as deeply as possible. Then the most miraculous thing happened. Wonderful pulses shot up from his body into hers, joining their ecstasy together in beautiful harmony.

"Oh, woman," he muttered after the pulses died down. "My

woman."

"Yes," Muriel said on a sigh. "I am yours and you are mine."

Eleanor shouted the incantation but it made no difference; she could not find the sniveling Fosset boy in the scepter no matter how hard she tried. The vision was blurry as if blocked by some kind of powerful magic.

"Why must you be so loud?" her brother complained as he motioned to his valet to set another platter of sweet meats on the table beside his throne.

"I do not trust that whelp of an emissary to bring the child to me. He shall fail. Again. I should not wait to torture the remainders of his family."

The valet stumbled, dropping the platter and spilling food and broken crockery all over the flagstone.

"Forgive me, Your Highness," he whined as he supplicated himself in front of the throne.

"Allow me to put him out of his misery," Eleanor growled, raising the scepter above her head in order to strike a deadly blow. Bludgeoning the fool would ease her agitation. She was certain of it.

"Stay your hand, Sister. You have frightened poor Fosset with your beastly behavior."

With scepter still aloft, she turned to her sibling, unrecognizable in the manly guise she spelled upon him. How she should like to strike him down. Club his smug smile from his face, bash in his skull and watch his brains ooze out upon the floor. Yes. The act would give her great satisfaction.

So she swung.

But the scepter flew from her grasp and skittered across the floor to the opposite end of the hall.

"Sister..." Elwood shook his head in boredom. "You embarrass yourself."

Fiery rage coursed through her reptilian form and she erupted, spewing flames at her brother, though it was no use. The gift the magi bestowed upon her family was also a curse. They had great power, wealth and the ability to control dragons, but they could not kill one another.

Elwood's blond curls flamed into a halo of embers before sputtering out, leaving him intact apart from minor singeing. He turned his attention to his valet who was now writhing on the floor engulfed in flames. Tossing his glass of wine upon the man did little to help the situation.

"I command you to save my valet."

"Why?"

"You cannot simply kill my servants willy nilly."

Fosset screamed as the flames licked up and down his body, eating his clothing like a ravenous beast.

"He is useless."

"No. He is not. I happen to like this one."

"You grow soft, Brother."

"I grow impatient with your outbursts."

A rumbling discontent gurgled up her esophagus until she was ready to spew fire once more.

"I shan't give you my virgins unless you save my man. T'is no jest."

She tilted her head back, pointing her snout toward the ceiling, and ejected her anger toward the already charred rafters. Then, as if her brother's exaggerated sigh did not offend her, she raised her talon, silently commanding the scepter to return to her, and once in hand, swung it in an arc over Fosset's blackened body. A blue light surrounded the man, easing his suffering, so that he lay curled and unharmed, though naked, upon the cold stone floor.

Elwood gestured to the guards who stood at the door to come take the valet away and Eleanor hurried the process by blowing puffs of smoke after them.

"You once found amusement in the suffering of your subjects," she complained once the double doors closed behind the men.

"Perhaps I long for other amusements. More subtle. Your overt viciousness grows tiresome."

"Give me what I want, and I shall leave you to your *own subtle amusements*."

"The bridal party shall arrive any day. Our cohabitation shall come to an end after my wedding feast." He refilled his wine glass and drank deeply.

Eleanor paced in front of the throne. She was so close to getting the thing she wanted that the sweet taste of revenge was upon her forked tongue. "What of the dragon-slaying slut? It has been a long time since I've eaten human flesh, but I shall enjoy picking the meat off her bones, if there is any there to pick."

Elwood narrowed his eyes at her. "She grows fatter, though not as plump as I'd hoped." He sighed. "She is as mad as they come, however. But, perhaps you already know this."

"How should I know this?"

He plucked a pie from the table and bit into it. "She rambles in her maddened state."

"Is that so?"

"Yes. Her ramblings include stories of you."

Eleanor stopped and tilted her massive head at her brother. "What are you insinuating?"

"You promised to leave her to me."

"And so I have."

"Have you?"

Hopping up to the throne, Eleanor thrust her head right up

against her brother's. His cringe of distaste gave her a modicum of pleasure. "I have done everything you asked. Built an army. Found your former betrothed, the Morainian bitch." She waved the scepter at him. "I have even provided you with a comely physique to entice your bride-to-be. All while you do nothing but sit on that throne and fill your gluttonous craw."

"We all have our vices, sister. Is your lustful nature more difficult to satisfy in a dragon's body, I wonder?" He guffawed and bits of food flew into her snout.

She hissed, flicking her tongue out at him.

"I'll take that response as a yes." Sighing and settling himself back in his throne, Elwood said, "We have no virtues, you and I, so it is pointless for me to ask that you be patient. Yet, the time for all our wishes to be granted, is nigh. You may despise me, but it does you no good to work against me."

How she hated it when her brother was right. It was perhaps the worst offense of all. But there were things that her self-assured brother did not understand. Magical, mystical things. Something was afoot, something powerful. And, as much as she wanted to believe her wishes were about to be granted, she also knew that the best laid plans could always fall apart.

This time, however, she would make no mistakes.

She would kill the child. Cahill too. All after feasting on the slayer-slut.

Then she would reclaim her throne in Lorentia, command the dragons and decimate her brother's kingdom.

Allan poured the last bucket of steaming water into the tub and wiped his hands before going to kneel beside the bed. Muriel slept more peacefully than he'd seen her sleep in weeks…months. It was a pity to wake her. But the moon was full, the time was right and there were some things that simply could not wait.

Gently, he caressed her cheek, smoothing a red curl from her brow. She sighed and smiled sleepily before opening her eyes.

"Is it morning already?" she asked with a yawn.

"Nay, not quite."

She covered his hand and brought the tips of his fingers to her lips, pressing delicate kisses there. The action was so sweet and tender yet also completely arousing that A'Dale nearly crawled beneath the bedclothes himself. But that would not do.

"Come, my love." He held out a hand to help her up.

Muriel pushed herself into a sitting position and when the bedding slipped away revealing her naked flesh, she glanced down at herself in surprise before meeting Allan's heated gaze.

"I did not dream what happened between us, did I?"

"No. You did not."

She blinked.

"You do not regret it, do you?"

Her reply was a simple shake of her head, causing her glorious hair to bounce messily across her bare shoulders.

Relief swept through Allan, for while he was exultant with having finally consummated their love, if Muriel regretted it...

Allan shook the thought from his head and reached for his wife, gently urging her out of bed so he could lead her to the steaming tub of water.

"A bath? Rather extravagant for the middle of a winter's night."

"It will help ease any discomfort." He aided her while she stepped over the edge of the tub and settled into the bottom.

She sifted her hands through the water, letting droplets trickle down her bare arms. "You used lavender oil."

"I did." Allan dragged a stool up to the side of the tub and sat. He dipped a rag into the water and then dipped it into a pot of soap, lathering it between his hands.

"You spoil me," Muriel whispered as he began to wash her.

"You deserve it."

"Why?"

"Because you are my wife." His hands stilled as he soaped the length of her arm. "And tonight, under the light of the full moon, we shall be handfasted." He clasped her now soapy hand in his, marveling at the appearance of their entwined fingers, a sight he had often contemplated but never imagined he'd experience.

"Oh, Allan…" Muriel's smile wobbled.

With the utmost care, he wiped a tear off her cheek. "Tell me these are tears of happiness."

"They are, but…"

"But?"

Again she brought his hand to her lips. "But I miss Hope. She should be present for something so important."

"Aye." Allan leaned close so that his forehead touched Muriel's. "Aye."

After a moment of silent thoughts, Allan left Muriel to complete her bath. Leaving her a wool blanket to dry herself, he waited by the fire. The sight of his wife, naked in the tub, tempted him too much.

While she dressed, he bathed, a much quicker procedure for him as the tub was a tight squeeze for a man his size. Once dried and dressed, Allan joined Muriel by the fire for a cup of mead and then, wrapped in cloaks and hand in hand, the two of them went outside to the little circle of stones that Muriel and Hope had erected for Hope's training.

The moon was large and still high in the sky, casting an ethereal glow upon the forest around them. Though a cold night, the air was still and the snow shone like crystals, as if surrounded by fairy jewels. In silence, Allan took Muriel's hand in his and with his other wrapped a length of rope around them, binding them together.

Once done, he gazed down upon her upturned face. "For all the gods to witness, I bind thee together with me, husband and wife."

"Husband and wife," Muriel repeated, her soft voice wavering.

"Two becoming one."

"Two halves of one whole," she murmured.

"Together."

"Together."

"So that we might live long and happy lives, side by side."

"Side by side. Forever, together." Her large eyes glowed like liquid silver in the moonlight.

"My love. My life. My Wife."

"My one true love. My Husband."

From the ground, a bolt of white light shot up into the sky, fusing their hands and then encircling them so that Allan felt as if he was truly one with Muriel, their hearts beating in unison, their souls joined for eternity.

Nothing had ever felt more right.

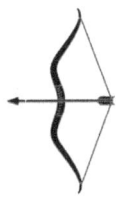

CHAPTER 25

While the family had undergone a metamorphosis, the great magician had fashioned a scepter out of precious metals in order to hold the dragon's egg stone. Using the rod, he beckoned the family forward...

— FROM THE LEGEND OF THE DRAGON CLAW SCEPTER

for the first time in forever, Duncan felt that all was right. A magnificent stag walked regally across his path and Duncan followed the animal through the trees. The sound of a soft, feminine voice filtered through the cool air, as did the pleasing scent of burning cedar. Winter meant the trees and underbrush were devoid of leaves and taking cover in the forest was not an easy task. He'd left his horse loosely tethered a good distance away for that very reason. And now he listened. Quietly, he moved out from behind a fallen log and trod softly and carefully across the snow-hardened ground. If he was not mistaken, the temperature grew warmer with each step he took and he had an urge to remove his outer garments.

Just as he unpinned the clasp of his cloak, he stilled, for through the bare branches of the trees, Duncan caught a glimpse of a startling sight.

A girl stood in a pool of steaming water, hands outstretched, head tilted skyward, eyes closed, chanting, and…

Utterly naked.

Water swirled around her legs as she stood there surrounded by white light.

The girl was part child, part woman, part mythical creature. The most beautiful being he'd ever laid eyes upon, yet his gaze did not linger and he turned away out of respect for something more beautiful, more powerful than anything he could imagine.

This was the girl he sought. He knew it as surely as if Eleanor was in his head, screaming at him.

However, the dragon sorceress had been silent ever since he'd come across the Seers. Taking a seat upon a nearby boulder, hidden in the trees, he let his chin fall against his chest, bowing his head in reverence. Now that the object of his quest was in sight, he felt no urgency to capture her.

He felt only warmth, love and peace.

Time stood still as he sat concealed from the girl, listening to her chant to the accompaniment of songbirds. Night fell, but she continued her song as moisture crystallized in the cold air, making the ether glisten with dancing diamonds. Day broke and the girl continued to sing while Duncan sat immobilized by her voice and her presence, as if suspended in a daydream.

The dragon-queen was a distant memory. Dunvegan did not exist.

Only this place, this girl, this voice.

All Duncan felt was goodness and lightness and love and the wonderful feelings sustained him for the next day and night as if he was not a living, breathing entity that required sustenance, but part of the earth: a tree that slept during the cold months, dormant, no longer in need of sun, the soil or water.

Perhaps I am dead, he thought, slowly lifting his face to the sky. *If so, death is a blessing indeed.*

It was after these thoughts settled around him that Duncan realized the singing had ceased. He blinked and gazed about him, feeling stiff and...thirsty.

"You may come out now," a girlish voice called.

Frowning, Duncan pushed to his feet. Unused for so many hours, his legs wobbled and he had to reach for a branch to steady himself.

The breeze shifted and the girl appeared from behind a large coniferous tree with the reins of his horse in her hand. Her skin was the color of fresh snow, pale and pure. Her hair was so black it was almost blue, save for the streak of white in the front. Her eyes were violet, shining out of her delicate face almost like the gemstone-eyes of the people of Dunvegan.

She had not been a dream.

"You are Duncan."

"And you are Hope."

She nodded as she stepped closer. "This is your horse." She made as if to pass him the reins.

"Aye."

Two steps closer and she handed the horse over. "You have been searching for me for a long time."

"I have." His brows drew together as he tried to take a faltering step. "How did you know?"

"I saw your journey in a vision."

"I see," Duncan said, without understanding in the least. "Is that what this is?" He gestured in the direction of the pond. "A spiritual journey?" He cleared his throat and hurried on. "Not that I was watching you."

Her laughter rang sweetly through the trees. "This was my initiation into the *Sisterhood*."

"You are a witch?"

Her smile was wide and beaming.

And beautiful.

"I am." Then her smooth forehead creased and darkness came into her eyes. "Not like the witch you serve."

"You know of her?" He leaned into his horse.

"I do." She touched his shoulder, the barest contact, and yet he felt it through his jerkin all the way to the innermost part of his bones. "I know you are a good and honorable man and that you have no choice in this task."

He gazed into her unusual eyes.

She moved her hand from his shoulder in order to pat the animal and the horse nickered contentedly under her touch.

"I have been ordered to capture you and take you to Dunvegan," Duncan said, unable to lie to her.

"I know."

Up close, Duncan realized just how young the girl was. Suddenly all his good feelings slipped away as his dilemma rained down upon him like hot ash from a volcano. In order to save those he loved, he had to sacrifice this girl. This pure and exquisite creature.

She smiled and began walking in the opposite direction.

When he did not follow—could not follow—for he could not bring himself to kidnap the girl, no matter what it cost his family, she glanced over her shoulder. "Are you coming?"

"Where are you going?"

"Home." The word brought a smile to her face, and yet for some reason, that smile was filled with melancholy.

With each day that Hope was away, Muriel became more agitated. Even spending time beneath the bedclothes with Allan did nothing to curb the anxiety.

Beneath the bedclothes.

On top of the bedclothes.

Upon the table...

Mercy.

She gave her head a shake.

Lovemaking was such a distraction—a welcome one—but a distraction, none the less. Kneeling in the snow outside the rabbit hutch, Muriel bowed her head and whispered a prayer to the sisters, that they might protect Hope and bring her home safely.

As if in answer, a warm wind swirled around her, lifting the tips of her hair and tickling her cheeks. A flock of starlings gathered in the tree overhead, singing sweetly. Rising to her feet, Muriel turned. A stag stood in the lane that led away from the cottage. It gazed at her, tail twitching before bounding off into the trees. That's when Muriel saw them.

Two figures approached, one leading a horse, the other leading the way. It was a woman out front, her bearing tall and proud. The wind tugged on the figure's hood, pulling it from the woman's head and Muriel recognized the black hair with the white streak of her adopted daughter.

"Hope?" she whispered.

Dropping the basket of feed, Muriel started off in the direction of the lane and soon found herself running and calling, "Hope? Is that you?"

Her daughter did not scamper toward her as she would have done before she'd left. Her pace remained constant, her head high, her face pale except for her bright eyes and red lips.

It was as Muriel feared. Hope had departed a girl and returned a woman. What had she seen during her vision time to effect such change? What had she done? What did she have yet to do?

"Hello, Mama," Hope said when she was near enough to be heard without shouting.

Muriel rushed up to her and clasped her hands before

pulling the girl against her bosom and hugging her hard. "I was so worried," she whispered against her hair. "You were gone so long."

Hope pulled back. "Oh, Mama. You needn't have worried."

"Aye, but you have never been out of my sight for even a day. I am a mother. It is my duty to worry."

A small smile touched Hope's ruby lips and she pressed a hand to Muriel's belly. "Yes, you *are* a mother."

A voice inside of Muriel's head—no, not a voice, *Hope's* voice—whispered, *You are with child. Only just. You must take care, Mama.*

Muriel gasped, placing her own hand on her belly. With child? But...oh *sisters*! She covered her mouth as the idea of being with child—with Allan's child—filled her with the most wonderful sense of love and joy.

"Hey, ho!" Allan called as he rounded the cottage, coming toward them, ax in hand.

Her first thought was to rush up to him and share the joyous news.

"Who is this?" He used the ax to indicate the man and horse.

Muriel had been so taken with Hope that she'd completely forgotten about the man who followed her. Peering over Hope's shoulder, she squinted, trying to get a glimpse of his aura, though auras were not her specialty and typically required her spectaculscope. From first glance she could see that the man was young, surely less than twenty summers. His face reminded her of Allan's, ruddy cheeks, kind eyes, strong jaw.

"Papa, this is my friend. His name is Duncan."

"Friend?" Allan bypassed Hope and strode right up to Duncan, chest puffed, eyes narrowed, ax gripped fiercely at his side. "Where did you meet him? What lies has he told you?"

Glancing nervously at Hope, the man remained silent.

"Speak," Allan growled, leaning in aggressively.

Hope moved gracefully to her father's side. Placing a hand on his ax-wielding arm, she said, "Fear not. He will not harm me. For our destinies are intertwined."

The newcomer regarded Hope with a shocked and questioning gaze, but remained silent.

"Papa, please." Hope spoke softly yet there was a firmness to her tone. "Let's go inside for I have much to tell." She walked right past the pair of them, heading for the cottage.

"I shall wait outside," Duncan said, nervously.

Hope stopped and turned. "No. You must come in and sup with us for it has been too long since you have had a proper meal." She focused her gaze on Allan. "Papa, would you tend to Duncan's mount? The animal is weary."

Allan frowned as if he wished to argue, but then held out his hand for the horse's reins.

Muriel was torn over whether to follow Allan in order to tell him the news, or to follow Hope and inquire about her initiation. The result was that she stood frozen, not moving at all.

"Come, Mama, we have a feast to prepare."

How long had it been since he'd eaten a home-cooked meal? Longer than Duncan could remember. Delicious venison stew upon a trencher of bread accompanied by mead. It was a feast indeed and it took effort to keep from stuffing himself.

"Where are you from, Duncan?" the woman of the house asked.

He looked up from his trencher, prepared to tell the truth. These people deserved to know who he was and what his intentions were. However, he heard a voice inside his head whisper, *Do not mention the sorceress.*

It was Hope's voice.

How much the sound of her sweet voice differed from that of the dragon queen. Soft, gentle…kind. Such a welcome relief from the piercing, painful sound of Eleanor.

He cleared his throat. "I was born in Darnell, the youngest of seven brothers."

"What are you doing so far from home?"

"I have been seeking…" He glanced at Hope. She smiled with encouragement. "…Peace."

Hope's father narrowed his eyes. Her mother tilted her head and frowned.

"Is Darnell at war?" Hope asked.

"Yes." He kept his eyes down, certain the pair would see the truth in his eyes. "Though Queen Elena is sister to Elwood of Dunvegan, the two have been at war for longer than I have lived."

"And have you ever happened to meet the king?" the woman of the house asked, her voice sounding strained. "Or…his other sister?"

He tore off a gravy-soaked piece of trencher and shoved it in his mouth, not wishing to answer.

Lies beget lies, a sweet voice whispered inside his head. *Fear not, for I will distract them.*

After a moment of silence, Hope reached across the small table and patted her mother's hand. "Mama, you are looking well."

"Thank you, my pet."

"Have you told Papa the news?"

Duncan stopped chewing.

"What news?" Hope's father asked gruffly.

"Oh, the very best news, Papa." Hope giggled and the sound reminded Duncan that she was little more than a child.

"You are to be a father…" she paused and then whispered,

"...finally."

"A father?" Allan stood, his stool toppling behind him. "But it has only been—"

"Hush, Allan," the woman said, glancing in Duncan's direction, a becoming blush staining her cheeks. "It is not yet confirmed."

"Oh, but it is," Hope insisted. "I saw it all during my vision time."

The large man came around the small table and dropped to his knees before his wife. "My love...is it true?"

Duncan had to look away. The moment was too moving to witness and his true mission poisoned the poignancy. He pushed himself to his feet and hurried for the door. Once outside, he vomited everything he'd just eaten, as if his body felt he didn't deserve to be nourished. Leaning against the wall of the cottage, Duncan heard the door open and shut quietly.

"You are unwell."

He raised his head in order to gaze at Hope. "It is merely self loathing."

As she stepped toward him, her lips moved silently and the snow crystals in the air shimmered around her. Even on a winter's eve she shone like an ethereal being.

"You must be strong." She put her hand on his chest. An innocent touch, yet so very powerful. "You are strong."

"Tell me what to do."

"You'll know what to do when the time is right."

She gazed into his eyes and miraculously, the weight of his quest lifted from his shoulders and blew away on a warm gust of wind. Slowly, she withdrew and once at the door, turned and said, "Come back inside."

Duncan did not get a chance to question Hope further, for she went back into the cottage before he had a chance to ask her what she meant.

When the two of them returned to the table, it was as if nothing had happened. Hope's mother and father chatted gaily, unaware of who he truly was or what he meant to do. Hope served him another helping of stew, winking, like they shared a common secret—a happy secret. Yet, he did not understand, for the only secret he had was that he meant to steal Hope away and take her to Dunvegan.

After he managed to eat for the second time, the women cleared the crockery and the four of them moved their chairs by the fire.

"Tell us a story, Papa."

"Which one, my love?"

"The Maiden and the Miners."

Duncan knew the tale, for it had its origins in Dunvegan and told the story of a beautiful maiden who had fled from Queen Elena's assassins in Darnell to Dunvegan where she was protected by the little folk who resided there.

During the telling, which had more detail and embellishments than any other version he'd ever heard, Duncan found his eyelids growing heavy. He was not the only one who fought fatigue, for the woman of the house laid her head against her husband's chest and was soon snoring softly.

When A'Dale got to the part about the maiden eating an enchanted apple, Hope put a hand on her father's arm and said, "We are all tired. Perhaps another time."

"Aye," the man said, gazing fondly at his wife. "I shall finish the telling tomorrow."

"I look forward to hearing the ending," his daughter replied. For the first time that night, her smile faltered.

Standing with his sleeping spouse in his arms, A'Dale carried her to the bed where he laid her down and covered her with a quilt. Then he motioned for Hope to follow him.

"You are a woman now," he said gently, taking her hand and

leading her to the ladder that led to a loft. "I built a bed. It's time you had your own."

Lifting her skirts, Hope hurried up the ladder to take a look. "Oh, Papa!" She came back down and hugged her father. "It's wonderful. I shall sleep as if I never wish to wake, just like the maiden in the story."

A'Dale hugged his daughter, watching Duncan warily over the top of Hope's head.

"I can sleep in the stable, if you wish."

"It's too cold," Hope said, gazing up at her father with a sweet smile. "He may sleep by the hearth, right Papa?"

With a growl, A'Dale threw a rough woolen blanket at Duncan. "For tonight."

"Thank you, sir. I am forever in your debt."

The man glowered at him and then his eyes squeezed shut as he fought a yawn.

Duncan finished the yawn. Gods, but he'd never felt more tired in his life.

He did not even remember lying down, nor covering himself, but suddenly a soft touch awakened him and Duncan rolled over to find Hope gazing down at him, a finger held to her lips. A soft voice inside his head, said, *Quiet now. We must hurry.*

He rose to his feet and tiptoed to the door where Hope had gone to wait for him. Once outside, Duncan was greeted by a soft nicker from his horse, who was already saddled and waiting. Provisions filled the saddle bags and the horse pranced as if impatient to be on the road.

Was he dreaming?

It felt like it, for the sky was painted in vibrant pinks and golds and birds chattered gaily from the trees, as if in greeting.

But the most surprising and dream-like occurrence was when a magnificent stag stepped out from the forest and pranced right up to Hope, bowing before her, its front legs stretched out as if supplicating before a sovereign.

Or a goddess.

Duncan rubbed his eyes.

When he reopened them, Hope sat astride the beast, beckoning for him to follow. Then the animal turned and bounded off through the forest with Hope on its back.

Still not convinced he wasn't sleeping, it took him a moment to move and two tries to mount. He didn't even need to urge the animal to run, for his steed took off after Hope, like it was playing a game of chase. It was sometime before he caught up to her, only because the seven point stag had stopped to wait.

Hope's cheeks were flushed and her eyes shone with joy. "You must try this." She hugged the animal's neck. "It is a thrill, indeed."

Duncan turned his horse in a circle. There was no path, no trail, no road to speak of. "Where are we going?"

"What do you mean?"

Duncan swept his hand, indicating the forest around them. "Is this another of your spiritual journeys?"

"Oh no." Hope laughed. "This is a short-cut."

"To where?"

"Why, to Dunvegan, of course."

CHAPTER 26

"Kneel," the sorcerer commanded.
Touching the scepter to their mother's shoulder first, he said,
"You shall be called Ninn-Arach, the Dragon Queen. You will
be feared among mortals. In exchange you have given up your
humanity."
He touched the rod to the woman's other shoulder and she rose
up, transforming into an enormous, fire-breathing dragon, the
likes of which had not been seen since Cragmar the Great...

— FROM THE LEGEND OF THE DRAGON CLAW SCEPTER

A llan held his wife close as he listened to her breathe the deep sighs of sleep. One hand lay softly upon her belly, a part of her that would soon grow as the child inside of her grew.

His child.

What miracle had taken place, to have brought all this to fruition?

He thought of Hope, the daughter of his heart, and eyed the ladder to the loft, wondering if Hope had slept as soundly as they had.

His mind wandered to the young man who had followed her home, so like the animals she brought back from the forest, injured and needing attention. The problem was, the boy was not a woodland creature, he was a man and Allan didn't trust him. They'd allow him to rest at the cottage for another day at most and then send him on his way.

With eyes closed, Allan imagined the young man setting off along the road, looking back with longing. Allan would follow shortly after, telling his womenfolk he intended to hunt. It would not be a lie.

He would be hunting...the boy.

Muriel made soft sounds at the back of her throat as she gradually roused from sleep. "Gods above," she said on a yawn. "I can't recall when last I slept so soundly."

"Aye," Allan whispered, placing a kiss upon her forehead. "Me as well."

"Is Hope awake?"

"I haven't heard a peep."

Muriel nuzzled her face into his shoulder. "She is exhausted, poor sweet. The initiation takes a toll on the body."

Smoothing tangled hair from her face, Allan asked, "You went through the same process, did you not?"

"I did." She smiled in remembrance. Then frowned. "It is a wonderful, terrible trial." She rested her hand against his chest. "I slept for a week afterward, or so my superior always teased."

While he knew Muriel better than any other person, there were still so many things he did not know. She had never told him about her magical training, or her life as a witch. They had avoided the topic because of Hope. Things would be different now.

So different.

Pushing back the bed clothes, Allan got up to tend the fire.

He stared down at the blanket upon the floor, blinking as if magically turned to stone.

But a fire, brewing in the pit of his belly, stirred him and he ran to the ladder, calling Hope's name. What he found at the top was the bed he'd made, quilts in place, the carved wooden dove he'd whittled for his daughter lying in the center of the bed.

No.

"What is it?" Muriel called from the foot of the ladder.

"He's taken her." Allan roared. "That blasted boy has stolen our Hope."

It wasn't the serving maid that brought her second meal, it was a soldier. What did that mean? Was the maiden dead? Had Eleanor sucked her soul out of desperation? Or was it something else…had the wedding party arrived and the girl was busy attending ladies in waiting?

"Who are you?" Lolling her head and squinting her eyes, Breanna asked the same question she asked of the maiden at every meal.

"None of your bloody business, bitch." The guard dropped the bowl of soup—mostly fat—beside her and said, "I'm not about to feed you. If you're hungry, eat it like the dog you are."

Right.

Bre had been stalling because her heart had softened toward the young Dunvegan maid and had not wanted to incriminate her and cause her pain while escaping. She cared naught for this guard, giving her leave to do with him what she would. She whispered the magic words.

The man made a strangled sound and dropped to his knees."What…have…you…" Clutching at his throat, his eyes bulged, rolled back into his skull and he fainted. She had to be quick. She'd only practiced the suffocation spell on rats and they were only unconscious for a few minutes. How long would the spell hold a man the size of this soldier?

Loosening her unlocked shackles, Bre worked quickly to chain the soldier in her place. Oh, it felt good to finally be doing something, to be putting her plan into action. The thought of seeing the sky, breathing air that didn't stink of foulness and rot, of going home to Lorentia, to her husband and waiting for Hope's return—less than three years, hence—gave her renewed vitality.

After gagging the slumbering man, Bre removed the keyring from his belt, his sword from his hip and his dagger from his boot and then tiptoed to the door.

"Hello?"

What was that?

"I demand to see the king." The voice was thick from disuse, but deep...and familiar. "I am a royal emissary. Please."

Glancing at the too-large sword in her hand and recalling her loss against a mere boy, Bre took only a moment to consider before moving quietly down the corridor to a cell at the end. Behind the bars was the man she'd seen dragged unconscious a sennight ago. He was large, but probably weak from his time in the dungeon. Pity. She could have used his brawn, but a weak giant was only going to hinder her escape. She turned to go.

"Breanna?"

It was as if she had been dunked in a tub of cold water.

Her name.

That voice.

It had to be a trick. Some nasty deception orchestrated by the queen.

"Bre. It's me. Tell me I'm not seeing things."

She ran to the bars of the cell. Trick or no, she had to make sure. "Cahill?"

He tugged against his chains. "Yes, 'tis me."

The voice was his, but the man looked nothing like her

husband, whom she had not seen in…Oh gods! The last recollection she had of him was from Hope's christening, over a decade ago. "Prove to me you are who you say you are."

"When we first met, you rode a horse named Elrond."

It was true, but that was a fact that Eleanor also knew. "What else?"

"You have a scar upon your thigh, given to you by the mother-of-all dragons."

Again this was information that Eleanor was privy to, making Bre even more suspicious. She turned to leave.

"Wait."

She stilled.

"We named our daughter after a stillborn child. Your sister. No one knows about that child save your family, who are all gone."

Breanna clutched at the bars. Oh Gods!

Fumbling with the keys on the ring, she finally found one that fit and twisted it in the lock before opening the door and rushing to her husband's side. She grasped the sides of his face and peered into his eyes. His skin was darkened, his hair shorn in a strange style she'd never seen before. But his eyes, oh, those eyes. There was no mistaking them.

Pressing her cheek against his, she whispered, "I thought I'd never see you again."

"Nor I, you."

With a shuddering exhalation, she pulled back. "We have no time for sentimentality, husband. We must move quickly and quietly." She whispered the words she'd spoken every day for months and the iron around Cahill's wrists and ankles sprung open.

He pulled his hands free and gazed in awe at what his wife had done. "How?"

"I shall explain later." She waited for him to clamber to his feet, cringing when she saw how unstable he was. There had to be something she could do.

There was the bowl of untouched food in her cell, but she didn't want to take the chance of the soldier waking up. She wracked her brain for something that might help. Suddenly, words formed on her lips. "*Victum, fortitudine, salutem…*"

A green light swirled around Cahill, making him glow and stand so tall, he truly appeared gigantic in the tiny cell. Once the light faded, Cahill remained, staring at her as if he'd never seen her before. "Bre? How…?"

"Once we are safe, I promise." She handed the large sword to Cahill. "Come."

Together, the two of them crept down the corridor. The dungeon was large and maze-like and they took a few wrong terms before finally coming to the entrance where a guard sat upon a stool, leaning against the wall, asleep. Bre was just about to cast a sleeping spell upon him when Cahill crept up and cracked the man on the back of the head.

"That should keep him down long enough."

Gazing up at her husband in wonder, still not convinced she wasn't dreaming his presence—though her madness had been feigned, there was a strong possibility her mind was not completely intact—Bre was reminded of years before, when they courted. A strange courtship for sure, for it had involved him capturing her and then the two of them teaming up to slay a horde of dragons.

Ah. Those were fine times, indeed.

But now was not the time for fond reflection…

They made their way up the winding stone steps, listening for anyone who might be approaching. However, when they got to the top of the stairs, and peered out between the bars of the locked gate, they found the outer courtyard teeming with people.

The wedding party had arrived.

"What now?" Cahill whispered.

"We slip out in plain view."

Cahill glanced down at her, eyeing her tattered garments before his glance quickly went to his own clothing which were dirty but still intact. "You wait here while I find a horse and something for you to wear."

Bre grasped her husband's arm for now that she had him close, she did not want to let him go.

"Bre," he said softly. "I am dressed as a Semetian. I shall pass unnoticed."

"Be careful."

"Of course." He grazed his fingertips against her cheek before motioning to the key ring in her hand.

With shaking hands, she found the large key that unlocked the gate.

"Lock it behind me."

She nodded for she did not trust her voice.

But when Cahill turned to walk away, she found her voice and whispered, "I love you." Then she whispered words from Muriel's memories—a protective spell.

The only evidence that he heard was the slight pause in his step for he did not acknowledge her words, nor look back.

Being cordial was a strain, indeed. Blasted guests from a foreign land.

Bah!

Elwood forced yet another smile before striding to the kitchens—one of the many advantages of his sister's sorcery, the ability to move with ease—to see to the wedding banquet. He did not wish to delay. Semetian tradition demanded that the betrothed did not meet until their wedding night and Elwood wished to meet his bride as soon as possible.

Another advantage to his new physique was a renewed drive to copulate. He licked his lips, for his appetite for flesh had expanded to include all manner of desires. Images of a painted bride intermixed with the delicious aromas in the kitchen had him salivating as he strutted through the rooms, the small servants scurrying out of his way as he searched for the cook.

"Remus?" He bellowed when the master chef did not make himself immediately known.

"Sire?" Remus ducked out from a store room. He was a tall, wiry man and while some might find such a physique suspect in a great cook, to Elwood it was proof that man did not pilfer foodstuffs from him.

Remus bowed low before Elwood, as if he might kiss his slippered toes. While Elwood normally demanded deference, on this day he had no patience for it, so he kicked Remus under the jaw, resulting in the cook falling on his bony arse and sputtering in shock.

"Get up, man. There's no time for sniveling."

Remus clamored to his feet, trying to suppress a choking cough.

"How much time is needed to prepare the main course?"

Blinking rapidly, Remus managed to find his voice. "The… er…" He coughed. "Morainian Mutton?"

Rolling his eyes, Elwood said, "Yes. The fucking mutton."

"For best results…" Remus stretched his neck, his over-large Adam's apple bobbing up and down. "The mutton should be gutted and hung to bleed for at least two days. The longer the better."

When Elwood growled impatiently—he had no intention of waiting more than a day or two for the feast—the cook hurried on, "But I will slow-roast the…carcass…with flesh on, the skin scored and basted with a molasses and brandy marinade over a cedar fire. It should be most delicious."

Elwood smacked his lips, imagining Breanna's corpse, spitted and cooked to perfection and presented to his bride on a platter. By that time it would be too late for the Semetian to back out. She would be his and she would know he could do with her what he wanted. Oh to see the fear in her eyes as he bedded her.

Saliva trickled from the corner of his mouth, hunger for all that he imagined, overpowering him. Empowering him.

When the cook did not make a move, Elwood growled, "What are you waiting for? Fetch the mutton. For I intend to be the one to gut the bitch."

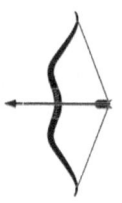

CHAPTER 27

Next the wizard touched the eldest sister. "You are the most beautiful woman in all the land, but though you will have many suitors, you will never find love."
The girl nodded and smiled, touching her face, for since emerging from the earth, she did not care one whit about love...

— FROM THE LEGEND OF THE DRAGON CLAW SCEPTER

The plan was to act as if he belonged, so that is what Cahill did. Striding toward the stable, intent on finding his horse—any horse—or two and some sort of disguise.

"You! Hand over your weapon."

A king's guard strode toward him, sword drawn.

Cahill stopped, empty hands up and speaking in Old Lorin, he said, "I am sorry, I do not speak your language." While he did not want to cause a scene, he also did not want to give up his sword. They would surely need it once out on the open road.

The guard nudged Cahill with the tip of his sword. "Eh? What was that?"

"He said, he does not understand your language," a deep voice spoke from behind Cahill.

Turning slowly, Cahill saw Arthur Bland standing behind him, a sardonic look upon his face.

"Well, tell the foreigner to give up his weapon and I'll let him be," the guard replied, standing tall in the face of Arthur's great height.

"I'm afraid I can't do that."

"You best, or it'll be the dungeon for the both of you."

Arthur sighed with great exaggeration. "While your invitation is ever-so-inviting, I shall have to decline."

The guard frowned, clearly unaccustomed to sarcasm. "It weren't no invitation. I'm a man of the king and his laws are clear. No weapons inside the castle." He pointed the sword at Arthur. "Both of you, give them up."

Bland withdrew his sword slowly and it became clear that the guard was frightened of him, for his sword hand shook so badly, he had to take hold of the haft with both hands. Arthur feigned a jab at the man, who stumbled backwards. With a suppressed smile, he presented the weapon to the guard haft first.

The soldier snatched the sword and then pointed at Cahill. "His too."

"Oh very well."

In Old Lorin, Bland said, "Give the man your sword, I shall get you another."

Cahill bowed his head at Bland as if he was a servant of the man and handed his weapon over to the guard, who scowled at the both of them before carrying the weapons off to dump into barrels that would end up in Elwood's armory.

"The guards are not accustomed to men of our stature," Cahill said in the ancient language of his homeland.

Replying in the same language, Bland muttered, "They are weak-willed bullies who prey upon the small inhabitants of this land."

Cahill glanced up at Bland, surprised by the man's empathy.

"How I long to teach them a lesson. But this is not the time." Gesturing subtly with his head, he indicated for Cahill to follow him. "Tell me, did you locate the thing you sought?"

"I did."

Bland stopped, his contemptuous expression replaced by one of legitimate surprise. "And is she—?"

"Alive. Very much alive."

"I admit, I did not believe it possible. Neither did I think I'd ever see you again."

"I had my doubts as well. Yet here we stand. Perhaps we ought to thank the gods."

"The gods—if there are any—care not for mortal hardship. They revel in it."

Cahill frowned, wondering what had happened to make this man so bitter.

Changing the subject, Bland asked, "What is your plan?" He cast a surreptitious glance over his shoulder.

"We hope to escape in plain sight. All we require is the cover of distraction." Motioning to the flurry of activity with the arrival of the foreign wedding party, he said, "This is ideal."

Removing his helm and cloak, he secreted a small sword that had been hidden at his back, inside the bundle and handed everything to Cahill. "See to my horse." His single raised brow told Cahill that he was giving him his steed to escape.

"Thank you."

"I wish I could do more."

"You have done more than I could ask," Cahill said. Then, before Bland could walk away, he whispered, "You cannot trust the king. His sister is far worse. Come with us. I shall pay you handsomely for your assistance. I am always in need of merchant ships."

Bland's jaw tensed and his eyes strayed to the colorful

caravans carrying the painted ladies of Semetia. "I cannot."
His smile was filled with regret and something else, something
wistful. "I too distrust the king, but I have vowed…" he did
not finish his sentence. He simply glanced once more at the
caravans and then turned to Cahill, subtly bowing his head in
respect. "Godspeed…Your Highness."

Cahill made for the side of the castle to the barred door
that led down to the dungeon. Breanna had been watching
for him and as soon as he appeared, she slipped out, locking
the door behind her. He wrapped her in the cloak, making
sure the sword was hidden beneath and then handed over
the helmet to cover her head and face. Though it was much
too large, once she sat upon the horse—with the stirrups
shortened for her frame—she was passable as one of Arthur's
men. Cahill led the horse back toward the front gate, through
the throngs of people, hoping to simply slip out while others
were coming in.

"Hand over your weapons. Horses to the stables." Two
guards greeted all who came through the gates with the same
command until they noticed the two of them heading in the
opposite direction. "You! Where do you think you're going?"

The man withdrew his sword and Breanna waved her hand
in the direction of the colorful caravan. "We are one wagon
short." Her voice sounded deep and unrecognizable. "How
do you think the king would feel if his wedding gift was lost?
Hmm?" She pointed to the castle walls.

The man fit his sword back into his sheath and waved
toward the drawbridge. "Gates close at sundown. If you're not
back before then, you'll be out for the night."

"Very well."

And like that, they were outside the castle walls.

It was too easy.

Cahill controlled the urge to glance over his shoulder at the guards, not wanting to give off any sign that they were escaping, for the urge to run was overpowering.

"We need another horse," Bre whispered from above once they were across the dry moat and on the road that led away from the castle. "Once they realize I'm gone, Elwood will send out his fastest men to recapture me."

"They will be far too busy with the wedding party to even notice."

"You are mistaken, I was to be at the wedding feast."

He glanced up at his wife.

She'd lifted the visor of Arthur's helm and gazed down at him, eyes wide as if seeing something he could not. Her lips twisted. "As the main course."

Cahill's empty stomach revolted at the sudden image of his beautiful wife, cooked and prepared like an animal. "There is no humanity in the pair of them."

"No. There is not. And they will stop at nothing to get what they want. They seek revenge upon both of us. They will not stop until we are dead."

The compulsion to hurry as far from the castle as possible struck with even more force. "Where will we find a mount in this desolate place?"

"There." Bre pointed down the road where a group of soldiers patrolled.

"Are you mad? We have one sword between us."

"And a dagger."

"Killing the king's men will only result in backlash."

"Who said anything about killing?" Bre took the reins from Cahill and kicked the steed into a canter as she approached the unit. He ran to keep up and when the men circled Bre with swords drawn, he cried out.

What were the chances that after all they had been through: the years of waiting, the years of searching and now, after finally finding his beloved, that he should witness her death?

The seed of doubt that had sprouted, whispered malevolently in his ear, *The chances are good, for the gods do not care one shred for the plight of mortal men.*

"Where is she?" Elwood shouted, pacing the flagstone of the Great Room, his face red, his hair in disarray as he swung the scepter against the wall, tearing a five hundred year old tapestry.

"Give me the scepter. She can't have gone far." Eleanor lifted her taloned hand and intoned a spell that wrenched the rod from her brother's grasp to hers.

"If I am not married by the end of the week, all subjects in the land will die a slow and horrible death."

"Brother," Eleanor tsked, rather enjoying his outburst. "While I would gladly help to decimate your kingdom, with no peasantry, you have no kingdom. You must not overreact."

He growled and made as if to charge her. With a sigh, she blew a puff of smoke in his face, sending him in the other direction, coughing and holding his nose.

"Now," Eleanor whispered as she gazed into the crystal inside the dragon claw. "Where are you, you dragon-slaying-slut? Where have you gone?"

Smoke swirled inside the crystal and she saw the outline of a figure on a horse surrounded by soldiers, but before the image could fully materialize, the crystal went blank.

"What mischief is this?" Eleanor muttered as she whispered a spell to break through the barrier that kept her from seeing Breanna clearly.

"What is it?"

"There is magic at play. Strong magic."

She tapped the crystal with a curved talon and for a brief moment, everything cleared, Breanna and another, riding hard for the border. But as quickly as the image materialized, it faded out again.

"Curses!" A burst of flame flew up her gullet, and lit up the scepter, making the rod glow red from the heat. The part of her that was yet human cried out, and she dropped the heated staff.

"Tell me where she is," Elwood demanded, his hair smoking from her outburst.

Growling, Eleanor bared her teeth at her brother. "There is only one way to break such a powerful spell."

"How?"

"The blood of an innocent."

"Don't look at me, sister. You know you cannot kill me."

She bounded up to her sibling and brought her snout close to his face. "Even if I could, *you* are no innocent." Smacking her scaly lips, she said, "Fetch me your princess."

As they rode hard toward the border of Dunvegan, Cahill had but one thought on his mind. How had Breanna done it? She'd been circled by soldiers, all with swords drawn, yet somehow she had talked the biggest one into handing over his horse. There had been no battle, no bloodshed.

Everything had been too easy.

"This way," Breanna called over her shoulder, pointing to the fork in the road, the path on the left leading to Darnell, the other leading to Morainia.

"No," Cahill called. "Take the other."

She brought her horse up to a halt and waited until he was beside her. Shaking her head, Bre said, "*She* cannot follow us into Darnell. And as we both know, *she* may come and go past the border of Morainia, as she pleases."

It was true. They had learned that lesson thirteen years ago and it was the reason they were in the position they were in today. Yet, Breanna needed to see what lay beyond the ruins. She needed to witness her homeland coming back to life.

She needed hope.

"Trust me," Cahill said.

"Cahill—"

"I must show you something."

"I have vowed never to set foot in Morainia again."

Quietly he said, "It would not be the first vow you have broken."

She reacted as if he'd slapped her and Cahill immediately felt sorry. But he spoke the truth and he needed Breanna to trust him. Not only for her, but for his sake. From this moment forward, they had to work together or they might never regain the trust and love they once shared.

He gazed into his wife's eyes, realizing they had spent more time apart than they had ever spent together. The anguish of all they had been through, all their family had suffered, passed between them in the heavy silence of their unspoken communication.

His wife's chest rose as she broke his gaze and stared in the direction that would lead to her homeland. The conflict taking place inside of her was evident as expressions of grief and anger warred across her features.

"Please," he said.

Eventually, she nodded and motioned for Cahill to lead the way.

The road was in disuse and the way was rough. However, it was only a few hours later that the crumbling remnants of a fortification could be seen on the horizon. It was all that remained of the guard tower and wall at the border between the two kingdoms.

"Cahill…"

He halted his horse and turned. Breanna sat atop her mount, staring wide-eyed at the ruins. Her face was ashen and a tear made a track down her grimy cheek.

"Come," he said. "Ride with me."

He waited, fully expecting his wife to turn the horse around and ride back the way they had come, but she didn't. She dismounted and tethered her horse to his before holding out a hand in order to be helped up onto the saddle in front of him.

They never rode together like this. The last time had been before they were wed, when Breanna had run away from Lorent Castle and Cahill had captured her, forcing her to join him as his army rode to war.

How different things were now.

Her body was as tense as it had been then. Her will even more steely. Yet there was a softness to her now, not just physically but in other ways too, as if something in her had changed.

As the horse neared the top of the rubble that marked the border, Cahill whispered, "Close your eyes."

They had barely spoken for the entirety of the trip. With a hand to her belly, Muriel glanced at Allan who rode ahead, navigating the steep trail with less caution than was wise.

Sadness pervaded. How was it that she regretted something that had been so beautiful? A loving act that resulted in something as wondrous a child—a gift she'd never dared to wish for? While barely more than a seed, now that she knew, Muriel swore she could feel it growing inside of her.

Yet still she regretted it. Lovemaking had distracted her. It wasn't just that chastity made a witch more pure, it was that it made a witch more focused and she had lost focus during Hope's most important trial.

She had failed as a superior.

I will kill him.

Muriel heard Allan's voice as if he'd shouted from the mountain top. The phrase had been his unspoken mantra throughout the journey. The first thing he thought when he woke in the morning and the last thought he had, before drifting into troubled sleep.

Muriel's mantra?

I have failed.

"Another day and we shall reach the border," Allan said gruffly over his shoulder.

They had traveled quickly, using the coins they'd saved from all those years ago. They'd been cautious, needing to keep up the pretense of being a peasant family. Pretenses no longer mattered. At every town they came to, they traded their horses for fresh mounts, traveling faster than Muriel thought possible. The one thing she and A'Dale had in common was the need to travel as quickly as possible and the lack of desire for food or rest.

And, of course, their desire to find Hope alive and well.

Beyond that…?

A lancing pain caught Muriel off guard and she clutched at her chest before toppling from her mount onto the stony ground. Writhing, she rolled over and over, unable to escape the searing heat inside her chest.

"Muriel, what is it? What is wrong?"

Allan's face materialized above her.

"It hurts." She clutched at her neck but it gave her no relief.

"Oh gods. Is it Hope?"

"She is more powerful, more evil than I ever imagined."

"Who? Who is it? What's happening?"

"The blood of an innocent has been shed. We are doomed."

CHAPTER 28

The sorcerer moved on to the boy. "You shall have
a never-ending supply of the most mouth-watering fare.
However, you shall never be satiated."
The boy smacked his lips, already imagining the taste of sweet
meats and pigeon pie, not caring that he wouldn't feel full for
that meant he could eat to his heart's content...

— FROM THE LEGEND OF THE DRAGON CLAW SCEPTER

D uncan sat on a boulder eating a stale crust of
bread—the last of their provisions—while Hope
ate a handful of dried berries, lost in thought.
"We are close," she said eventually.

"Yes." He drank from the goat's bladder that had been filled
with water at the last stream they'd crossed, and passed it to
Hope. "So are your parents." He glanced over his shoulder.
"When your father finds me, he will kill me."

She smiled, as if finding this thought amusing. "He may
wish to." After taking a sip, she said, "But they are a day or two
behind us." She motioned to the faint game trail they'd been
following. "Our path is quicker."

Duncan nodded. It was true, they had taken game trails the
entire way, steering clear of roads and towns, cutting cross-

country. After the first day of travel, the stag Hope rode had wandered off and Duncan had been about to give her the horse when a bear had ambled into the clearing where they'd been resting. He'd pulled the bow off his back and an arrow from his quiver when a soft touch on his arm forced him to lower.

"Put it away. He's a friend." She walked straight for the bear, talking to it in a strange, guttural language, and by the way the beast turned its head one way and then the other, Duncan would swear the bear had listened.

He shouldn't have been surprised when she climbed upon the animal's back and motioned for him to follow. But he was. He'd never seen the like, nor would he ever have the privilege of witnessing something as magical as Hope's control of animals again. When the bear stopped at a river, Hope dismounted, waiting in the shallows while the bear fished. It left the first kill at her feet before hunting for itself.

The remainder of the journey followed a similar pattern: when one animal tired, another appeared to take its place and between Hope's knowledge of edible plants and roots to be found, even in the dead of winter, and with the provisions they had brought, they never went hungry.

"The castle is less than a day's journey from the border," he said quietly. "What is the plan?"

Hope sat staring sightlessly at a point beyond the horizon. "We are not going to the castle."

"Where are we going?"

"There is something I must do first."

"But I must take you to the queen."

She blinked, turned her head and gazed at him. "We will see the queen, do not fear."

Do not fear? The very thought of the evil sorceress struck fear to his core.

Fear, disgust, hatred…

"You must promise me something."

"Of course."

"Come close, take my hands."

He did as she asked, kneeling before her, like a subject before his sovereign.

But when she told him what she wanted, Duncan pulled his hands away. He stood, shaking his head. "No. Surely that will not come to pass."

"It may and if it does, you *must* do as I ask. Swear it to me, on all that is holy." She took his hands again.

He wanted to deny her, he wanted to beg her to reconsider. But her eyes shone with such clarity and her bearing was so calm and peaceful, that he had no choice. He could not refuse her. Not because she threatened but because she simply asked. "I swear," he said softly.

"Thank you."

Breath shuddered in and out of his chest as she released his hands, like he was losing a part of himself.

"We shall have to ride the rest of the way together, for I cannot ask a forest dweller to leave their home for the perils of Dunvegan."

Duncan mounted and then pulled Hope up to sit in front of him, surprised at how slight she was. Once again, he was reminded that this amazing creature was little more than a child. A powerful, beautiful, magnificent child.

How could he ever do what she'd made him swear to do?

Duncan's only recourse was to ensure that the eventuality she spoke of never came to pass.

They rode in silence as they neared the border, the forest dwindling as they went. Trees became low bushes and then grass, until there was nothing but sand and rock beneath the horse's hooves.

Suddenly Hope's body stiffened in front of him and she

gasped, clutching at her breast. "No!"

He halted the steed. "What is it?"

Turning toward him, her lips trembled as a fat tear slipped down her cheek. "Oh Duncan, I am sorry." Her hands shook as she covered his with hers.

Since he'd met Hope, she had exuded a knowing sort of serenity. This was the first time he'd ever seen her troubled or upset and an icy finger circled around to the back of his neck. "What did you see?"

She shook her head, placing her warm hand upon his cheek.

"Hope, you must tell me. What is it?"

"It is your brother." She covered her mouth, her eyes going wide.

Duncan stopped the horse, his heart turning to stone in his chest. "Which one?"

"Dixon."

After his brother Dawson, whom Duncan had been forced to slay, Dixon was the next youngest. A shy, introverted man who had always been the peacemaker in his family.

"How did he die?" he asked, his voice sounding oddly flat to his ears.

She shook her head.

"Tell me."

"It was a sacrifice." Her eyes welled with unshed tears "She is evil incarnate."

Suddenly, like a dike being breached by a wave, Duncan was flooded with images and feelings. He saw what happened, experienced the whole thing as if he had been there, been the one to brandish the weapon, been the one to have had his throat cut, feeling his life force ebb away, his blood gushing out upon the flagstones.

"No."

He dismounted and fell upon his hands and knees, seeing

nothing but crimson. He staggered to his feet, hands clenched. "No!"

"Duncan…"

He drew his sword and swung it haphazardly at the nearest boulder; in his mind's eye, it was a dragon, a stinking, filthy beast that was cruel beyond comprehension. "You will die. I will kill you!" He swung and swung until his arms burned and he could no longer see straight.

Do not let her evil into your soul. For that is the very thing she wants.

It was too late for that. Eleanor had been his unwanted companion for so long that he could taste her brimstone breath, feel the scratch of her taloned claw down the inside of his gullet. He was her pawn and he was helpless to do anything about it.

Your sword is broken. The voice in his head was soft and consoling.

The broken blade dropped at his feet and Duncan fell to his knees, shaking. Hope stood behind him, he could feel her there, even before she laid her hand upon his back.

After a time, she whispered, "I am so sorry, Duncan, but we must carry on."

He drew a deep breath and rose. Ready to move. Ready to fight.

Ready to die.

Eleanor prepared the cauldron in her spell room at the back of the castle. Her brother lounged in the corner, eating a leg of mutton while he waited.

"How long is this going to take? I have guests to entertain."

She ignored his impatience, throwing ingredients into the

pot: eyes of owls, the skin of a snake, powdered night shade and the thorns from the black locust tree. "Now, for the final ingredient."

The body was still warm, the blood still flowing. She ripped the head from its shoulders, turned it upside down and squeezed so that the blood flowed directly into the cauldron.

When the flow began to cease, she tossed the corpse aside and stirred the pot with the butt of the scepter. A burst of flames, aimed at the kindling beneath the pot, hurried the fire that would combine the ingredients.

"She has magic," Eleanor mumbled.

"Who?"

"Your former betrothed, you dolt."

"How does she have magic?"

"I do not know." The blood coagulated on the surface of the cauldron, forming vague shapes that should have continued to grow and become clear, but instead separated so that the image was lost, the blood floating benignly upon the surface.

Eleanor grunted in frustration. "Prick your finger. I need your blood too, brother."

"Why?"

"I must create a bond. As you were her intended, once upon a time, you will have to do."

Elwood made a show of reluctance before allowing his sister to prick his finger with her razor sharp talon and squeeze three drops of blood into the magical brew.

"It stings," Elwood whined, sticking his finger into his mouth and then spitting it out again. "Horrible, horrible." He gagged and spat upon the floor.

"Shush," Eleanor said, as she waved the scepter over the steaming concoction and whispered the spell that would help her find the one who had wronged her family too many times. An image formed, a strange landscape that grew clearer and clearer. "Yes. Oh yes."

"Where is she?"

"Ahh." She leaned over the pot. "She has returned home."

"Impossible. She only just escaped. Lorentia is too far."

"Lorentia is not the home I speak of, brother."

"Morainia? Tell me you jest."

"I do not. She plans to reclaim the kingdom."

"That kingdom is as barren as her womb." He came to stand beside her in order to gaze into the cauldron himself. "But 'tis to our advantage. *You* may cross that border, sister. Go. Bring her back, for I must have her." He smacked his lips. "Basted and roasted upon my table."

"Her magic is powerful. More powerful than she realizes." Eleanor gazed into the cauldron as images flitted across the surface. "I am vulnerable in her homeland and she is not afraid of me." She tapped the staff upon the cauldron and sparks flew, causing the scene she'd been gazing upon to separate.

"So, the bitch has bested you once more?"

"Bah!" Eleanor said. "Not even close." She raised the scepter and brought it crashing down on the edge of the cauldron, causing the contents to jump and reform. "Hmm..." She gazed into the resulting pictures—a fortune-telling of sorts. "Tonight we feast. A welcome banquet for the foreigners. Tomorrow we will invite your Semetian guests to witness a display of the power of our family. What do you think?"

"How will that bring the Morainian slut back?"

"She will also observe this display—I will ensure it—and then she will return of her own free will. Once a slayer, always a slayer." Eleanor's tongue flicked out as if to taste the images she saw below. "Mark my words, brother, by tomorrow, you shall wed your Semetian bride and I shall liberate her of her innocence, all after feasting upon the flesh of our enemy. Tomorrow we shall return to our rightful forms."

Morainia did not look as she remembered, not from when her family ruled—certainly—when the kingdom was lush with forests and pastureland, full of inhabitants both animals and people. But, neither did the land resemble the barren place where they had christened Hope.

This Morainia was brand new. An oasis of summer in the middle of winter. The blackened ground had a lime green carpeting of grass and sprouts. Steaming pools of water were rimmed with low bushes and thigh high trees.

She and Cahill rode for over an hour, slowly, so that she might take it all in, not speaking except for Bre's exclamations of surprise and delight.

When they came upon a particularly pretty spot, where young Dragon Trees shaded a clear pond, Bre asked Cahill to stop. She slid off the horse and approached the water. "Is it more palatable than last time?"

"It is. I drank from the waters of Morainia when last I passed through."

She knelt by the side of the pond, dipping her hand inside. "So warm."

"The warmth from the ground must be the thing that keeps this place green."

Cupping her hands, Bre dipped them into the water and drank. A tang of sulfur, but nothing more. She drank again, not realizing how thirsty she was. After her fourth mouthful, she looked down at her hands, clean for the first time in months.

"Ugh, I am a filthy beast." She raised an arm and sniffed. "And I stink." She stood, stripping off the rags that barely covered her and left them in a pile in the grass, before walking straight into the pond.

"Ahh!" She lay on her back, the warm water soothing her

aching muscles. "Join me, husband. For I have not felt this good in what feels like an eternity."

"I am not sure lingering here is the best course of action." Cahill cast a glance southward in the direction of Dunvegan.

"Don't worry. I shall protect us." Bre closed her eyes and whispered a spell. Muriel had said it so many times, the memory was one of the clearest Bre had. Once she was done, she stood and waded to a shallow spot so she could scoop mud into her hands in order to use the grit to scrape away months of grime that clung to her skin.

"What have you done?" Cahill asked.

"I have invoked a protective spell. *She* shall not find us." She rubbed her arms and chest. "Now, husband, why are you still dressed?"

Absently, Cahill removed his vest. "How do you know magic?" He dropped the garment beside hers before untying the knot at his waist.

"It is both a happy and sad story that I shall relate, once you are by my side."

Dropping low into the water, Breanna dipped her head beneath and scrubbed her hair, by the time she came up for air, her husband was wading toward her, gloriously naked.

He was exactly how she remembered him. And yet, it was as if he was a stranger. A handsome, wonderful, loving stranger. Queer little throbbings tugged on the deepest part of her belly.

It had been so long...

"You look well, Bre." His gaze took in her physique, lingering at her chest, before rising to meet her eyes again. "How is it you appear more at peace than before you left Lorentia? You have been held captive..." He gently turned her around in order to gaze at her back. The sensation of his finger tracing the lines that criss-crossed there, sent delightful shivers, despite the memories of what those marks represented.

"You were tortured. Oh my love…"

Cahill wrapped his strong arms around her and Bre leaned back against his broad chest. This was where she belonged. Here in her homeland, with her husband. The only thing missing was Hope. Bre easily called up memories of their daughter. As a babe—cooing, as a toddler—laughing, as child—dancing when she ought to have been practicing.

Her heart filled with love and joy.

Her heart was full of hope.

Bre turned within the circle of her husband's arms, and gazed up at him. "Take my hands," she said, softly. "For there is only one way to share my story with you."

"How?"

"The way it was shared with me."

"I do not understand."

"You shall." She lifted her palms up, presenting her hands to her husband. Oh how she loved him. While her memories from the last decade were not her own, she still had other memories of him preserved inside of her: their courtship, their marriage, the battles they fought—side by side—the birth of their daughter…

She loved this man more than life itself and she had only one thing to give him to show him how much she loved him.

The best gift she could think of. A gift that was given to her, out of love.

The gift of memory.

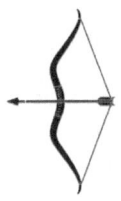

CHAPTER 29

*Finally he came to the youngest. "And you." He gently touched
the scepter to her shoulder. "You shall attain great power as
you move through life but you shall exchange it for happiness."
The child met his gaze, for she could already feel the power
growing inside of her. When the magi went to touch her on
the other shoulder, she snatched the scepter from his hands and
bashed in the side of his head, killing the ancient one without
conscience or shame...*

— FROM THE LEGEND OF THE DRAGON CLAW SCEPTER

The bed was too small making it impossible for Allan
to get comfortable. Now that they had reached
Dunvegan, he did not want to stop, but Muriel
had insisted they take a room at the inn in Dunvale, a strange
village hewn out of rock, a short ride from Dunsmoor Castle.
Allan had been here before, years ago. It seemed like a lifetime
ago, when he'd traveled with Lord Hood and the *Merry Men
Players*.

"Something is about to happen," she'd said.

"What is it?"

"I do not know, but I hear whisperings of it in the wind. I
can feel it."

He slipped out of bed and paced the tiny room of the inn. The place was not made for men his size and the result was he felt constricted, like a caged bear that was poked and prodded until spoiling for a fight.

"No..." Muriel moaned in her sleep.

Allan stood over her, watching her flail beneath the bedclothes. His hands opened and closed as if longing to grasp the weapons that hung beside the door.

"Allan?" She was awake.

He sat beside her on the bed and she reached for his hand. "What is it?"

"I am sorry."

This was not what he'd expected to hear. The word was like a balm to his soul and he found her face in the darkness and stroked her cheek. For the first time since setting out on their quest to find Hope, he felt an emotion other than desperate rage.

"What are you sorry for, my love?"

She covered his hand and brought it to her lips.

"For failing you. For failing the queen and..." she paused to take a shuddering breath. "For failing Hope."

He reclined once more on the bed, pulling his wife down beside him. "Nay. None of this is your fault. 'Tis I who failed. I had one job, to protect our..." A'Dale cringed, unable to say the word daughter aloud. His hand slid from Muriel's shoulder to her belly. "We will find her. And when we do, I vow I will protect all of us."

Muriel shifted beneath him. "What will come to pass will be beyond your skill as a soldier, A'Dale."

Just as her apology warmed his heart, her use of his surname chilled him. "How do you know?"

"The magic here is strong and I feel it from every direction. There is war in the ether." She let out a long exhalation. "There is only one way to do battle with magic."

"With magic, I know, and yours grows." He rubbed her abdomen, as if he could feel what lay, deep inside her belly. "Day by day, I see it. It is as if you are your old self."

"I shall never be my old self." Taking his hands, she removed them from her stomach so that she could sit up. "I am no match for the power of one so evil."

Allan pushed himself upright again, caressing Muriel's back. "Is there nothing we can do?" he asked quietly.

He felt her still beneath his touch and then slowly, she turned to him. "These things we are feeling? Anger. Fear. Shame? They all add to her power. Hate begets hate." She spoke in a strange, flat tone, as if reciting the words from a tome that was difficult to decipher. "There is only one thing that is more powerful."

"What is that?"

This time it was she who reached for his face, tracing his features in the darkness. "We must control these emotions. When things are most dire and when our natural inclination is to be ruled by hate, we must not allow it."

"How?"

"Love. Love is the only way."

Cahill woke up feeling disorientated.

Where was he?

He pushed himself into a sitting position. The sun rose over a strange, yet familiar landscape, steam rising from a pond nearby where the figure of a woman crouched. The woman turned, saw him and smiled.

For a fleeting moment, it was as if he was looking in a mirror. Then he noticed his hands…man's hands.

He rubbed his eyes. What in the name of all that was holy...?

"You're confused."

Bre walked toward him, wearing the washed rags that were so familiar. As if he'd worn them himself only yesterday.

"It's okay. I feel the same way." She stood over him, hand outstretched, as if to pull him to his feet. "Come."

Still bewildered, he took her hand and stood, allowing himself to be pulled in the direction of the pond.

"Look." She pointed.

A strange reflection stared back at him. Shorn hair, darkened skin, clothes that belonged to people from across the Selward Sea. He touched the surface, noting how his hands were stained dark in places with a lighter skin tone showing underneath.

"Who am I?"

She crouched beside him. "You are Cahill."

He turned his gaze from his strange reflection to Breanna.

"You are in disguise." She touched his clothes, before continuing softly, "You did it so you could infiltrate Dunsmoor Castle." She paused, her chin quivering. "You sacrificed all...to save me."

A strange memory surfaced of being chained in the dungeon of Dunsmoor Castle. Of the beatings and whippings he'd suffered, of longing for death. No, not his memories.

Hers.

He touched her cheek. "You endured so much."

"So have you."

"You gave me your memories."

"Yes. And I have yours."

"How?" Before she could answer, the answer came to him, as if he'd known it all along. "Muriel showed you. Because she gave you her memories."

Bre blinked, as uncertainty flitted across her features. "The red-headed witch?"

"Yes. She…" Cahill stopped speaking, for in his mind's eye were images—memories?—of living in a small cottage in the forest. Of a girl with violet eyes and raven black hair broken only by a streak of pure white across her forehead. "Hope?"

With the utterance of her name came multitudes of memories of his daughter, from infancy to young womanhood. He shut his eyes, relishing each and every vision. "Oh my child…" he murmured. "Oh gods, thank you."

"You see her?"

"Yes."

"How is she? Is she well?" Bre demanded, pulling Cahill's hands from his face. "Tell me. Tell me all."

Sitting side by side, on the banks of the pond, Cahill relayed all that he could, a mishmash of memories from their daughter's childhood. Nearly all of which were happy. Memories that were not his but felt so real that they had to be true.

Finally, after hours—Cahill could not tell—the images began to fade, as if the memories were no longer being viewed for the first time, but were becoming stored in his mind. That was when he noticed his wife with tears on her cheeks. He wiped the moisture away with the pad of his thumb. "Thank you. Thank you so much."

She nodded and smiled. Her lips quivered. They sat in silence for a time, Cahill lost in his own thoughts—his new memories—while Breanna seemed to be lost in hers. She reached for his hand and squeezed. "You remained faithful to me," she whispered.

Turning toward her, he frowned. "What do you mean?"

"Giselle."

"What of her?"

Breanna shook her head. "Never mind. It doesn't matter." She leaned toward him, hand on his cheek, and kissed him. "I do not deserve you," she whispered.

"Nor I, you."

Breath shuddered in and then out of her chest. "I should not have left. I should have stayed with you."

Pulling back, Cahill said, "If you had not left, I would not have this." He tapped the side of his head. "Now wife, there is no need to explain for I understand why you did what you did." He wrapped his arms around her and held her close. "I understand completely."

How strange it was to know his wife so well. To feel her inside of him—even though much of the memories belonged to the witch—it was as if they were scenes viewed through Breanna's eyes.

Clouds covered the sun, casting shadows over the pond so that the steam that rose created nebulous shapes vaguely resembling human and animal form. As if in unspoken communication, they lifted their heads to the sky.

"Gods of old." Breanna stiffened within his arms. "How could I have forgotten?"

It was not clouds blocking out the sun, but hordes upon hordes of dragons, flying in formation, led by the largest dragon he'd ever seen.

"She is creating an army," Cahill said, recalling the information that he'd learned from the serving maid in the dungeon.

"Aye," Breanna said through clenched teeth. "I saw them myself. Or rather, you did, when you crossed the kingdom to save me."

"She means to attack," Cahill added, as he watched the hordes disappear over the horizon. "Your escape is the perfect excuse to wage war."

"Then there is only one thing to do," Breanna said softly, already making her way to the horses.

"We return."

"Yes. I know where they sleep. You saw the place."

Blocking the sun from his eyes, Cahill said, "We arrive at nightfall and, under the cover of darkness…"

"We kill them all."

Once Hope was satisfied with the circle of stones she'd erected, she motioned for Duncan to join her within the circle. His horse stood hobbled nearby and after giving the animal a pat, he entered the circle in order to kneel beside Hope.

"Take my hands," she said, her face serene.

Duncan hesitated. He wasn't sure why. The rage that had eaten him up all night, making it impossible to sleep, particularly on the hard, stony ground, had grown until he tasted rage on his tongue, felt it boiling in his blood and churning in his stomach.

"Why?"

"Because you must clear yourself."

He held his hands against his chest. "What if I don't want to clear myself?"

"Your hatred is like a signal fire, and the stronger it is, the easier for her to sense your presence."

Duncan considered all the years he'd lived with Eleanor in his head, taunting him. Baiting him. She purposefully caused his hatred for her grow so that she would always be able to find him.

"To hide from her, you must feel nothing for her," Hope continued. "It is the only way."

He took Hope's hands and, though her touch was warm, her hands radiated a cooling effect, climbing up his arms, through his chest, down his torso and into his legs. Her touch was a balm to his overheated body and he closed his eyes, giving himself over to the pleasant sensation.

Suddenly her hands trembled within his and Duncan opened his eyes. Hope's gaze was skyward, her ruby lips shaped in an O. He knew what was there without even having to look for he could smell them—dragons gave off a strong stench—and hear them: the beasts squawked and blew fire, their wings creating loud disturbances in the air.

"There are so many," Hope said, once the last of the beasts were long gone.

"She means to invade Lorentia. I've heard her speak of it."

Hope nodded.

"But first, she requires the soul of an innocent." Duncan bit his lip because Hope was the innocent Eleanor most coveted.

"I know," Hope said softly as she reached for Duncan's face. "Do not be afraid for me."

"She is powerful."

"There is something even more powerful."

"What?"

She did not answer, except to take a deep breath and say, "Now, get down on one knee."

"Why?"

"I need you to swear your allegiance to me."

"You do not need me to swear. You already have it."

"An oath is a powerful thing, Duncan, and I will need your help. Please. If you cannot swear then I must ask you to leave. It is your choice."

How different this girl was from the dragon queen. Though there were similarities—both were powerful—where one was dark, the other was light. Where one forced fealty through violence and cruelty, the other asked for allegiance out of loyalty and goodness. The result was that he would do whatever Hope asked and he was honored that someone as powerful as she would wish it from someone like him, a mere soldier, one who had been charged with doing her harm.

He dropped to a knee and gazed up at her. "I am yours."

"Swear to me you will do exactly as I say."

"Of course."

Hope lifted her face to the sky, whispering magical words that floated down, surrounding his face and shoulders like gently falling snow. When she was done, she gazed down at him. "Repeat these words, *I am bound to you and you to me, wherever you are, so I shall be.*"

Duncan gasped, for the words were similar to a hand-fasting ceremony.

"Yes," Hope said. "This ceremony is very much like the rite of hand-fasting, except that it unites our souls, not our bodies."

How had she read his mind?

The same way I can speak to you without words, came the silent reply.

From Duncan's vantage point, Hope was an ageless goddess, glowing in the sunlight, the bringer of peace and light. He repeated the phrase, binding himself to Hope and the glow that surrounded her reached out to encircle him, as if it had arms, holding him in an embrace. A beam of light pierced his chest and from his heart rose a shimmering cord of braided gold. The same happened to Hope, though hers was a ribbon of white. When the ends of their ethereal cords were tied into a knot, Duncan experienced a snapping sensation—not unpleasant—as the cords drew back to their rightful place, a piece of Hope inside of his heart, a piece of him, tied to her.

"Rise, Sir Duncan. My knight. My protector."

He rose to his feet, his legs feeling powerful beneath him.

She pointed in the direction the dragons flew. "Our journey is not over. Come. Let us do the very thing Eleanor least suspects."

"What is that?"

"Go to the source of all her power."

All day she and Allan searched for Hope, but to no avail. No one had seen her or Duncan in the village of Dunvale, at least not those who took the moment to stop to talk. Neither had the pair been sighted on the road to Dunsmoor Castle. However, they were close, Muriel could feel them—Hope in particular: a subtle warmth on the wind, a soft scent in this harsh landscape.

"Muriel. Look!"

Allan sat, mounted a few paces in front of her, pointing at the sky.

Gasping, Muriel covered her mouth in horror. She'd lived in Lochsend during the dragon invasion of Lorentia, a battle that took place before Hope was born. She thought she'd never see the likes again, but that number of dragons did not even compare to what she witnessed now. Hundreds upon hundreds of fire-breathing beasts filled the sky, blotting out the sun and raining ash upon the land below.

"Oh *sisters*," Muriel whispered. "This is why she came, isn't it?"

"What did you say?" Allan asked.

She buried her fingers in her mount's mane. "Do not blame the boy, Allan. Hope brought him here. This is Hope's test and I know exactly where she's going."

"Where?"

Pointing in the direction that the dragons flew, she said, "We must follow them."

"Are you mad?"

"No, Allan. I wish I was, but I'm afraid I'm not."

"Muriel…"

"Come, Allan. We must find the dragons' nest."

CHAPTER 30

The child rose up, the potency of her transformation coursing through her veins like hot lava inside a volcano. Where only a day before she had looked to her family with love, now all she saw was a threat to her power.
In a fit of rage, she raised the rod above her head, intent on murdering them all...

— FROM THE LEGEND OF THE DRAGON CLAW SCEPTER

O f all the battles he'd fought, all the dangerous situations he'd been in, Allan had only felt similarly consumed by rage and fear two other times. The first was coming upon the family cottage before he knew Breanna was their visitor and the second was in the Thieves Forest. His throat was filled with acid, burning him from the inside. His head was filled with angry hornets and his muscles ached with tension and inaction.

Love. Love is the only way.

That was fine for Muriel to say. Even after all that had happened, she was still the purest woman he knew. Allan was not pure, and despite Muriel's warnings, all he could think about was finding Hope and killing that wastrel boy and whoever else got in his way or tried to harm his daughter.

"Halt, who goes there?"

They had ridden up to a checkpoint a few miles from the castle where five soldiers from the Dunvegan guard were posted.

A soldier rode straight toward Muriel, sword drawn. "You. Remove your hood."

The barely tethered rage inside of Allan caused him to draw his sword in response.

"Eh, this big one wants a fight."

Within moments they were surrounded by soldiers, demanding that Allan drop his weapon. Begrudgingly he did, ignoring Muriel's pointed look as she removed her hood, revealing her mass of red curls.

The first soldier sidled his horse right up beside Muriel so that he could touch her hair. Allan squeezed the reins so tight, his fingers turned white.

"Nah, this isn't the one." The man tugged cruelly at Muriel's hair and then pinched her cheek. "Too plump."

"Let's take 'em back, anyway." A second man came up on Muriel's other side, close enough to pinch her thigh. "She looks like she'd roast up nice and tasty. The king will never know the difference."

Allan growled.

"Who is it that you seek?" Muriel asked, quickly. "We have been traveling for days. Perhaps we have seen this person."

"A thief."

"A prisoner."

"A Semetian."

At the very least, they did not seek Hope. That was a relief. Not that Allan felt it. His anger still boiled, his rage still rang between his ears and hatred coursed through his veins.

"Let them go," the first soldier said. "But take their horses and supplies."

The desire to fight overwhelmed him, and after dismounting, he stooped to pick up his sword to do just that. But Muriel's hand on his arm momentarily quelled the need. "We must be on our way."

He glanced up at his wife, saw the worry in her clear eyes. After a deep breath, he rose, leaving the sword on the ground and watching passively—with hands clenched at his side—as the soldiers pilfered their belongings.

Once the men rode out of earshot, Muriel said, "The anger consumes you."

"Yes," he said through clenched teeth. "I have tried to do as you say, but…it overpowers me."

"It is because she once controlled you, do you remember?" Muriel faced him.

At first Allan did not recall what Muriel spoke of.

"The potion," she clarified.

Years ago, Allan had inadvertently consumed a potion that had been intended for Cahill. The dragon queen had controlled him until he'd confessed his one-true love. Muriel. Though the object of his affection did not know about his feelings until much later. "How is that possible?"

"Until Eleanor dies, you will always carry a part of her inside of you. It is magnified because we are so close to her. So, you must understand that what you are feeling is not you. It is her."

"How do I stop it?"

Muriel reached up and stroked his cheek. Her touch soothed him, allowing him to breathe through the tightness in his chest. "Tell me stories."

"Stories? What good—"

"Of Hope."

His daughter's name was like a tonic and a memory from

her childhood came to mind. "Did I ever tell you about the time she built herself a nest beside the woodshed because she wanted to lay an egg?"

The sweetly surprised look on his wife's face helped ease his suffering. "No. You have never told me that story."

"Ah, I think I forgot until just now…"

As they walked, Allan spent the remainder of the journey relaying stories of Hope and with each story his heart eased, his blood moved through his veins at a normal rate and the area between his eyes stopped throbbing.

Just when the sun dipped beneath the horizon, their path steepened and the scent of sulfur intensified.

"We are close," Muriel whispered, taking his hand as they climbed the slope of what must have been an old volcano.

As they neared the rim, they heard the rustling of the beasts below.

"Get down," Muriel whispered, tugging on his arm.

"Wha—?"

She pointed to the other side of the volcano where riders were silhouetted against the setting sun.

The dragons slept, Hope had made sure of it as they picked their way to the base of the volcano. In a small, unoccupied space, she created a circle of blackened stones around them much like Duncan had seen her do before, whispering magical words in a sing-song voice. Once her task was complete, she took his hands.

"As long as we stay inside this circle, nothing will harm us, do you understand?"

"Yes."

"Do not leave this circle. No matter what happens."

"But—"

A soft touch upon his cheek. "Trust me."

"I trust you."

"And in the event that things go awry, you must do the thing I asked."

Duncan dared not think of it, yet he replied, "I promise."

Her smile made his heart soar and when Hope came up on tippy toes and kissed his cheek, Duncan felt lighter and happier than he'd felt in years, despite the terrifying situation he found himself in. "Why are we here?" He motioned outside the circle. "Surrounded by evil?"

Gazing out at the sleeping beasts, Hope murmured, "Dragons are not evil."

"But they are. I have seen the devastation they have wrought."

"They only do as they are bid." She turned back to Duncan. "If controlled by evil, they will do evil. I am going to give them another way."

"How."

"You shall see." The full moon had risen over the rim and moonlight bathed Hope's face in a pale glow.

Turning her back on him, she faced the sleeping beasts and began to sing. It was a lullaby of sorts, though he did not understand the words. However, if she meant to lull the creatures into a deeper slumber, the song had the opposite effect. The dragons roused, one by one, hopping closer to their circle of stones, though never crossing. Eyes of various colors shone in the dark as massive heads tilted from one side to the other, as if they listened. Puffs of smoke rose from the snuffling huffs coming from the restless beasts.

No, not restless…

Curious?

Hope's sweet voice rose and swirled amid the smoke from the dragons' breath and the most amazing thing happened.

First one dragon, and then another and another, opened their mouths and made a sound that Duncan had never heard dragons make before. They cooed and warbled, like doves, joining their deep voices with hers.

Hope was so intent on her mission and Duncan was so captivated by the scene before him that at first he did not notice the massive shape that momentarily blackened the moon. It was perhaps the second or third pass of a shadow over Hope's features that Duncan tilted his head skyward.

Not a cloud, no, an enormous dragon—one Duncan was too well acquainted with—glided overhead.

Eleanor.

Allan lay beside her in the dirt, peering over the rim of the volcano, his body shifting and twitching restlessly. There was only one way to alleviate his suffering. Eleanor had to die.

But how?

The full moon shone so brightly, they were able to clearly see into the base of the volcano, the sheer number of vile beasts. Muriel shivered.

"They rouse." Allan was right, the beasts had begun to stir…and congregate.

Wait. What was that?

Muriel tilted her head and listened. Without thinking about why she was doing it, she reached out to touch a wisp of smoke that rose from the beasts below. It was almost as if there was a song hidden in among the tendrils. A sweet song.

A magical song.

"She is here," Muriel whispered, pointing a shaking finger. "She is in their nest."

"Where? Do you see her?"

"No. I hear her."

"Come." Allan rose and held his hand to help her up. "We must go to her."

"We cannot. The dragons will tear us apart."

"There is a way to walk among the beasts without them smelling us." Allan took her hand and led her to a pile of dragon excrement. He stooped beside it, scooped some up in his hands and covered himself in dung.

"Of course," Muriel said, a vague memory—not her own— confirming Allan's actions. She only gagged once as she covered herself in filth, for her attention was not on the revolting task, but on the song that whispered to her from within the smoke.

"Look," Allan whispered. "There is a path."

Stinking of dragon, she followed her husband down the narrow path, moving as quickly as possible while careful not to make too much noise. The closer to the base they got, the stronger the stench of brimstone and filth until her own awful scent was overpowered by the other.

Thankfully the moon was full, for it would have been an impossible path to navigate on a dark, moonless night.

As if in response to her thoughts, a cloud covered the moon and she stumbled into Allan in the sudden darkness. Moments later the moonlight reappeared and, with a finger to his lips, Allan motioned for them to continue and they stealthily made their way to the bed of the volcano. It was more than a nest, it was a hive, home to a multitude of beasts, all of which were awake and gathering at one end.

Muriel tugged on Allan's shirt and pointed to the opposite side, thinking the words, *She is there.*

Allan must have heard, for he nodded and with her hand held firmly in his, began to navigate them in Hope's direction.

A loud squawk split the night, followed by a rush of wind and a blast of fire. Allan pulled her close as they both looked up to see the largest of all the dragons gliding overhead, circling the volcano and finally alighting upon the rim.

"You think you can hide from me, you stupid cow?"

Allan pushed her down behind a pile of bones and sunk beside her, dagger in hand.

By the light of the moon, the dragon's snout was silhouetted and its long tongue flicked out like an asp, curling and hissing. "I tasted you that day. You cannot cover your scent from me."

The dragon's taunts enraged Muriel. Oh, she'd told Allan that love was the only way, but now she wondered if she had been wrong. Now that she had Breanna's memories, Muriel knew how to slay a dragon. She would not have to rely on memories alone, for hadn't she taken life herself? Wouldn't the death of Eleanor bring peace to the continent?

Love and peace were cast aside at the sight of her nemesis, who leapt from her perch and glided down to the base, landing with a soft thud a few paces from where they hid.

"You try to turn my pretties against me?" The dragon hopped toward them. "There is only one way a witch can be so strong, so daring...so stupid."

Two more hops and she stood on the other side of the pile of bones. Muriel could hear Eleanor smacking her scaly lips. "You are an innocent. And, as it happens, an innocent is *exactly* what I need."

The dragon's snout appeared above, its nostrils flared—sniffing—its tongue moving side to side, tasting the air.

A dagger stuck into the slit of the eye, that was all that was needed.

Before Muriel could act, Allan lunged, driving his weapon into the exposed snout and the dragon cried out in shock and pain. "You foolish mortal!" She ripped the dagger from her nose and flung it away then reached over the pile and plucked Allan from where he crouched, flinging him much like she'd flung the sword.

"No!"

Muriel jumped to her feet in alarm. The dragon turned, only two feet away, examining her with its blood-red eyes. "You may be powerful, but you are no match for me."

It was true.

Muriel tried desperately to think of a spell, but she was hypnotized by the creature's bejeweled eyes, immobilized by the evil that surrounded the beast like a cloud of smoke, entering into the lungs, tainting the soul.

When the dragon-sorceress leaned down, her snout touching Muriel's nose, Muriel lifted her face, resigned to the fact that she had failed.

Utterly and completely.

She did not deserve happiness. She deserved death and her unborn child—the product of her failure—deserved to die with her.

CHAPTER 31

The rod flew out of her grasp. Her mother seized it and swung, meaning to crush the skull of her eldest. But once again the rod would not cooperate, slipping from her grasp and rolling away. This time, the brother lunged for the thing, using it as a shield from his family members who meant him harm. All three attacked at once, trying to wrestle the rod from his grasp. The four fought for hours, biting and punching, tearing and scratching, but no harm came to any of them...

— FROM THE LEGEND OF THE DRAGON CLAW SCEPTER

Mortals were so predictable.

Breanna had returned, as Eleanor had foretold, and she'd brought the *good* witch with her. How fortuitous. With a talon wrapped around the witch's waist, Eleanor drew her close and breathed into her face. When the mortal opened her mouth to gag, Eleanor covered her mouth and nose with her opened muzzle and...sucked.

The best part of sucking the soul of an innocent witch— beside regaining her human form—was that her magic would be added to Eleanor's and she would be even more powerful.

At first the woman fell limp from unconsciousness. Then, as was always the case, the body fought to hold on to what it stubbornly believed belonged to it, its soul.

Foolish, laughable mortals!

Like an urn, the physical body was a vessel for the soul. Nothing more. When the urn was dashed upon the floor, whatever was inside could be swept into another vessel.

She was that other vessel.

Only, she was stronger.

Larger.

More powerful than any other vessel.

And the witch was sweet. So gloriously, deliciously sweet: tasting of goodness, and magic. Reminding Eleanor of the delights of the flesh, the taste of food, the sensation of the sun on one's skin, the touch of a man...

But wait!

What was this?

The touch of a man?

No!

Eleanor ceased her sucking just as rage consumed her. She lifted her head and bellowed.

Over her own cry could be heard the sound of another shout, plaintive and pure.

"Mother! No!"

Covered in dung, Breanna slipped between the gathered beasts, piercing the eye of one and then another, slaying them easily. The dragons had to be enchanted, for they did not move when one of their flock burst into flames beside them. Whatever the reason for the lack of fight from the brutes, it mattered not, for she and Cahill had one purpose, to kill them all. The easier it was to accomplish the task, the better.

She pulled the sword from yet another fiend, jumping back

before the thing burst into flames when a dragon roared and a flash of white ripped the sword from her hand.

"Mother! No!"

Pulling the dagger from her belt, Breanna turned, expecting to see Eleanor standing before her. In fact, Breanna *longed* to face the dragon queen once more. She hungered for such a confrontation, envisioning herself stabbing the sorceress in the slit of her eye—killing her immediately.

She had killed Eleanor once before and she would do it again, and again and again…

Bloodthirst pounded through her and Breanna bared her teeth as she lunged but it was not Eleanor who came toward her. It was a woman.

No…not a woman. A girl, who glowed like a celestial being. A ghost?

Or, more likely a specter conjured by the sorceress to confuse and waylay her.

Breanna would not be fooled.

While she had slain ten, maybe twenty beasts, there were still so many more to kill and she would not be hampered by Eleanor's trickery.

She feigned left and then lunged for the dragon on her right, stabbing the passive being in the eye, not even waiting for it to crumple before turning to the next.

"Stop!"

Just as she leapt, a magical force held her in place, immobilizing her a foot off the ground, her arm outstretched in a stabbing motion.

"Why must you be so cruel?"

That voice? It was familiar and yet…

Some wisp of a memory tried to form inside her head but broke apart, like a tendril of smoke dissipating on a breeze, leaving her confused.

The ghost approached, cloaked in moonlight, her hair black except for where a silver lock glowed upon her forehead. Her cheeks glistening with pearls. No, those were not pearls, they were tears.

Hope?

Cahill sprinted over, sword drawn, and then stopped short, staring at the girl in surprise. Upon his lips was the very same name Bre had heard inside her head.

"Hope?"

"Father." The apparition clasped Cahill's hands. "Do not kill them. Please. They mean you no harm. We must…"

A blast of fire rained ash upon them as Eleanor touched down between her daughter and husband. "What do we have here? A family reunion? How quaint."

Breanna struggled within her magical bubble, but her body did not respond, only her mind.

No!

When Cahill thrust his sword at Eleanor's head, she swept her tail, knocking him flying. She could not see where he landed but she heard the sound of his body crashing against something. Rock? Bones? Another vile beast?

"Hello Hope," Eleanor warbled in mock pleasantness. "My name is Eleanor and I am your grandmother."

Oh gods, no!

"I know exactly who you are," Hope said, not cowering but facing the dragon, her chin lifted with poise and grace.

"As you should." Eleanor's massive head tilted to one side. "I am delighted to see you again."

"I imagine you are."

"Tell me child, how old are you, now?"

"Old enough."

"But not yet sixteen, am I right?" If dragons could smile, Eleanor smiled, her tongue flicking out and grazing Hope's cheek.

Free me, my daughter. Please. You must free me! Breanna screamed inside her head.

For a brief moment, Hope's gaze left the winged beast and met hers over the lumpy shoulder. *I cannot, Mother. I must do this alone.*

Breanna revolted against such a notion but it did no good for her body was frozen and could do nothing but watch the scene unfold before her.

Save yourself, Hope. You must do whatever you can to save yourself.

"Don't worry, Mother," Hope said aloud. "I will."

Then she stepped into Eleanor's ugly embrace, lifted her face and opened her mouth.

Aghast, Duncan observed the horror before him. Everything told him to break his promise to Hope. Fury and fear tore his heart apart in equal measure and yet somewhere inside of him, a piece of Hope lived.

He would not break his promise to her.

Not when he saw the dragon queen attach her snout to Hope's upturned face.

Not when he witnessed the sorceress suck the life from Hope's body.

Not even when Breanna fell to the ground in a heap once Hope's magic was broken by her demise.

He did not leave the circle when Eleanor keened with glee, her horrible body transforming before his eyes from dragon to human.

"It is done!" she cried, raising human arms to the sky. "I am free! And I am the most powerful being in the land!"

She rose up upon dark magic and transformed once more into dragon form. Her shouts of triumph rang out across the desolate land as she soared high overhead, only to plummet for the crater once more, opening her wings at the last second to alight beside Breanna, who knelt with the limp body of her daughter in her arms.

"I have promised my brother that I should find you and give you to him. Alive." The sorceress ripped Breanna from her daughter's corpse and then fluttered to the crumpled form of the man Hope had called Father.

"The two of you together shall be a feast, indeed."

Cackling, the beast rose for the final time, captives squirming from her talons, as she took off in the direction of Dunsmoor Castle.

Duncan fell upon his knees, tearing at his hair.

This was not how it was supposed to go. Hope was not supposed to die. Eleanor was not meant to become more powerful and Hope's parents were not supposed to be captured and dragged off to certain death.

He should have done something. He should have broken his oath.

He should have…his oath!

Duncan rose, stepping from the protective circle of stones. He had a job to do and…he glanced up at the moon. It had traveled across the night sky, resting like an egg—a dragon's egg—on the opposite lip of the crater.

"I will not let you down," he whispered as he began to dig with the sword he found discarded by Hope's mother. It was difficult work, for the ground was fire-hardened and rocky and soon his hands slipped from the sweat that dripped down his arms.

He fell on his face just as a sword slashed at the spot where he'd just been kneeling.

Hope's other father, A'Dale, stood over him, his face covered in blood, a sword held aloft by both hands. He was about to bring it down on Duncan's head, when Duncan rolled, retrieving the fallen sword before scrambling to his feet.

When next Allan swung, Duncan deflected, though the force of the blow caused him to stumble back.

"It is your fault Hope is dead!" the man bellowed. "For that you must die."

The clashing of metal on metal brought Muriel back to awareness. She crawled to her feet, her legs wobbly, her head swimming from the encounter with Eleanor. There was something else beside the sound of the skirmish that alerted her to danger. Multi-colored eyes blinked at her from the heads of beasts tilting one way and then another, as if also confused by the sound of swordplay.

Rubbing her eyes, Muriel weaved her way toward the noise and then tripped. Something small and soft lay at her feet. Using her hands to see, Muriel gasped for she knew immediately what it was.

Hope.

She pressed an ear to her daughter's breast, but she heard nothing but emptiness.

"No," she wailed, searching for Hope's hand in the darkness. "No. Please. No."

Her daughter's skin was cool to the touch, her fingers beginning to stiffen in death.

She rocked over Hope's corpse, crying and wailing, no longer caring if they roused the beasts from their enchantment.

"We must not fight," a youthful voice cried, panting and out of breath.

"There is nothing left to do, but fight. And die."

"You don't understand…oomph."

The boy, Duncan, landed on his arse right beside Muriel. Seeing her there, he turned to her, squeezing her shoulders, his eyes wild. "Tell him to stop. I must bury her by the light of the full moon." He pointed at the rim where the moon hung suspended. "It must be done now."

"Who told you to do such a thing?" Muriel demanded, shrugging out of his grasp. "For what you suggest is an abomination." She slapped the boy before turning her attention back to Hope, stroking the white lock from Hope's forehead and closing her unseeing eyes.

Duncan grabbed a handful of hair and yanked her head back as he brandished a dagger at her throat. "Hope made me swear to do it." He glanced up to where Allan stood above him, prepared to decapitate him. "It is a sacred oath and I *will* bury her, even if it means I must kill you first."

Muriel blinked at the boy, then turned her gaze back to her adopted daughter.

Though Hope did not move, Muriel felt something on her face, the whisper of a caress?

"Sisters, why?" she asked, shutting her eyes, not wishing to acknowledge what lay in front of her. "Why did you allow this to happen? Where is the balance?"

Do as the boy says, for Hope is with us and has much to learn on this side of the veil.

Muriel opened her eyes and a shadow crossed Hope's slack features.

"*Satis est!*" she commanded before she even looked up. Her husband's arm remained aloft but his sword clattered on the hardened ground beside her where she'd made him drop it. Duncan's dagger fell as well.

It was then, with her head lifted skyward, that she realized that the moon was in the process of descending past the crater's rim.

"Quickly, A'Dale, we must bury her. We don't have much time."

"But—"

"Do not argue. It is ordained."

A whispered incantation sped up their efforts and the shallow grave Duncan had started grew until there was enough space for Hope's slight corpse. Together, the three of them tossed handfuls of dirt and rock upon her curled form until not one part of her remained visible.

Was that because they had succeeded or because the moonlight was gone? Muriel raised her face to the sky to find it black as pitch, studded with stars...but no moon.

Squawking and honking, erupted amongst the beasts as they closed in around the trio, suddenly curious, their nostrils flared and their tongues flickering in awareness.

"Come," Duncan said, motioning to Muriel and A'Dale to follow him. He stepped into a circle of stones and disappeared.

"A fairy circle, of course," Muriel whispered, taking Allan's hand and pulling him inside. "They cannot see us nor sense our presence as long as we remain inside."

"Why does it matter?" Allan asked, a look of wearied sorrow on his face. "All is lost."

"All may not be lost." Muriel put a hand to her belly, reminding herself that she had life inside, a life borne out of love.

She glanced at Allan, her husband, her one true love.

Why, if not for him, she would be dead right now and so would Hope. How could she have doubted the power of love?

She took her husband's hand and held it. He squeezed in return.

"Tell me stories of Hope," she said softly.

Allan grunted. "I cannot."

She placed a hand upon his cheek. "Please. You must."

"Why?"

"Because I have forgotten so much." Gently she touched his jaw. "I need to remember because your stories may be all that remains of our Hope."

EPILOGUE

"We cannot kill one another," the youngest said.
"Such a pity," replied her sister.
"We must work together," the brother said.
Their mother took the scepter in her talons and gazed upon
the beautiful stone that had been the source of all their good
fortune. "Together we will conquer the continent, becoming the
wealthiest, most beautiful and powerful family in the land."
She turned to her children. "But first, we must build an army."
"An army? How?" The eldest asked.
"With this." Their dragon mother waved the scepter
at the barren land upon which they stood.
"For we shall build an army of dragons."

— FROM THE LEGEND OF THE DRAGON CLAW SCEPTER

She floated down a long path, surrounded by trees that
closed in the further she went. Voices accompanied
her the entire time. Friends. Ancestors. Sisters.
She had learned so much of both good and evil.
A lifetime of knowledge.
A hundred lifetimes.
You will forget much when you cross the veil.

Then what was the point of all of this?
You will remember what you need, when you need it.
There is another reason you are here.
What is it?
She took a part of your soul.... One lifetime. You needed to retrieve what was left.
So, part of me is missing?
Only until you take it back.

She walked until she came to the end of the path where there was a tiny hole, no larger than that of the entrance to a rabbit's burrow.

"I'm too big."

You are not too big, for you may take any form.

Hope looked down at herself. In place of hands were paws. A glance behind revealed a silvery-cotton tail. She made a motion to move, and instead of walking or floating…she hopped, easily navigating her new body into the narrow burrow.

But the burrow was enclosed and Hope needed to move through. She turned her body around and, using her powerful hind legs, dug and dug until she pushed through. Turning once more, she saw light.

The bright light of a new day.

She reached out a paw—no a hand—toward the light and felt someone grasp her on the other side. A familiar hand.

"Look, she's alive!"

"Oh, thank the gods."

"Sisters! Thank you, thank you!"

Rubble and rocks fell away from her body and with each removal, the sun shone brighter, forcing Hope to turn her head away and blink.

Strong arms lifted her from where she had lain, and dragged her to the circle of stones, the ones she had erected when she had been mortal.

The man held her close, softly singing a lullaby. A familiar song.

Another set of arms encircled her from behind, soft and sweet. Her scent so familiar and comforting.

These were her parents.

No. Not her parents. But they loved her as such and that was all that mattered.

"Mama. Papa." Her voice felt rough, as if she had not spoken in forever.

"Our darling girl."

The three rocked together until finally the man said, "He was right. The boy was right."

Ah, yes. Duncan.

Opening her eyes, Hope turned her head, sensing his presence as clearly as if he'd spoken to her. "Hello Duncan."

"Hello." Duncan dropped to one knee and bowed his head.

Extricating herself from the mortals who loved her was difficult, for their warmth was nourishment to her cold body. She stroked the head of the young man who had saved her and with a finger beneath his chin, lifted his head to meet her gaze. "You have done well, Duncan."

He blinked at her, as if seeing her for the first time. "I feel…" He wet his lips. "As if I failed you."

Shaking her head, she smiled. "No. No, you have done exactly what needed to be done."

His smile wavered and he reached a tentative hand to her hair. "You have changed."

Glancing down, Hope saw that her once black hair had gone completely white. She stood, turning a circle and observing her body anew. It was not the body of a child, it was that of a woman.

However, it did not matter what physical form she took now, for this body would not last.

Her gaze rose as she breathed deeply, forcing air into her deadened lungs. Outside the fairy circle, a commotion started. Dragons, dragons and more dragons milled about, squawking and crowing.

Her dragons.

Hope moved outside of the protective circle and clapped her hands, garnering the attention of the animals. "You follow me now."

Much like Duncan had done, one by one, the dragons supplicated themselves before her and Hope walked among them, like a sovereign amongst her subjects.

"You are no longer under evil's spell."

The beasts cooed, a lovely scratchy sound that resonated inside of Hope's chest. "I shall give you the freedom you deserved, but first…"

She turned toward her mortal friends. "Mama. Papa. Duncan. Come." She beckoned them to join her.

Tentatively they did, casting distrustful glances at her reptilian friends. She whistled and three smaller dragons hopped forward. They bent low, exposing their long necks.

Hope went to the first and patted it. "Papa, you shall ride this one."

"Ride? Are you mad?"

"You are a warrior and I need your sword."

She beckoned her father forward and helped him mount the dragon, showing him how to sit across the shoulders and wrap his arms around the creature's neck.

Leaving her adopted father, Hope turned to the woman. "Mama, do not be afraid. You shall ride this one. She is gentle and sweet."

"Hope…"

"I have need of your magic." She smiled at the woman who had cared for her and loved her like a mother.

Muriel cast a worried look at her husband, who sat uneasily atop the first beast.

"It's okay."

With courage, the woman came forward and allowed Hope to help her onto the back of the female dragon who cooed when Muriel wrapped her arms around its neck.

Hope turned to face Duncan. She whistled and the third dragon hopped forward, bowing its head and lowering its body so that mounting might be easier. "This one is yours, Duncan."

The young man came forward hesitantly.

"What is it you need from me?" he asked.

She did not answer until she handed him up onto the dragon's back. "Wherever I am, so shall you be. Do you not recall the vow we made?"

"Of course."

She smiled. "Good." She met each of the mortals' gazes as they sat uncomfortably upon the reptiles' backs. "Do not fear, my friends."

"Daughter, what are we doing on the backs of dragons?"

"We are going to pay my grandmother a visit."

"Your grandmother?" Duncan asked slowly. "Eleanor?"

"Is there any other?"

"It is folly."

Hope shook her head. "It is as it should be. For I have need of my royal parents."

Muriel gasped and Hope made her way over to her.

Taking her hand, she said softly, "I know who I am. I also know that you and Da will always be my mother and father."

Suddenly Hope raised her head and sniffed. There was foulness in the air. They had no more time to discuss matters, they had to hurry or the king and queen of Lorentia would die.

"What about you?" Duncan asked. "Will you ride a dragon too?"

"No. I have no need." Hope shut her eyes, whispered the words the sisters had taught her and rose up, high out of the volcano. Her newly sprouted silver wings unfurled behind her, her blonde tail whipped in the wind and her reptilian mouth smiled.

For she was flying and there was nothing more glorious in all the world.

THE END

slayer
tales

THE SAGA CONTINUES IN…

A PIRATE'S BRIDE

(slayer tales #5)

BEAUTY REBORN

(slayer tales #6)

ABOUT THE AUTHOR

DL has a passion for bringing myths to life. Whether it's stories about time travel, reincarnation, Robin Hood or any number of legends, she believes there's magic to be found in the world around us even if we only experience it through our imagination. DL lives in the foothills of the Rocky Mountains with her two dogs, two cats, two children...and one husband. To learn more about her, visit www.dlsnow.ca.

For new releases, free books and contests,
SIGN UP FOR DL'S NEWSLETTER:
http://eepurl.com/CN9g5

DL'S BLOG:
https://dldsnow.wordpress.com

DL ON TWITTER:
http://twitter.com/DaireStDenis

DL ON FACEBOOK:
https://www.facebook.com/pages/DL-
Snow/160192040731844

DL ON GOODREADS:
https://www.goodreads.com/author/show/2783651.D_L_
Snow

TURN THE PAGE FOR MORE FROM DL SNOW

ALSO BY D.L. SNOW

ENJOYED THIS BOOK?
CHECK OUT OTHER BOOKS BY D.L. SNOW

SLAYER

Slayer Tales begins...

Marriage? No, thanks. She'd rather kiss a dragon.

All Prince Cahill needs to assume the throne is one simple thing: a wife. Except every virgin princess in the kingdom has turned up deflowered before the deal can be sealed. The very next maiden to cross this threshold, he vows, will be his bride.

When she appears—injured, half-frozen and reeking of dragon dung—he holds to his promise and puts her to the final test to prove her worthiness. A test that involves a mattress and a pea.

Breanna couldn't be less interested in marriage, especially to a cocksure royal like Cahill. Since losing her family to a dragon horde, she has become the continent's finest slayer—a job she doesn't plan on giving up until the last dragon's blood drips from her sword.

Yet her sleepless nights are plagued with visions of Cahill doing wicked things to her untutored body. And when she fights at his side to repel a dragon attack, her visions become delicious reality.

But Queen Eleanor, whose reign is about to end, has no intention of giving up her power. Not to Prince Cahill, and certainly not to some young upstart…

✦ ✦ ✦

praise for DL snow's SLAYER

"This was a wonderful break to my every day life and if you enjoy adult fairy tales this is one you will enjoy."
— Theresa Joseph, *The Romance Studio*

"This was a great story with a sense of humor….A fairy tale of sorts that is definitely worth the read…Loved it!"
— Sabine, *Manic Readers*

THIEF OF HEARTS

slayer
Tales

ONCE A PRINCESS, NOW AN ASSASSIN...
HOW'S THAT FOR A HAPPILY EVER AFTER?

The Princess: Happily ever after? Zaina doesn't believe in it. Now revenge on the other hand...All she has to do is: cut her hair, dress up as a boy, call herself Little John, join the traveling circus, guard her soul against the evil sorceress, battle dragons and avoid the lethal tip of the mysterious Lord Hood's blade. It's perfectly easy. Oh, but don't forget the potion, the one that's intended for the villain who ruined her. It ends up in the wrong hands, causing anyone who touches it to fall in love with her except, of course, the one she desires most.

The Outlaw: If there is one thing Lord Hood is good at, it's sniffing out a lie. And the newest member of his troupe, the lad Little John, is lying about something. Hood just has to figure out what. In the meantime, he will continue to steal from the rich and give to the poor and evade the bounty hunters who pursue him. For one day soon he will return home to avenge the murder of his betrothed and perhaps that will ease the dark stain upon his heart.

ALSO BY D.L. SNOW

SIREN'S SONG

A Time Travel Romance

After giving up fame, Joss Jones wants a normal life. Maybe she'll find it in Bandit Creek. Or…maybe not.

From the moment she moves into the old mansion she inherited, she's stalked by a ghost who torments her before dragging her back in time to Bandit Creek, 1899. Has she gone crazy or is this old mining town, full of saloons, gambling, whoring and fortune seekers her new reality?

It feels real enough as does the ghost who brought her here. His name is Morgan Hawes and he is very much alive. Is Morgan the key to Joss finding her way home or is Joss stuck for the rest of her life as the Siren of Bandit Creek?